NEARER THAN THE SKY

ALSO BY T. GREENWOOD

Breathing Water

NEARER
THAN THE SKY

a novel

T. GREENWOOD

St. Martin s Press ≈ New York

This is a work of fiction. All characters and events portrayed in this novel are either fictitious or are used fictitiously.

www.stmartins.com

Book design by Michelle McMillian

Library of Congress Cataloging-in-Publication Data

Greenwood, T. (Tammy).
    Nearer than the sky / T. Greenwood.—1st U.S. ed.
    p. cm.
    Sequel to: Breathing water.
    ISBN 0-312-26503-4
       1. Munchausen syndrome—Fiction. 2. Problem families—Fiction. 3. Women—Psychology—Fiction 4. Arizona—Fiction. I. Title.

PS3557.R396 N4 2000
813'.54—dc21   00-027852

First Edition: August 2000

10 9 8 7 6 5 4 3 2 1

For Mom, Dad, and K.K.

Acknowledgments

Writing this novel was, at times, like being caught barefoot in a storm. For umbrellas and other shelters, I'd like to thank my family, the Stewart family, and the Sherwood Anderson Foundation. For making me weather the storm and examine the thunder, my gratitude to Lon deMatties, Nicole Norum, Christy Fletcher, and Lori Applebaum. For showing me the break in the clouds, my appreciation to Joe Veltre and Erika Fad. And for teaching me how to dance in the puddles, my *always* to Patrick.

The farthest Thunder that I heard
Was nearer than the Sky
And rumbles still, though torrid Noons
Have lain their missiles by—
The Lightning that preceded it
Struck no one but myself—
But I would not exchange the Bolt
For all the rest of Life—

—EMILY DICKINSON
(from poem 1581)

ONE

I UNDERSTAND LIGHTNING. I am not afraid of the rumble, gentle as an empty stomach but powerful enough to shake the ground beneath my feet. I'm not afraid when the sky opens up and blinds my eyes with rain. And when its cold white fingers reach down, looking for someone to touch, I barely shudder anymore. I have an agreement with the sky. An understanding.

It happened when my mother ran back inside the Foodmart with my baby sister, Lily, on her hip. She'd forgotten to buy baby aspirin and Lily had a fever. I was in the shopping cart; at four years old I was still small enough to fit in the front basket with my mother's purse. She parked me and the groceries next to our orange Chevy Nova and said, "Indie, honey, I'll be right back. Don't you move." As she hurried back across the parking lot, I busied myself with a package of cookies I found poking up from one of the bags. I remember they had chocolate stripes and holes in the middle I could fit my thumbs through. The chocolate melted on my hands. It was 1970, August, and our first summer in the mountains of northern Arizona. We didn't know then about the monsoons.

I can only imagine what the other Foodmart shoppers must have thought about me out there in the parking lot like any other bag of groceries. No different from an abandoned carton of ice cream, cardboard growing soggy in the sun. Maybe if someone had paid more attention then it would have stopped with this. If someone had wheeled me into the Foodmart, down the aisle where my mother must have stood browsing the shelves of medicine as if the bottles were magazines she might like to read, then maybe she would have realized that you don't leave four-year-old babies in shopping carts in parking lots. Not even when your youngest has the pink raspberry flush of a fever.

But no one did. After the electric doors closed behind her clean white heels, I sat eating cookies while the other Foodmart customers bustled about opening trunks and wiping the crusty noses of their own children. Every now and then one of them would notice me and smile, probably at the chocolate mess I'd made, but not one person looked for my mother. They must have thought she was inside the Nova somewhere, preparing the car seat or looking for a lost toy.

I knew she would come back. I wasn't afraid of that. I do remember the sudden chill in the air, though, and the long shadows that fell across the parking lot as storm clouds moved across the sky. I remember the sound of shopping-cart wheels moving quickly across the pavement, and the first few drops of rain on my face.

I must have eaten five or six of those cookies, each one growing soggier and soggier in the drizzle. I remember the way my hair tasted. The way the rain beaded up on my bare arms. The smell of wet pavement.

The first rumbles of thunder could have just been my stomach.

It could have been hunger instead of a threat from the sky. But then the thunder rumbled again. Louder this time. Insistent. But it wasn't until the sky exploded, threatening and angry, until it opened up and the rain came down in sharp slivers, soaking the brown paper bags and the cookie in my hand, that I started to feel afraid. The next crack of thunder made the shopping cart roll a little, and I felt panic for the first time, the dull thudding of my heart, the heat rising to my ears, as I looked toward the doors of the Foodmart in the distance.

Every time the doors opened, I expected to see her. But it was only a Foodmart cashier in a red apron, a lady with a yellow umbrella opening above her like butterfly wings, a man with a long gray beard and a bag brimming with green leaves. And then, just as the heat in my ears started to bring tears, the glass doors opened up again, and I saw my mother in her crisp polka-dot sundress and Lily still safely nestled on her hip.

"Ma," I cried. Relief like cool rain.

She stood in the doorway, not moving. Not coming. I watched her struggle with the baby aspirin bottle, and the soft puff of cotton inside. Through the rain, I watched her put the tiny orange pill on Lily's tongue. Watched Lily shake her head. Tighten her lips over my mother's finger. I watched her kiss Lily's head, brush her white-blond curls out of her eyes, and adjust her position on her hip.

Thunder rolled through my body, rolled under my skin like waves. She looked up from Lily then and remembered me. What happened next lingers in my memory like an electric current that refuses to leave the body. The details circulate from fingertips to fingertips, toe to nose to toe.

The thunder cracked again; it sounded like a slap. Like a giant hand hitting skin. I watched my mother's steps quicken and then I put my hands up to my ears and closed my eyes. *One . . . two . . .*

three. I imagined I was counting my mother's steps toward me. *Four . . . five* and I opened my eyes.

Everything was white. Metallic and cold. My skin felt like it had been stung by a thousand bees. And my heart was suddenly still. No beating, only buzzing. Only the hum of an electric lullaby.

When I could see again, I realized that I was no longer in the shopping cart. I was lying facedown on the hood of the Nova, staring down at the spilled groceries on the ground. At a hundred pink tablets of baby aspirin, at the polka dots of my mother's dress. The shopping cart was in the next parking space, and glowing red.

The rain wasn't coming down so hard anymore. But I was cold, freezing cold, and I couldn't hear anything except for the buzzing of my body. When my mother's free hand found me, I shrank away from her touch. Her wide blue eyes grew wider, and Lily cried. When she finally spoke, her words tasted like sour milk. And Lily's cries were the bitter of unripe berries.

They say that two things can happen to you if you are struck by lightning. The first is that you will die. The second is that you *won't* die and that you will be left with few (if any) injuries, no lingering symptoms or souvenirs from your encounter. But even now, so many years later, I can't hear well with my left ear, and with the other one I can still taste sounds. Music and wind. Voices and lies.

My mother says it didn't happen this way at all. She says that she *was* inside the Nova, buckling Lily into her car seat. Finding my lost Crissy doll. She says she would *never* have left me alone in the parking lot. But I remember the click of her heels, the pinkish orange aspirin melting in the rain. And when she tells the story her way, her words taste like asphalt. Like aspirin. Like anything but the truth.

My mother has never been able to take the blame. Not then

and not later. The way she tells the story, she's the one who kept me from turning into a blackened version of my former self. The way she tells it, she saved my life. In her version of this story, of *every* story, she's always the hero.

In those days, there were no words to describe the nature of my mother's tales. No diagnosis for her tendency toward fiction. No names for women who make accidents happen to their children, no terms for imaginary heroes. And so we listened to my mother's stories in silence and tried to believe. That she brought my brother, Benny, back to life when he stopped breathing in his crib. That she saved me from the lightning. That Lily's illness was real instead of something Ma put inside of her. We listened in silence and waited for the words that might explain.

I understand lightning. I know the cold taste of light, the inevitable paralysis of its touch. I know how deceiving an empty sky can be, and I understand the consequences of thunder. But sometimes, I still dream the gentle thrill of electricity, and stand in open fields during storms with my arms raised. Because illumination of this intensity is apt to show you something you might not see otherwise. In the white cold light moments of a storm, you're bound to get at least a glimpse of the truth.

PETER AND I WERE NAKED and intertwined when the phone started ringing. Because before the shuddering afterglow, while muscles and bones, tongues and lips and hips still rang metallic and taut, my mother's blood was filling with poison. When the soft skin of his back yielded to my sharp fingers and all of him quickened, her own quicksilver, arsenic dance had already begun, and with this crescendo came her crescendo of lead. I didn't pick up the receiver. But after, while he slumbered, I shuddered still. That moment was over, but my mother's poison lullaby was just beginning, and some part of me knew. The phone started ringing again.

It was Lily who called. It was always Lily who called, her whispers as deceptively sweet as Nutrasweet, leaving me with a bitter aftertaste and a slight headache.

"Ma's sick," she said.

"What's the matter?"

"They don't know. It's real bad. She called an ambulance."

Despite the fear in her voice, ambulance sirens (the harmony of high-pitched squeals and the sonorous chords of *fear* and *accident*) were not unfamiliar sounds to either of us.

"Where is she?"

"Down here. At St. Joseph's."

"Why is she in Phoenix?" I asked. My mother lived more than two hours north of Phoenix, in the mountains.

"They transferred her, Indie. It's real bad this time," and then sweetly, "Can you come home?"

"Is she going to be okay?"

"She's filled with poison. It's in her blood," she said softly. I imagined Lily winding herself up in the phone cord, the blue light of the TV shining through her transparent nightgown. Her baby, Violet, raspy-breathed inside the rented oxygen tent in the living room. "They can't figure it out. Maybe lead poisoning. The blood tests haven't come back yet."

I tightened my grip on the phone. "I spent six hundred dollars the last time on an airplane ticket, and there was nothing wrong with her."

"I really think you need to come home this time," she said, twirling me inside a cotton candy swirl. "I'll pay."

When I hung up the phone, I watched Peter's chest rise and fall. He sleeps so deeply sometimes that his silence wakes me up, and I'll press my ear against his chest to make sure that he's still alive. Tonight, he was smiling. Sometimes he even laughs in his sleep. I envy his dreams. I curled against him, pressing my body against his until there were no spaces between us, until his skin became my skin. Until the cadence of my breaths matched his.

This had happened so many times now, I wasn't worried about falling asleep again. Another frantic call from Lily wouldn't keep me awake all night. I grew up in the village where the little boy cried "Wolf!" I was a local. I knew these streets like I knew my own name, and Lily knew them too. After she hung up the phone she would return to the couch where she'd been sleeping since Violet got sick. She would toss and turn, of course, each rumble of her daughter's chest waking her. But Ma would not enter her mind again until morning, until after the rituals of coffee and bacon and newspapers and her husband's kiss good-bye. Only then would she begin to wonder if the Wolf was really hiding under our mother's bed or if Ma had made him up. Fabricated him like so many school projects, out of chicken wire and papier-mâché.

I didn't want to go back to Arizona now. It was autumn, and the woods around our house were on fire. I had asked Peter not to rake the fallen leaves around the cabin, enjoying the way the rust and gold and purple carpeted the yard and driveway. The sky had been bright and blue and cold lately; the heat of the summer had finally relented.

This summer had been particularly hot and difficult to endure. I lost my job in April, and without it, I hadn't known what to do with my time. I'd been writing for the local paper for almost ten years. I wasn't a good reporter, I knew this, but I had loved my job. I didn't even mind that I usually got assigned to the dullest stories. Dog shows and 100th birthday parties. Big fish and ballet recitals. I never thought the paper would let me go, but when they lost their lease on the building, they had to pick *someone,* and I guess I was the logical choice. I missed the cool blue office, the whirr of electric fans and the clicking of typewriter keys. I missed driving to one town or another for a story, the windows of the truck rolled down and the radio turned up. I missed the interviews conducted on porches, and later transcribing the stories about UFO sightings or the new school principal's recipe for potato salad. Summer days are long in Echo Hollow. And even longer without anything to do.

So when the air began to turn cold, and the first bloom of red appeared in the maple tree in front of the house, I felt a certain sense of purposefulness. It was as if that red signified that the stagnant heat of summer had finally broken, and that in its place was something brighter. I had felt so optimistic that Peter was even able to convince me to come to work with him at his café. He promised he'd teach me how to make muffins, how to busy my hands and my mind. For a month now, I had been waking up with him at two o'clock in the morning. We had to be there to start baking at three, and we live deep in the woods, an hour's drive from town. I had been learning how to navigate in the darkness of early morning, how not to be afraid. The stillness of this hour surprised me, when the only sounds were wet leaves crushing beneath our feet and our screen door closing. I loved the way our headlights were the only lights on the interstate at that time of night. It felt like we were alone in the world, as if no one existed anymore but us.

Even in town there is a certain peace at this hour. We would park on the empty street in front of the restaurant and sit for a few minutes before going inside. Sometimes Peter would put his arm over the back of my seat, and look at the small brick building, at the new awning: THE SWAN SONG CAFÉ & THEATRE, painted in white block letters. After ten years of working for other people, Peter finally had his own restaurant. In all the time we'd known each other, I'd never seen him so happy. And in these half-light moments before dawn, I felt happy too. Like we were sharing something. Of course, then the spell was inevitably broken by the reality that muffins and bread needed to be made, that the industrial-size dishwasher in the kitchen was probably on the fritz again, that morning would come if we waited too long inside the truck. But for a little while, anyway, the world belonged to us.

He had taught me my way around the basement bakery, how to maneuver the giant silver bowls and long wooden spoons. How much batter would make the perfect muffin. The intricacies of sugar and flour and why butter is so important. He made the bread and rolls, which were much more complicated than my muffins. Part science and part philosophy. There was as much to be learned in this basement bakery as there was at the university, I supposed.

After the loaves of bread were in the oven, Peter would leave me to make the muffins and go upstairs to start the coffee and unwrap the salads in the deli case. Joe, the cook, would get there at seven to start making lunch. And two of the girls from the college would be in to open up shop at eight.

I was still learning, and my muffins were completely unpredictable. Sometimes they came out hard and small, burned at the edges. Other times the batter grew so high that the muffins looked like small mountains but were still sticky and wet inside. My favorite part of the day was after the muffins were made, when I carried the heavy trays, stacked four or five high, up the stairs. I used thick white dish towels to protect my hands from the hot pans, and the steam from the muffins made the hair around my face curl. Joe and Peter and whoever was working the counter that day would all gather around one of the tables, and we would break open the wild blueberry or banana and chocolate chip muffins before the onslaught of customers. We used a plastic spatula for the butter and Peter poured everyone coffee. No one ever complained about my baking.

We were usually interrupted by some impatient businessman or other regular who felt somehow entitled, peering through the locked door, asking to be let in. Peter never turned them away, though. He always went to the door and smiled, unlocking it and opening the floodgates.

After the morning rush, Peter and I would go up to the theater he had just built on the second floor of the building. He had dreamed about this ever since he opened up the restaurant a year ago. Here he could run his favorite movies, all day long, every day. Most of the multiplexes were on the outskirts of town, and none of them showed the obscure foreign and art films or the quirky movies that Peter loved. He also let people bring their food and drink from the café into the theater. It made for a longer clean-up time after each show, but it also made people feel like they were at home. Or like they were breaking rules.

The brick walls kept everyone cool in the summer and warm when autumn came. Some of the seats were from the college, sold when they renovated their auditorium. Others were just chairs we found at garage sales that weren't too beaten up. Sometimes, Peter and I would sit in the back and watch movies all afternoon, leaving only for the lunch rush or to use the restroom. With the smell of yeast and a dusting of flour in my hair, I could forget for a while that I'd lost my job. That all the work I'd done for the past ten years had resulted in nothing.

I lay on my back and looked up through the skylight at the starless sky. Peter rolled over and put his arm across my chest. I had come here, to Maine, almost fifteen years ago for college. It had seemed the natural thing to do, because it was so much like my childhood home in Mountainview yet somehow strangely and safely different. The thick woods of Ponderosa pines became the white labyrinth of birches here. The snow looked the same, but the cold was deeper. It resided less on your skin and more in your bones. There were similarities, but there were great differences, particularly in the skies. Here, in Maine, the clouds protect the stars at night. They are only fuzzy spots of light in the distance.

In the mountains of northern Arizona, they are exposed. Vulnerable and bright. You could reach up into a blue-black night like this and steal them.

I laid my head against Peter's chest and fell asleep, forgetting my mother for a while. But when the alarm started buzzing at 2:00, it was thoughts of her that pulled me into the world.

Peter's hand shot out and turned the alarm off as soon as it first buzzed. He moved slowly out of bed, and I watched him pull on his jeans and a T-shirt. He was so quiet, his waking a familiar dance; each movement was refined and perfected so as to be completely noiseless.

"Hey," I said.

"You startled me," he said and sat down next to me on the bed. "You're taking the day off today, aren't you?"

"Lily called while you were sleeping," I said.

Peter raised one of his eyebrows despite himself. He knew these streets too. We had been together for fourteen years now, since we were nineteen years old. The midnight phone calls failed to even wake him anymore.

"Ma's in Phoenix this time," I said.

"Phoenix?"

"They transferred her down. Lily says there's poison in her blood or something. She wants me to come home," I said.

He nodded.

I sat up and waited for Peter to respond, to lay his head on my lap and say, *Don't go.* That way I wouldn't have a real decision to make. If he needed me then I wouldn't have to leave. But he only turned away from the window and bent down to kiss my forehead, gently touching my naked breast with his hand.

"It's okay, you know." He smiled. "If you need to go."

I nodded and waited for his words begging me to stay. Jealous or selfish or needy words. But he would be fine here alone. I could leave for a month and nothing about these mornings would change except that he wouldn't have to wait for me to wash the sleepy seeds from my eyes or find a clean pair of jeans. He could return to his usual morning routine, the one he'd had when I was still at the paper. I waited for him to ask me to stay, to say that he really needed me at the Swan, but instead he only put his long, thin fingers into my hair and made circles on my scalp, making me drowsy and weak. When Peter's father brings us lobsters, Peter does the same thing to them. He turns them upside down and rubs their heads gently until they are anesthetized, hypnotized. Only then does he drop their limp bodies into the boiling water.

"I'll give it a few days," I said. "We'll see how she is in a couple of days."

I closed my eyes while he finished getting ready. He came back in and kissed me softly. "Go back to sleep," he said. His wool jacket was scratchy against my skin and smelled like pine. It was as much a part of these woods as the trees were, as we were becoming.

After Peter left, I put on a pair of his flannel pajamas and wool socks. Even in October, the early mornings here are wintery. He had turned on the small reading lamp next to the couch, and the living room felt warm. I opened up the door on the woodstove to add another log to the fire, but he had already taken care of it. I stood up, brushed the ashes off my knees, and sat down on the couch, pulling the quilt Peter's mom had made for us last Christmas around my shoulders.

All summer I had sat like this, reading the want ads, trying to figure out what to do. I didn't know anybody else who didn't have to go to work every day. Even our friends who had started having babies worked. And having decided a long time ago not to have children, my sense of being adrift and without purpose was compounded by all this free time. Carefree. There was not a thing in this world that needed me. Peter certainly didn't need me doting on him. Our cat, Jessica, was also independent, needing only a bowl of water and food, a spot of sunlight on the floor to survive.

At first, I tried planting things. But I was overzealous, impatient. The ground hadn't even thawed yet before I started poking holes and planting seeds. A hard frost in late May killed even those few little green shoots I had managed to coax from the soil. I thought about art and music. Bought equipment to make stained glass, thought I might be able to sell my work at the artists' gallery in town. But I could never choose from the sheets and sheets of colors. I was too overwhelmed by the possibilities. I bought a guitar at a pawn shop in Portland. It came with a slide and a stack of Mel Bay sheet music for beginners. I sat on our back porch while Peter was at work and strummed "Au Clair de la Lune" until my fingers ached, until the neighbors' dogs down the road started to howl. Finally, Peter built a study for me, and suggested that I try to write again. Stories or something. Become a freelance writer. But in that beautiful attic room, surrounded by my favorite books, an old red oriental rug beneath my feet, every word I wrote sounded like a tired newspaper article.

OCTOBER 9, 1999. INDIE STACKS ONE CORD OF WOOD, SPLINTERS AND BLISTERS RESULT. Backwoods, Maine. *Indie Brown, showing remarkable grace wielding an ax, split and stacked an entire cord of wood this sunny afternoon. A gentle breeze and a blazing autumn backdrop made the scene both poignant and picturesque to pas-sersby. Chuck Moony arrived upon completion of the task with steaks for the barbecue and a potato salad from Shaw's. Peter arrived soon after. Dinner was cooked on the hibachi and served on a makeshift table made of unsplit logs and a piece of plywood from the garage. Religion was discussed, and all came to the conclusion that God must reside in these autumn leaves.*

Peter built this house when we were twenty-three years old. He picked this spot of land because of autumn. He chose this place because of its semblance to fire. He drove me here from our little apartment in town and made me stand in the exact center of the four square acres he had purchased. "Listen," he said. "You can hear the leaves turning."

Two days later, Lily still hadn't called back and I thought that it had passed. That the Wolf had returned to the woods of my mother's imagination.

After we turned off the whirring projector and swept behind the seats, covered the salads and bundled the day-old bread and muffins for the women's shelter, Peter and I sat at one of the tables in the empty café.

Joe slung his backpack over his shoulder and turned off the lights in the kitchen.

"You guys want to go get a beer?" he asked. "It's still happy hour at Finnegan's."

"No thanks." Peter smiled. "Maybe tomorrow."

Joe shrugged and went outside where his bike was locked to a parking meter. He lives almost as far out of town as we do, but he makes the trek by bicycle from April, when the snow starts to melt, until late October or November, when snow starts to fall. Joe is a funny character. He's as thin as an adolescent boy. He wears thick glasses, and his clothes never seem to fit quite right. He likes heavy metal music, but he reads Russian novels. Sometimes in the mornings he insists on AC/DC instead of the public radio station. We have known Joe as long as we've known each other. We all met that first summer after freshman year at the Birches, where Peter made ice sculptures and I waited tables. Joe had gone to a culinary school somewhere in Vermont and wound up at the Birches as an apprentice. That was the summer that Peter had his accident and we fell in love.

"You okay?" Peter asked, rubbing his thumb across the back of my hand.

I nodded.

Joe tapped on the glass and waved before he started to pedal away. We waved back and Peter squeezed both of my hands, leaning forward to whisper in my ear.

"You wanna watch a movie?"

This was something we usually reserved for special occasions, for anniversaries and birthdays. It was exactly what I needed; Peter always knew.

"What about Julia?" I asked.

"She's downstairs doing the money. It'll be at least a half hour before she's done."

He took my hand and led me through the doors and up the stairs again to the theater. He still has a small limp, even after all these years, but I love the way it makes him move slowly, with care. I can see in his walk the old man he will become.

While he readied the projector, I took off my dress and folded it neatly, unrolled my socks and untied my shoes. I sat on the floor in front of the screen with my knees up under my chin. When the lights began to flicker across my body, I closed my eyes and waited until I felt his hands on my shoulders. Until I tasted his words, as familiar and comforting as a wood fire in winter. The soundless film made ghosts across his chest, across the scars that ran along his naked legs. Even hair and muscles could not disguise the old wounds, but the black-and-white pictures could. I think that's why he loves this place. Our bodies only a screen, a moving canvas.

18

After, I lay with my head across his thighs, my bad ear pressed against him.

"Are you happy?" he asked. He always asks this after. To make sure.

I nodded, lifting my head to look at the pictures moving across his face.

After I slipped my dress back on and tied the laces on my tennis shoes, as we were walking up the dark theater aisle, Julia opened the door tentatively and peered into the darkness at us. I felt my face turning pink.

"Indie, your sister's on the phone. She says it's an emergency."

Peter squeezed my hand. We followed her down the stairs into the café. I went into Peter's office and closed the door. The phone was resting on his desk, and I thought, *I could leave you there, Lily. I could leave you and Mom on the other end of the line. I could never answer the phone again. What would you do then?*

The phone was cold against my ear. And I wondered for a moment, before Lily knew that I was there, if it might be over.

"Indie?"

I nodded my head silently, waiting.

"I think you should come home now," she said.

"Is she . . ."

"They put her in the psych ward last night. They say she's become a danger to herself," she said, her voice shaking.

I almost laughed. A danger to *herself.* "What are you talking about? I thought you said it was lead poisoning or something. Can't they just treat her for it?"

"It's complicated."

"You mean the treatment?"

Lily's breath was quivering. I imagined her pale and fragile on the other end of the line. A gust of wind could make her whole body tremble.

"Lily?"

"They say she's been doing it to herself."

"What?"

"They said that she's been poisoning herself."

"I don't understand," I said.

"The doctors said that it's nothing environmental, that it's *her*. That it's intentional. They found rat poison in the tests. And other chemicals, things you don't just eat or breathe by accident."

"What does *she* say?" I asked.

"She says they're full of shit. But she's really out of it."

I tried to imagine my mother in a psychiatric ward of a hospital, but when I closed my eyes, I only saw Jack Nicholson in *One Flew Over the Cuckoo's Nest*. My mother didn't fit into this picture, except maybe as Nurse Ratchet, in a starched white uniform, her graying blond hair coming loose from the tight braid she usually wore.

"Last night she started talking to Benny."

I felt as though my heart had become detached from all of my veins and muscles and was floating upward, pulsating in my chest, my throat, my head.

"What do you mean?" I asked, knowing exactly what she meant.

"They called to ask me who Benny was. They told me she was talking to him. Like he was in the room with her," Lily said. I could hear the pain of this catch in her throat.

"How long is she going to be there?"

"I don't know. They want to send her back up north once she's stabilized physically. They want to get her set up with a psychiatrist in Mountainview, to get her on medication, into counseling.

But she can't go up there alone. Somebody has to go with her."

"What am *I* supposed to do?" I asked.

"*I* can't go with her. I need to be here with Violet." She sighed heavily, the weight of a thousand worlds on her shoulders. "I can't do this by myself. I need your help."

Anger welled up, and my dislodged heart found its way to my hands, which throbbed as I squeezed the phone. "Lily, it's not as easy as that. I'm all the way in Maine, for Chrissakes—"

"—and our mother is talking to our dead brother. Not to mention that she's been drinking rat poison with her tea and swallowing eyedroppers of Draino *for Chrissakes*," Lily hissed.

"Fine," I said. "I'll bring her home, but I'm not staying."

"Soon?"

"It's just because of Benny," I said. "I want to hear what she has to say about Benny."

At home, Peter made tea for me and grabbed a beer for himself. We put on mittens and sweaters and sat outside watching the sun melt through the leaves that still clung to the trees. The end of autumn is precarious. A simple storm could rip the colors from the trees, leaving the dull branches exposed.

We'd made a harvest dummy and carved jack-o-lanterns that shared the porch with us. We didn't get trick-or-treaters, but Peter had insisted on a punch bowl filled with candy.

I sat on the step below Peter, holding my mug with both hands, and he wrapped his legs against my sides to keep me warm. The loons that live at the pond up the road had left already. All summer they had called out to each other desperately in prehistoric voices. It was quiet without them.

"What are you thinking?"

I shrugged. There's no way to explain some things to Peter.

No way to articulate the twisting feeling my nerves get every time I am suddenly and involuntarily connected again with my past. My childhood is like an amputee's phantom limb. It's not something someone intact can understand.

"Will you come with me?" I asked and immediately wished I hadn't. I felt his legs stiffen against my sides.

"Ind," he said. "I would, but the restaurant . . ."

"Forget it," I said. "It's fine. I know."

"If you need me to, I suppose I could have Joe watch the place for a few days."

"I *said* it's fine." I turned to look at him.

He lowered his head and kissed my hair. "I'm sorry."

I nodded and suddenly felt guilty. Peter was afraid of flying. It was almost cruel to request this of him. Besides, I didn't really want him to come, didn't even know why I'd asked.

After Peter went to bed, I crawled up the ladder that pulls down from the ceiling in our bedroom and sat at my desk. I picked up the fountain pen that he gave me for my birthday and opened the sketch pad I'd been using to write things down in. The light from the shed shone through the window onto the open pages.

OCTOBER 31, 1999. LOCAL WOMAN ATTEMPTS SUICIDE BY POISON, SURVIVES. Phoenix, Arizona. *Judy Brown is in the hospital tonight after an apparent suicide attempt by ingestion of poison. Detectives found a "virtual arsenal" of poisonous substances in the cabinets of the woman's Mountainview home. Mrs. Brown survived the nearly lethal dose and rests tonight in the psychiatric ward of St. Joseph's in Phoenix. Mrs. Brown is the mother of three children: Miranda Brown, Lily Hughes, and Benjamin Brown, deceased. It is reported that Mrs. Brown was heard speaking to her dead son last night. She was seen, perhaps, staring into the orange glow of the hospital parking lot muttering excuses.*

I tried to picture Ma in some hospital room now, talking to

Benny, but I couldn't imagine what she might have to say to him after all this time. For more than twenty years now she hadn't even said his name, and *sorry* had certainly never been uttered. She probably knew I would be able to taste her lies. More bitter than lead or arsenic on my tongue.

I wasn't born yet when Benny stopped breathing. That was when Benny was a baby and Ma and Daddy were still living in California. She says that Benny got himself tangled up in his blanket. That he was blue. She says that it took her almost twenty minutes to get him breathing again. That if she hadn't been trained in CPR, he was sure to have died. That she breathed her own life into him, and that it was her breath that brought him back.

I imagine my mother, twenty years old, in a nightgown someone gave her for her bridal shower. The nylon probably hadn't worn thin yet. The elastic in the cuffs still tight around her small wrists. I imagine her bare feet on the cold linoleum floor of Benny's room. A mobile with impossibly colored plastic butterflies spinning over his head. I can hear my father snoring softly in the other room, the insistence of mourning doves in the tree outside the bedroom window.

She says she found him blue inside that blue room, the one I vaguely remember sharing with Benny before we left California.

The air was probably heavy that day, a thick marine layer like a gauzy blanket over the rented bungalow. It might have been thick enough to choke a child. At first she might have thought he was only being smothered by the haze. That it had filled his lungs like smoke.

If she hadn't been in nursing school, if she hadn't studied that chapter in the book (each time she tells the story she pauses here), *he would have died*. But what she always leaves out is that her breath wasn't enough. That when she closed her lips over his and blew, part of him was already dead. And the part the sea air killed was the part that would have kept his head from lolling to the side when he was tired. The part that would have kept him from sucking on the edges of his T-shirts or falling down whenever he tried to run. That missing part would have made him like any other kid instead of a *retard*. That word rang in my ears long after I left the playground, holding Benny's hand and making sure he used a tissue to wipe the snot from his nose. *Retard* tasted like the smell of Lily's diaper pail.

The reason we were at the diner was because we had just gotten haircuts. Promises of tuna melts with sweet green pickles and va-nilla shakes were the only way she could convince Benny to hold still, not cry, not scream at the sight or the sound of the scissors. For me, she promised chicken-fried steak and mashed potatoes in return for my long thick braid. For the curls that had become so tangled that summer she couldn't comb my hair without eliciting piercing screams and tears. After the hairdresser cut through the thick rope, my head felt wobbly and light, and I put the braid in the glove compartment of the Nova.

At the diner, Ma gave Benny a quarter to ride the motorcycle out front. He climbed on and pretended to rev the engine. He was big for his age, too big for the ride, but he loved this more than the cold thrill of a vanilla shake on the back of his teeth. When the motorcycle stopped rocking back and forth, Benny's lip started to quiver.

"Let's go in," I said. "You can pick the table."

Ma was in the bathroom with Lily, trying to get her to go. Since Ma had started potty training her, Lily wouldn't go anymore. She'd hold it until she got stomachaches, until Ma would have to take her to the doctor. Lily said she was afraid she'd fall into the toilet. She was also afraid she'd get sucked down the bathtub drain.

"Which one?" I asked Benny.

"The window one!" he said, pointing at a table where three teenagers were sitting, smoking cigarettes.

"We can't sit there. Pick an empty one."

"I want that one," he said, rocking back and forth.

"How about that one over there? You can see the fire station from there."

Benny nodded and went to the booth. Ma came out of the bathroom with Lily, whose face was puffy and red.

"Good girl," Ma said, reaching across the table for a napkin from the dispenser. She blotted Lily's eyes, even though she hadn't been crying. "Lily went number two all by herself," she said proudly.

"Number two, number two!" Benny hooted.

"Shhh," Ma said and put Lily in the plastic baby seat.

"My head feels wobbly," I said, moving my head back and forth. I felt light.

"It looks pretty, honey," Ma said.

"Do *I* look pretty?" Benny asked, shaking his head back and forth. Little pieces of hair that the hairdresser missed fell from his shirt onto the table top.

"*Benny,*" she said.

"Pretty, pretty, pretty," Lily said.

"Yes you are," Ma cooed and pulled a bib out of the blue baby bag. "A pretty, pretty girl."

"I want liver and onions," Benny said to the waitress.

"Benny, why don't you get a tuna melt?" Ma said, tying the bib around Lily's neck.

"Daddy gets liver'n onions," he said.

"I want chicken-fried steak with mashed potatoes," I said. "And a vanilla shake, please."

"I want liver'n onions and pickles," Benny said.

"He'll have a tuna melt," Ma said.

The waitress looked at Benny and then back at Ma. "I think he wants liver and onions," she said.

Ma scowled at the waitress. *Please don't, Ma,* I thought. *Please don't yell at the waitress. Let him get his stupid liver'n onions.* I stared at the checked pattern on the linoleum until I was almost dizzy.

"Fine," Ma said. "And I'll have a tossed salad with cottage cheese. Italian dressing on the side. And some sliced peaches for the baby."

"Pretty," Lily said, pointing one of her chubby fingers at the waitress.

"Thank you, sweetie-pie," the waitress smiled.

Ma snuffed and turned her head, staring out the window at the fire station.

"She's adorable," the waitress said to Ma. Magic words.

Ma turned away from the window and smiled. "Thank you. You know, she's only two and a half but she's already got quite a personality."

After the waitress brought our food, the door opened, jingling, and I looked up from the Arizona map on the place mat. I had been counting all of the places I had been. *Flagstaff. The Grand Canyon. Montezuma Castle.* It was a man and a lady I recognized, but I wasn't sure why. Then I remembered it was one of the nurses who worked with Ma at the nursing home. Ma called her "Miss Snotty-Pants" behind her back, but "Karen" to her face. She was holding hands with some guy with black, black hair. She looked different in bell-bottoms than she did in the starched white uniform she wore at the nursing home.

"Hi Judy," she said and came over to the table. "This is my boyfriend, Larry."

"Nice to meet you," Ma said, holding out her hand and giving one of her whole-mouth smiles.

"This must be Lily," Karen said. "Isn't she an angel? And how are you, Indie? I understand you've become quite a little bookworm."

I felt my face getting hot. Ma was always telling me I should get my nose out of my books and make some real friends. But the way Karen said it made it sound like I was just plain smart.

"And this must be Benny," she said. "Aren't you a fine-looking young man?"

"I got my hairs cut," Benny grinned, pushing his onions around his plate. Then he speared a long, wriggly piece of liver and shoved the whole thing in his mouth.

"I see, I see." Karen smiled and turned to Larry, who was studying the chalkboard menu on the wall. "Where do you want to sit?"

Ma watched Karen and Larry walk away. While she retied Lily's bib, her eyes never left them. Ma could do that—tie my shoes, make me a jelly sandwich, braid my hair, all without paying any attention to what her hands were doing.

I noticed before anyone else did.

Benny's eyes were watering and his chest was heaving. It looked like he was crying, but no sound was coming out. He dropped his fork and his hands flew up to his throat.

"Ma!" I said. She was scooping some cottage cheese onto Lily's peaches.

"Shhh, Indie," she said.

"Benny's choking!" I said, standing up because I didn't know what else to do.

Benny's face had turned from red to white.

"Ma!" I said again, panic like heat.

Ma was looking over toward the table where Larry and Karen were sitting. When she looked at Benny and saw him wriggling in the booth, her face flushed red. She looked quickly back across the room at Karen and Larry.

"Somebody help!" I cried. "My brother's choking!"

Then Ma was up and pulling Benny out of the booth. She got behind him and put her arms around him, balling her hands into a fist at his chest.

"I'm a nurse," Karen said, running back over to our table.

"So am *I*." Ma glared at her and squeezed Benny.

Benny made a horrible animal sound and then something flew out of his mouth and landed on the linoleum a few feet away. It was the piece of liver, gray and slippery. He coughed and cried. He was clutching at the place where Ma had squeezed.

"You may have cracked his ribs," Karen said, horrified.

"He's *breathing,* isn't he?" Ma said, brushing from her eyes a long blond piece of hair that had come loose from her ponytail.

The waitress was staring at the piece of liver like it was a piece of Benny's lungs. Ma bent over and picked it up. She stood there with it dangling between her fingers, like she couldn't figure out what to do with it.

"You okay, Benny?" I whispered.

He nodded, wiping at his tears with the back of his hand. A small, thin string of snot caught on his finger.

"Here, Benny," I said, pulling a handful of napkins from the dispenser and helping him wipe at his nose. I stole a quarter from the tip left in the next booth and handed it to him. "I'll be right out. Go ride."

Benny wiped his runny nose on his sleeve and walked out the door. I looked back to where the teenagers were sitting. One of the boys had his hands curled at his chest, making his face droop and his voice slur.

"You are so immature," the girl giggled and put her cigarette out in her soda.

"I'm retahded," he mumbled, drooling.

My eyes stung.

Ma was still standing in the middle of the floor holding the piece of liver. Karen was sitting down with Larry again. She shook her head and said loud enough for Ma to hear, "She's only a nurse's aid, I don't know what she was thinking."

Ma walked toward the teenagers. I waited for her to say something, to defend Benny. To make the acrid taste of *retarded* go away. But she didn't say anything. She just went straight to Karen's table and gently put the piece of liver down on her place mat. "I may not be an RN, but I can find a pulse. Difference between me and you is I'm not fucking everything with one."

Ma turned her back to them and came back to our table. All of the color had left her face; even her lips were pale.

"Let's go," she said.

Outside, she yanked Benny off the motorcycle ride and pushed him into the backseat of the car. Lily had fallen asleep in my arms. She was heavier in sleep, but I didn't dare to try to hand her to Ma. So I struggled to get her into the car seat all by myself while Ma lit a cigarette in the front seat. I got into the front next to her, and she turned the key. A fire truck turned on its sirens as she peeled out of the parking space. I opened the glove compartment, pulled my braid out, and held it tightly between my fingers.

SILENCE. PETER LEFT while I was sleeping, and in the stillness of early morning it was quiet in the cabin. I could hear Jessica purring at the foot of the bed, the refrigerator humming in the kitchen, a log shifting in the woodstove. The sky outside might have been filling with light, but here in the woods the light of dawn is not strong enough to penetrate the thick foliage. It would be at least eight o'clock before the sun would find me.

The pillow next to me still smelled like Peter, the unidentifiable scent that I might call *home* if I were to smell it outside of our cabin. I rolled over and held the pillow. I buried my face in the smell, and it immediately began to fade. He had left a note on his side of the bed. A yellow piece of legal paper torn carefully in half. I knew the other half was probably on the little desk in the living room. Peter is precise with his placement of things. Nothing is ever lost here.

I turned on the light and tried to decipher his handwriting. The scratches and elongated loops were as familiar to me as my own after all these years. Sometimes I even notice the slant of my own hand beginning to mimic his, becoming his when I am tired. The note asked me to make sure to tell the pilot I was on the plane—an old joke between Peter and me. A ritual to keep me safe. Peter doesn't fly anymore. He hasn't for years. We used to travel back to Arizona to visit Lily and my mother. That was when I was still able to make myself believe that there was normalcy in their lives, that I was just like any other college girl bringing her boyfriend home to meet the family. The last time we flew together was back to Maine after a trip to see my father in California.

It was spring, and below us, the Midwest was being ravaged by tornadoes. Entire neighborhoods were being lifted and spun and thrown down again. But we were high above the storm, resting on clouds. Despite the bumps and dips, I liked the idea of this, as if we might be able to look out the window and stare down into the eye of a cyclone. But Peter was terrified. I could see his lips silently counting the seconds between the bumps, as if counting might somehow help him predict the next jolt. It wasn't until the plane actually dropped, plummeting sharply, and even the flight attendants screamed, that my own heart buckled. In those terrible moments of falling, I recollect only the unfamiliar smell of hotel shampoo in Peter's hair and a small burn on his wrist when I clutched his hand, thinking, *This is the way it ends.* But after, when the plane had stabilized and the pilot came on to explain and apologize in that lighthearted way they always do, I let go of that feeling. It's something you have to do, I suppose. Something to keep yourself from paralysis. But Peter refused to get on an airplane again after that. He says that life is easier when you're afraid of flying. That the world becomes a much smaller and harmless place. Besides, *his* parents still live together on the coast up in Bar Harbor. We can get there in a couple of hours by car whenever we need to.

I got up and went downstairs to the kitchen. I opened up the cupboard and found the kitty treats. Jessica looked at me suspiciously, and I shrugged, tossing her two orange fish-shaped snacks. As the coffee brewed, I searched through the pile of junk on the back porch for my suitcase. I hadn't gone anywhere for so long, I couldn't even remember the last time I had used it. It was the same one I'd had since I left Arizona for college. Finally, I found it under our big red cooler, cobwebs binding it to a mess of cardboard boxes and unused junk.

I carried it into the kitchen and set it on the kitchen table. Only one of the clasps still worked, the lock was broken, and I vaguely remembered having had to duct-tape it together the last time I used it. Inside, the plaid lining was faded and soft. There was an elastic pocket along the back for toiletries, thin leather straps to hold everything in tight. I picked my favorite things from the laundry pile in the mud room. The suitcase was too small to fit even a week's worth of clothes inside, but there was something comforting in this lack of space. A pair of pants, a skirt, less than a week's worth of underwear and shirts. I wasn't planning on staying long. This suitcase wouldn't allow it.

As I closed the one functioning clasp, I thought about Peter's family. Visiting his parents is something we look forward to. Something we plan for. He never gets calls in the middle of the night, threatening calls that force him onto airplanes. The trips to Bar Harbor are something we happily anticipate. The recollection of his father's hands, fisherman's hands, reaching for mine at the dinner table to say grace fills me with longing. The way the doorbell rings and the patter of his mother's slippered feet behind the door, even the way she peeks through the gossamer curtains to see who's there affects a certain gravity on my heart. My favorite visits, though, are when his sister, Esmé, is home from Brown. When we arrive she is almost always sitting on the love seat by the fireplace, her knees curled under her, peering over the top of a book. But when she sees Peter, she tosses the book aside like a banana peel or crumpled-up piece of paper. She loves Peter more than anything in the world. You can see it in the length of her hugs, in the desperate way she clings to him each time we leave. In late August the fields behind their house are filled with blueberries that we bring back with us in his mother's Tupperware. Sometimes I can smell the salty air in my hair for days after a visit.

At night in Peter's childhood room, as we lie curled tightly into each other in the narrow bed, I pretend that this is my home too. After Peter has fallen into the deep abyss of untroubled sleep, I listen to the waves crashing against the rocks, and pretend that this family belongs to me. But every time we visit their little red farmhouse where you can see the ocean from the hayloft in the old barn, I feel unbearably sad. Longing that is deeper than *want*. It's not as simple as desire. It's more like missing something you've never had.

Now I pretended that I was only going to visit Peter's family. This was the only way to get myself through my cup of coffee and out the door.

Chuck Moony pulled up the driveway when I was checking to make sure I had my ticket and my toothbrush. Jessica begged for another treat, and I gave in. She purred and wound herself around my legs and I thought, ridiculously, that she was trying to keep me from leaving. That maybe she intended to tether me here with her fluffy tail.

"Ready?" Chuck asked through the screen door.

"Ready as I'll ever be," I said and joined him on the porch.

Chuck is Peter's best friend. They grew up together in Bar Harbor and moved here together to go to school. Chuck dropped out after freshman year, though, when his mother died. He went back to Bar Harbor to help his dad on the docks. He knows everything in the world about lobster and crabs. About the color of the horizon at the edge of the sea at any time of day or night. He says he could never have learned as much in college anyway. He only came back to Echo Hollow a few years ago after he and his wife, Leigh, got married. I think Peter likes having him close again. There's something nice about having a shared childhood with someone. You don't have to explain a lot of things to each other.

Inside the cab of the truck Chuck handed me a Styrofoam cup of coffee from the Dunkin' Donuts and gestured to a bright pink box on the floor. Inside were a dozen chocolate glazed donuts, my favorite kind. I leaned over and kissed his scratchy cheek. As we backed out of the winding driveway, I watched my red and gold world roll by, curl away from us like feathery smoke from a chimney.

"You need to stop at the Swan?" he asked, turning carefully onto the main road.

"No. We can go straight to the airport."

"Okeedokee," he said and rolled down his window to let some cold morning air into the truck.

"How's Leigh?" I asked. Leigh had just found out she was pregnant a couple of months ago.

"Good." He smiled. "She started making maternity dresses a week ago. There's not much of a point to it. She's still only a hundred pounds."

I laughed.

Chuck usually came by the house at least three nights a week. At the beginning of the summer he started working for a contractor building spec houses, and he would stop by on his way home, still covered with a layer of sawdust. Leigh worked nights, so he'd come alone, carrying grocery bags filled with beer and meat. It was the one thing I looked forward to on those miserable summer days. He and I would sit outside on the porch while Peter marinated the meat and then tended the barbecue. The cold beer cans were relief from the heat, and Peter's meals were small feasts. They would tell stories about growing up in Bar Harbor and I would laugh until my stomach hurt and my cheeks were tired from smiling. But sometimes when Leigh had a night off, he would bring her along too, presenting her to me as if she were a gift, as if female friendships were as easy as proximity. And inevitably she and I would stumble for things to talk about inside while Peter and Chuck sat happily on the porch. She was too quiet, and she never seemed to trust me. When she got pregnant, I was grateful for finally having something to talk about. She would bring along catalogs filled with baby things and we would sit across from each other at the table discussing cribs and bibs. Cloth versus disposable diapers. She even seemed a little less leery of me when I told her that Peter could probably help her make homemade baby food.

When we got on the interstate, my stomach turned from too much coffee and chocolate. It was a long way to the airport, and I hoped that the sharp pains in my abdomen would subside. I shifted around in my seat trying to make it feel better.

"Bellyache?"

"Yeh," I grimaced.

"You want me to stop at the rest stop?"

"Nah," I said. "I'll be fine."

"There's a Tums in the glove box," he said.

"Thanks," I said and found a family-size container behind a bunch of tools.

"Ulcer," he said, clutching his own stomach.

The Tums was chalky on my tongue. I leaned my head against the window and closed my eyes. The breeze from Chuck's open window blew across my forehead. When I opened my eyes, Chuck said, "How's your ma?"

"She'll be fine," I said.

"It must be hard for you."

"What's that?" I asked.

"The way things get switched around. I mean, my ma was the one who always made sure everybody else was okay. You take it for granted, you know? That she'll make cupcakes when it's your birthday. That when you've got a cold she'll put Vicks on your chest. I remember when she got sick it felt weird to have to take care of *her* for a change."

I nodded. Ma had never put Vicks on my chest.

"What do they say, *that's the way the world crumbles?*"

"Something like that," I laughed.

Chuck's mother died when he was only twenty. His father killed himself less than a year later. Chuck found him hanging from a noose made of fishing nets.

He insisted on parking at the airport and walking me to my gate. He even spent ten minutes trying to get through the metal detector. Watch removed, wedding ring, big silver belt buckle. Finally the woman with the magic wand figured out it was his steel-toed boots. He brought me two Egg McMuffins, but my stomach still hurt so he ate both of them. He also came back from the newsstand with a thick *Vogue* that smelled like the perfume counter at the JC Penney and a double-size pack of cinnamon gum. "For your ears," he said.

I opened up the pack and offered him a piece. He smiled and pulled one out. He rolled the silver foil between his thick fingers and chewed.

"How long are you going for?" he asked.

I shrugged. "Not long."

"Promise?" he asked. "You know we'll all miss you."

Until this moment, I hadn't felt like crying. But I could feel tears welling up in the corners of my eyes. He rubbed his knuckles gently across the top of my head. "You better be back before Leigh needs those maternity dresses."

We sat quietly then, watching my plane taxi slowly to the gate. Both of us chewing methodically.

"Look," he said, spitting his gum into his hand suddenly. "I made Jessica."

In the palm of his hand, his little pink wad of chewing gum had been transformed magically into a miniature sculpture of my cat.

"Party trick." He grinned. "I call it Oralgummi."

"I love it," I said, smiling, and he popped the miniature sculpture back in his mouth.

He waited for me to get on the plane, and even then through the porthole window, I could see him standing in the big glass window waiting to make sure the plane took off okay. I knew, too, that he would stand there until he couldn't see me anymore through the clouds.

There was no one waiting for me at the airport in Phoenix. Lily's husband, Rich, had to work, and Lily couldn't go anywhere since Violet got sick. She had suggested I take a taxi, recited directions to her house. I had only been there once, and all of Phoenix looks the same to me. There are no landmarks to help orient yourself. No distinguishing characteristics to differentiate this corner from that corner.

It was early. Because of the time change, it was only 11:00 A.M. I thought about going to the airport bar but then thought better of it. Better to get this over with, I figured. Instead I called Peter at work from a pay phone.

"Hey," I said. "I'm in Phoenix."

"Hi. I've been thinking about you all day. How was your flight?" I could hear kitchen noises in the background. The familiar whirr of the dishwasher. The clean steel sound of knives on butcher-block cutting boards.

"It was okay. I had a couple of Bloody Marys."

"I miss you," he said. "Can I call you later . . . from home? It's a madhouse here."

"Sure," I said. "Miss you."

"Okay, talk to you tonight," he said. His voice was muffled. I could see him with the phone between his ear and his shoulder as he pulled a full pot of soup off the burner using two hands.

When I walked through the sliding glass doors, the heat hit me like a wave. I gasped when the hot air reached my lungs. I had forgotten this intensity, the unbearable weight of the air here. Usually it isn't this hot in Phoenix in November. I felt nauseated and wished I hadn't had so much vodka earlier. The tomato juice was acidic in the back of my throat. Like vomit. The waves of heat and nausea were intensified by the smell of vinyl in the taxi. The sight of Lily's house at the end of a street of identical houses made me almost shudder with relief. I paid the driver and opened the car door, letting in the hot air again, and then walked up the concrete walkway to her door.

"Come in out of the oven." Lily laughed and held the door open for me.

Walking into Lily's house was like walking into a hospital. Everything inside was white. Clean and antiseptic. But beyond the clean bright of blond wood floors, white leather couches, and white curtains was the smell of something sickly. It was cold inside. Refrigerated as if to preserve.

I set my suitcase next to the couch, and Lily gave me a small hug. She was thinner than I remembered. I felt the sharp angles of her ribs against my chest, and the bones in her fingers when she squeezed my hand. Her hair smelled like the perfume she started wearing after she married Rich.

"I'm glad you're here," she said.

"Is she sleeping?" I asked, motioning to the bassinet in the corner of the room. The sound of the air conditioner wasn't as loud as the sound of artificial breath being pumped into Violet's oxygen tent.

"I just put her down a couple of minutes ago."

I walked over to the bassinet and looked down at Lily's baby. I had only seen her once, when Lily and Rich brought her to visit his mother in Boston and then to see us in Maine. She was eight months old now, but she looked as though she had just been born. Her hands were clutching the satiny edges of her blanket. The hair on her small head was only a few white feathers, her skin transparent. The only evidence of blood and breath were the thin blue rivers at her temples.

"How is she?" I whispered, afraid to startle her out of this temporary peace.

Lily shrugged. "The doctors are still doing tests."

"She's pretty," I lied. She looked like the ghost of a child. Like the abandoned cicada skins in the backyard of our Mountainview house.

"We got her pictures done at Penney's a couple of weeks ago. Remind me to give you one before you leave," Lily said, gesturing to a photo on the end table. In the picture, Violet was propped up against a white velvet backdrop. The navy blue dress, all ribbons and lace, contrasted sharply with her colorless face. Inside the bassinet her breath was almost as still as it was in this photo. Frozen.

I sat down on the couch, sank into the cold white leather like the soft palm of a hand. Lily sat across from me in a hardback chair. She looked strange in this room. Strange inside the thin, pale pink sweater and long skirt. No matter how much time goes by, when I think of Lily, I think of her wearing the homemade sequined costumes Ma made, rusty baton in her hand and white vinyl boots. Here, in this white place, she looked like she was playing grown-up.

"How's Peter?" Lily asked.

"Fine," I said. I glanced around the room. The forced air blew the thin curtains. "Lily, how serious is this stuff with Ma?"

Lily looked down at her hands in her lap. "I don't know."

"What exactly is the matter with her?" I sat at the edge of the couch and willed Lily to look at me. "It sounds like one of her games, Lily. It sounds like she's doing this for attention."

Lily looked at me then, her face strained. "It's real. Her doctor says it's *attempted suicide.*"

"Jesus," I said, snorting.

Lily's eyes opened wide. "How would *you* know? You don't live here anymore. You don't even know what's going on in her life anymore. You probably didn't know she's lost like thirty pounds. That she's been calling Daddy and hanging up. Maybe if you weren't so stubborn . . ."

"It's not my fucking fault," I said. "This is all about Ma. This has nothing to do with me."

"I'm just saying that she's depressed. Think about it, Indie. Everybody leaves her. Daddy left her, you left her. I'm the only one who stayed. I'm the only one who . . ." Lily sighed and shrugged her shoulders, a gesture that could have been Ma's. "She's lost everything. She lost Benny and then she lost everybody else."

Heat rose up the back of my neck. In the chill of this room, my skin was on fire.

"I'm just saying that it makes sense. She has nothing. She has nobody except for me. And now, with Violet sick, and me not able to go up there so much, she's alone."

"I'm not sure what you expect me to do," I said.

"I expect you to help her get back home. I expect you to keep an eye on her until she gets a doctor up there. I expect you to be a goddamn human being, to have feelings. She's our *mother*. It's *Ma*."

It sounded like a small explosion, like a firecracker or the sharp crack of thunder.

Lily stood up and walked quickly to Violet's crib. The sound came again, guttural and deep. Thunder, or the rumble of a train. Violet's lungs not strong enough to expel whatever poison was inside. Lily checked the gauge on the oxygen tank and put her hands inside the plastic cocoon to rub Violet's chest.

"Is she okay?" I asked.

"She's *fine*," Lily said, turning around and glaring at me. Standing in the middle of the white living room, she could have been some sort of suburban angel hovering above this sick baby. Her bare feet on the thick, pale carpet the only evidence of the child I once knew.

*H*ERE IS LILY: *grass-stained knees and purple shorts Ma got at the Methodist church rummage sale. Her halter top is stretched across her small chest and she is twirling her baton and walking on her hands. The portable record player is sitting on the front steps to the house, connected to the outlet in the kitchen by Daddy's thick orange extension cord. The record is spinning around and around; the 45 of "Grand Ol' Flag" is scratchy. I know exactly where it will skip. I know exactly how flustered Ma will look when she lifts the arm and sets the needle back down.*

Ma had dragged Lily's stairs from the garage. On the side of the wooden prop, she had used a whole bottle of Elmer's and a whole plastic container of silver glitter to write "Lily Brown" in her pretty handwriting. The steps themselves were covered in bright blue vinyl held down with shiny silver studs.

I was sitting at the kitchen table, trying not to get my legs tangled up the extension cord, pretending to do math. Benny was under the table, peeling the wrappers off of Lily's crayons.

Ma came in the room with a handful of mail. Through the

window, I could see the mailman pulling back down our long driveway, waving to Lily, who was standing on top of the stairs waving.

"Where's your brother?"

"He's not doing nothin', Ma," I said.

"Benny, come out from under there right now. I am losing my patience."

Ma was always losing her patience. I imagined it like a tennis shoe or an earring made of colored glass. Maybe she'd find it someday between the cushions of the couch or in the back of Benny's closet. I don't know why she needed him to come out. She was the reason he was there in the first place.

"Where's your father?" Ma asked, sorting through the pile of bills.

"He's out back," I said, glad she'd decided to leave Benny alone.

It was Saturday, the only day that Daddy didn't work. He owned a bar in town, called Rusty's, and he was at the bar every day except for Saturdays, and sometimes even on Saturday afternoons he'd go in just to check on things. Sometimes he'd bring me with him to play pool. Today, he promised both Benny and me that we could go with him to work. Benny liked the onion rings and the jukebox. I liked the way the sunlight fell across the green felt on the table. I loved the sweet red liquid of a Shirley Temple and the sound of the balls falling after you put a quarter in the slot.

But now, Daddy was in the backyard trying to tame the weeds. The couch that his best friend, Eddie Grand, had brought to us instead of to the Goodwill was still sitting in the backyard. We couldn't get it through the doorway, so Daddy put it out back. Sunflowers had first started to grow up around the couch in August, and by September had started to poke their way up through the cushions. It sat out there all winter and now it was completely tangled up in dead weeds.

Ma put all the mail down except for a manila envelope. She smiled and started to tear it open. She pulled out the contents and sat down at the table. She laid each sheet of paper out neatly across the table, making a shooing motion with her hand toward my math book. I slammed it shut and pushed it aside.

"What came?" I asked, trying to read upside down.

"Shhhh . . ." she said, scanning the first page and then the next.

"Ma . . ."

"It's the entry form for that pageant in Phoenix," she said. "Let me read."

I could feel Benny under the table, hear each wrapper being torn and then discarded. I hoped he wasn't eating the crayons again. Last time he ate Lily's crayons he threw up Burnt Umber and Sea Foam Green all over my bedspread.

"What's a pageant?"

"The Miss Desert Flower contest?" Ma said as if I were terribly dense or something. "For Lily?"

"Oh." I shrugged.

Daddy came into the kitchen then with an armload of tangled weeds. He wrestled them into the garbage and sighed.

"Did we get the electric bill yet?" he asked, noticing Ma and the mail.

"No," Ma said, distracted.

"What's that?" he asked.

"It's the entry form for that pageant in Phoenix I told you about," Ma said, smiling.

Daddy's chin jutted out sharply and he sat down next to me. He put his arm around the back of my chair and peered over my shoulder at the forms.

"When is it?"

"June," she said.

"You're going to take her out of school for this?"

"*No.* It's after school's out."

"I don't think it's a good idea," Daddy said and ruffled my hair as he stood up.

"They offer scholarships to the winners," Ma said loudly, shaking the letter at him. Her face was getting red. I felt Benny get still beneath my feet.

"And how much does it cost to enter this damn thing?"

Ma looked down at her hands, and said softly, "It's only three-fifty. That's for everything including the room."

"Forget it," Daddy said. "We haven't got it."

"Ben, if we cut back a little. I can work some overtime at the home," Ma tried.

"I said *no.*"

I could feel Ma shaking; the table was trembling ever so slightly with her anger. She put her palms flat on the table next to either side of the entry form and stood up.

"*You* said no," she said incredulously.

"Yes."

"You said *no.* And that's the final word?" Ma's voice was starting to grow. Like weeds growing around me, holding me in my chair. The sharp blossom of her words startling. "Asshole."

Daddy looked hard at Ma and then turned his back. Benny held on to my ankle. I could feel his fingers digging into the skin right above my tennis shoe. I reached for my math book, but Ma beat me to it. She picked up the book and waved it over her head and then hurled it at Daddy. It whizzed over his head and hit the wall where her collection of spoons from around the world was hanging. The wooden case rattled and then fell. There were spoons from Japan and Spain and Canada all over the floor.

"I'm going to work," Daddy said softly and kissed the top of my head. My eyes stung with tears. He'd promised he'd take me later so that I could practice my bank shots.

"You leave and I won't be here when you get home," Ma said, following him to the door. "I'll take the money, and I'll take Lily, and I'll go to Phoenix."

Benny's hand released my ankle and I felt my blood rushing hot out of my face, down my arms and legs. I imagined it spilling in a pool of Brick Red wax at my feet.

When Ma ran out of the house after Daddy, Benny scurried out from under the table. There were toast crumbs from breakfast still at the corners of his mouth.

"Ma's going to take Lily away?"

"Shhh," I said and took his hand. We scurried quickly out the back door and around to the side of the house.

Daddy got in the car and slammed the door shut. I heard the engine rev and then he was backing slowly down the driveway. Lily was standing at the edge of the yard holding her rusty baton with one hand, sucking her thumb with the other.

"I'll leave you!" Ma said. "I'll leave this shit hole. I'll go back to California!"

She stood in the doorway as Daddy and the Nova became just a small orange spot moving through the trees. And then she started to slam the screen door. Over and over. Each time it crashed against the door frame, Benny put his hands over his ears. Again and again she slammed the door until one of the hinges came loose and rattled down the front steps. She bent over and picked up the hinge. She looked at it for a second and then threw it into the driveway.

Ma sat down on the steps and Lily came over to her, still sucking her thumb, and curled up in her lap. She was too big for this. Her legs were long now; they dangled down to the very last step.

Benny had disappeared. Hiding, probably. I sat down with my back against the house, plucking at the thick blades of grass, listening to Ma croon, *We'll go away, Lily. We'll go away someday.*

L ILY HAS ALWAYS BEEN prettier than I am. I knew this from the time that I could differentiate her reflection from my own in the cracked mirror in the bathroom. Before I had the words, I knew that she was *beautiful* and that I was *plain*. But this was before I understood the implications of my plainness. Before I understood that despite attempts at fairness, parents are bound to love their beautiful children more. That homely children are not touched in the same way that their more attractive siblings are. That tenderness has less to do with love than with the softness of skin or with large blue eyes and cupid's-bow lips.

Even now as I watched Lily making dinner, I found myself making the usual comparisons, categorizing the differences between us. Hair, eyes, the gentle curve of her shoulder or wrist. Lily's thick blond hair was pulled up and tethered by a velvet scrunchy. Her neck long and her skin pale. Even at twenty-nine and only eight months after Violet was born, her body was still long and straight like a boy's. Her bones were small, like a bird's.

Her eyes were so large and deep-set, they might be startling to someone who wasn't so familiar with the intricacies of her face.

"Do you still eat meat?" Lily asked without turning away from the counter.

"Gawd yes," I said. The Swan was mostly vegetarian (that was the latest trend in town) but Peter and I were absolutely rabid when it came to a good steak.

Lily, like my mother, has always been a good cook. I remember my mother's futile attempts to teach me. It wasn't that I didn't like to; it was just that I was so easily distracted. She gave up when I first swore I'd remember and then promptly forgot to check on a tuna casserole we were making. She found me lying on my stomach watching TV nearly two hours after I was supposed to take it out. I remember her standing there with oven mitts on and the room smelling of burnt tuna. She dumped the whole thing into the garbage and never let me help her in the kitchen again.

But Lily loved to be in the kitchen with Ma. She even had a miniature apron that Ma had made with purple and white checks, purple rickrack trim, and a pocket shaped like a heart on the front. Lily made little loaves of bread and little pies. Daddy almost always ate at the bar, but on Saturdays Lily would present him with some sort of casserole or meat on a TV tray so that he could watch basketball and eat at the same time. I'd curl up next to him on the couch and we'd eat while Lily watched to make sure that he was enjoying it.

Tonight, the ingredients were more expensive. The pots and pans not the kind we had growing up: copper instead of the burnt-bottom stainless steel ones in Ma's kitchen. Lily's appliances were cleaner and shinier. Black espresso maker, pasta maker, Cuisinart. None of them looked like they had ever been used.

"Do you want a hand?" I asked Lily. She had finished making the marinade for three thick red steaks and was peeling potatoes.

"No thanks," she said.

"I've gotten better," I said. "Peter's been teaching me how to bake." I thought about the plastic containers in the bakery clearly marked *Wet* and *Dry*. I didn't have to do too much besides mix them together and then add berries or bananas to the mix. I don't know why they never seemed to come out right. "He still does all of the cooking, though."

"Why don't you open a bottle of wine or something?"

"Sure," I said. I needed something to do with my hands. I also needed a drink. "Red or white?"

"We're having steaks, so how about a Merlot?"

I glanced quickly at a row of wine bottles in a beautiful wrought-iron wine rack on the counter until I found the word *Merlot* on one of them. I removed it carefully from the rack and Lily handed me a corkscrew. We never had wine in our house growing up. Daddy drank beer, and when Ma drank, it was always bourbon.

"I've never been very good at this," I said. "But let me give it a shot."

I twisted the corkscrew and then started to press down on the silver arms like wings. The cork promptly dropped into the bottle. Pungent wine splashed into my face and on my T-shirt. "Shit," I said. "Sorry."

Lily turned away from the potatoes. "It's okay," she said, grabbing a sponge from the sink and wiping furiously at the counter top. Long after all of the wine had been soaked up, Lily kept running the sponge across the smooth granite surface. She made one last swipe and tossed the sponge into the garbage bin under the sink.

"I'm really sorry," I said.

"It's okay. I'll open another one. Are you hot?" She went to the wall and adjusted the air conditioner. I felt a cold gust of artificial air blow across the back of my neck. Then she gracefully and silently pulled the cork from another bottle of Merlot and poured me a glass. I took a long swallow and felt the wine warming me against the chill in the air.

Rich came home just as I was about to sneak upstairs and find a sweater in one of Lily's closets. Lily met him at the door and ushered him past Violet, who had finally fallen asleep, into the kitchen.

"Indiana Jones," Rich said and hugged me. I have always liked Rich. He reminds me a lot of Daddy. His family is from Boston, hard workers. He went straight to work after high school for his dad's construction company. He worked his way up until he was foreman and then when his dad died, he and his brother took over. He opened up the Phoenix branch of the company to be near Lily. He and Lily met on a cruise that he took his mother on after his father's funeral. The story of how they met is one of those stories that makes me think of a photo spread in one of the magazines Lily read when she was in junior high and I was in high school. It is dimensionless. Colorful and smiling, but flat and glossy. Forgettable. He simply saw her sipping on a piña colada at the end of an outdoor bar and thought she looked like an angel. He told her so, and one year later he had relocated to Phoenix and they were on the same ship on their honeymoon. It makes me laugh to remember how Peter and I met when I hear stories like these. The story of how we fell in love is more like the crackly black-and-white films that Peter shows at the theater than the pink, lavender, blue of Lily and Rich's romance.

"When did you get in?" Rich asked and pulled a beer out of the refrigerator.

"This morning."

He popped the top off and just as he was about to set it on the counter, Lily glared at him, and he scooted past her to put the cap in the trash. Lily was amazing. When Peter and I moved from our apartment into the cabin, I found about a hundred bottle caps underneath cushions and behind books on shelves.

"Have you been by the hospital yet?" he asked.

I shook my head. I watched Lily stiffen.

"Rich, can you get the candleholders out?" she asked. The steak crackled under the broiler. Lily emptied a pint of sour cream into the bowl of potatoes.

Rich smiled at me and squeezed my shoulder. He handed me the candleholders, which I arranged in the center of the table, and he set down three plates from Lily's china cabinet. They were white with the faintest raised flowers at the center. I couldn't imagine her letting red meat touch these plates.

"You're driving her up to Mountainview?" Rich asked.

"Yeh," I smiled. "I am *not* looking forward to it, either."

Rich has been in our family long enough to know about Ma's tendencies toward drama. I've always been able to count on Rich as an ally when Ma did this kind of thing. While Lily cried into her hands or took Ma into another room to calm her down, Rich and I would smoke cigarettes in Ma's backyard. We'd been through this before.

"Better not leave her alone when you stop for gas." Rich chuckled softly. "She might get thirsty."

I stifled a laugh. It felt good to make fun. It made this less absurd. Less insane.

Lily turned around. Her face was red, the platter of steaks was trembling in her hands. I concentrated on the meat so that I wouldn't laugh.

"Just kidding." Rich shrugged. "Sorry."

"How's the company doing?" I asked quickly.

"Great. Summer's over, so the guys are happy. You'd never

believe what a difference there is between a hundred-fifteen degrees and ninety degrees."

"I can imagine," I said.

Rich lit the candles with a lighter from his pocket. When Lily reached into the fridge for the butter, he pretended to suck out the lighter fluid.

Lily turned around and saw him. She slammed the mashed potatoes on the table. "Enough!"

She sat down and put her napkin in her lap. I watched her eyes brim with tears and then spill. She didn't move her hands to her face to stop them.

"This looks great," Rich said and reached for her hand.

Lily stared at her plate.

He cut into his steak. Red juice spilled out from the middle. He speared a thick pink piece and put the whole thing in his mouth. "It *is* great."

Lily wiped quickly at the tears and smiled at him weakly.

Then, in the other room Violet's chest rumbled and I watched Lily's glance dart quickly toward the living room. She lay her fork across the plate and strained her neck to listen. She stayed like this until the danger of another explosion seemed to have passed.

I feigned jet lag so that I wouldn't have to stay inside that cold living room after Lily had started the dishwasher and blown out the candles.

"You sure you don't want some bread pudding?" she asked, scooping a warm spoonful of our mother's bread pudding into a glass bowl. "It'll help you sleep."

"Nah," I said. "I'm pooped."

"I just made up the bed," Lily said. "Ma was the last one to stay here."

I followed her up the stairs, noting how she walked on the balls of her feet as she passed by the living room.

"Night, Rich," I said, peeking in at him. He was sitting on the couch next to Violet's bassinet, flipping through the channels. He was still wearing his work clothes. His tie was loosened, though, and he had slipped off his loafers. He had a new beer on the coffee table, resting carefully on one of Lily's marble coasters.

"Night, Indie," he said softly. "Sleep tight."

"Shh . . ." Lily said, pointing at Violet and shaking her finger.

Lily showed me to the guest room and waved her hands around, gesturing to everything I might need. "There are clean towels in the closet, extra blankets and pillows. If you get hot you can adjust the air here. I usually keep it at 65 degrees. I've been sleeping downstairs with Violet, so if you need anything, come get me. You might wake up in the middle of the night if you're jet lagged. Help yourself to some of the bread pudding. I don't sleep much, so you won't wake me up."

"Jeez, Lily, stop. I'll be fine. Thank you."

She looked flustered, and then she peered toward the open door.

"What's the matter?"

"Nothing," she said.

"Is this about dinner?"

"I'm *fine*." She pulled back the blanket and fluffed the pillow.

"Thanks," I said, yawning.

"There are more blankets in there," she said, suddenly irritated. "Sleep tight."

After she left, I lay down on the hard bed. The walls, even in the darkness, were bright, reflecting the street lamp outside. The sheets were crisp to the point of being uncomfortable. I imagined Lily spraying them with starch and ironing then stiff and flat. I closed my eyes and concentrated on the noises of this house. I missed the sound of the woods. The sound of Peter breathing and the smell of a fire burning in the next room. Above me, the ceiling fan spun the stagnant air. And beyond that, I could hear the whirring of the dishwasher, the whirring of the air conditioner, the whirring of their hushed voices indistinguishable from the voices on the TV. I fell asleep listening to the sound of oxygen being forced into Violet's lungs.

I woke up in the middle of the night to a familiar sound. It sounded like branches tapping against the windows of the cabin during a storm. I reached first for Peter and then, remembering where I wasn't, sat up disoriented and blinked my eyes until they focused in the dark room. The sound was coming from outside, but there were no trees in Lily's yard. There was only a cactus, and gravel scattered to fill the spaces where grass should be.

I got out of bed, covered my shoulders with a blanket, and walked down the hallway. The thick carpeting on the stairs was soft on my feet, different from the cold wooden floors of the cabin. But at least the floors at home were solid. I felt as if I might sink into the carpet here, that I might easily be swallowed in the creamy pile.

There was a soft light coming from the living room. I thought Lily might be feeding Violet, that I might be intruding. I was afraid I might have stumbled into that hour of night when Lily and her baby were the only ones awake in the house. It was difficult to imagine Lily cradling Violet in her arms, though. Even in pregnancy Lily had lacked that certain indescribable quality I have always equated with motherhood (the slight blush of a cheek, the certain swell and softness of the body). Leigh Moony's face was already beginning to turn that particular shade of blush, even just a couple of months into her pregnancy. Her bones were not so angular anymore. But Lily had retained her pale cold skin and sharp angles throughout. I saw her once in the early months when I came out for one of Ma's false alarms. Then later, after Violet was born and Lily brought her to Maine. By then the small swell of her breasts had already disappeared; she'd let her milk dry up, opting for the cans of formula and clean glass bottles instead. I had noticed after dinner that her dish rack was full of sterilized glass bottles and rubber nipples.

Lily wasn't in the living room, and Violet was silent in the crib. I peeked at her and watched her for several moments, looking for some indication that she was still breathing, for the faint rise and fall of her chest.

There was a light on outside, illuminating the back patio. Beyond the reflections the light in the living room made on the sliding glass door, I could see the faint outline of Lily's patio furniture. White wicker chairs and a glass-topped table.

I glanced at Violet and then slid the door open slowly. A rush of warm air hit my face. It had to have been thirty degrees warmer outside than it was in the house. It felt like going inside the cabin after sledding or skiing on a winter afternoon in Maine. At first I didn't see Lily, and thought that maybe she had just left the light on to ward off burglars. Maybe she was in the kitchen fixing a bottle or some warm milk for herself. Then I heard that scraping, brushing sound again and saw a flash of Lily's hair. What I hadn't noticed until now were the tumbleweeds, a virtual forest of mangled branches. The entire backyard was littered with them, some as tall as Lily. I could hear her grunting as she pulled them apart, cutting them with a pair of hedge clippers. From the patio I watched her fighting the tumbleweeds as if she were in the jungle instead of her own backyard. My heart started to beat loudly when I heard her cussing.

"Goddamnit," she whispered. "Fucking weeds. Shit."

I thought about turning around and going back inside the house, but she was so close now she would have been able to hear me sliding the door open again.

I coughed softly.

"Jesus," she said, startled, as she appeared from behind one particularly large tumbleweed. She held her hand to her chest as if to keep her heart from escaping.

"Sorry," I said. "What are you doing?"

She shoved the tumbleweed aside and came to the patio. Despite the heat, she was dressed from head to toe in black. Black turtleneck, black jeans, and thick black gloves.

"Trying to get rid of these damn things," she said pulling off the gloves.

I raised my eyebrows at her and motioned to her clothes. "Why are dressed like that? You look like a criminal."

"You wouldn't believe how prickly they are. The first time, I came inside all scratched up. My legs and hands were a mess for a whole week."

"It's one-thirty in the morning," I said.

"Did I wake you up?"

"No. But can't this wait until morning? Have you slept at all?"

"I have to wait until nighttime because it's too hot to dress like this during the day." She sat down in one of the wicker chairs and cocked her head to the side, to get a crick out of her neck.

"Lily," I said. "I'm worried about you."

"Don't be."

"I'm serious. You're all wound up."

"I am not wound up."

"What about dinner?" I persisted. "Rich and I were just kidding around."

"You and Rich are cruel," she said.

"It was all in fun."

"You think this is fun? You think any of this is fun?" Lily waved her arms toward the house, toward the tumbleweeds, toward me.

"I'm just saying that sometimes you need to let go for a second. You need to be able to step back. Rich is only—"

"Rich . . ." she started. "Rich isn't dealing with this very well."

"The stuff with Ma? Come on. He's been down this road before. This is classic Ma. Making fun *is* his way of dealing," I said.

"Not with *Ma,*" Lily said, her voice cracking. "With Violet."

"What are you talking about?"

"Nothing," she said and pulled off her gloves. Her hands were small and white on the glass tabletop. She looked at me intently. "He thinks I'm overreacting. He thinks it's not as bad as it is."

"I don't understand," I said. "He seems very concerned."

"He doesn't come with me to her appointments, he won't help with her medicine at home. . . ."

"I'm sure he's just scared," I said. I remembered Rich holding Violet right after she was born. At the beach in Maine, he shielded her from the cold wind with his whole body. I remembered the way her small fingers curled desperately around his thumb.

"And then that crap at dinner. It's like he thinks everything is a joke."

"That was about Ma, Lily. That had nothing to do with Violet."

Lily stared into the dark backyard.

"Besides, they'll figure out what's wrong soon enough and then she'll be fine," I tried.

"She really *is* sick," Lily said then, loudly. She turned to look at me and something like fear flashed across her eyes. Her hand flew to her lips and fluttered there, a strange, long-winged butterfly hovering in front of her face.

"I didn't say she wasn't, Lily. Jesus."

I left her in the backyard and returned to the cold room, cold sheets, cold air spinning over my head. Leaning over and picking up the phone, I knew that Peter would have already left for the café. I imagined he was probably deciding which films to show for the day. He might have had Joe mull some cider to ward off the autumn chill. As the phone rang, I closed my eyes and thought about cinnamon and cloves and sharp blue autumn skies. I imagined Jessica, woken from sleep, covering her ears with her paws. But when the machine picked up, I couldn't think of a thing to say and hung up the phone. I lay back down on the unforgiving sheets. Outside the tumbleweeds crackled and I perched at the edge of sleep all night, peering down at the dreams that would not come.

1972. I don't know now if this is true or only a vaguely recollected nightmare that has lingered too long. But I do know this: cold linoleum on my bare feet, the glare of the bathroom bulb in the middle of the night, and the way my mother's hair spilled like lemonade over her shoulder as she knelt next to Lily on the bathroom floor.

The maze of the Mountainview house is more complicated in my dreams. The hallways are wider and the doors lead to rooms that were never there. Shades drawn reveal landscapes inconsistent with the aspen, pine, oak of my childhood. Sometimes I see night through the glass, sometimes I see California ocean, desert red and long stretches of impossible green (and I don't know if it is grass or water or the velvet expanse of an old green dress of Ma's I found in the closet one day). I could get lost in this dream house, while in reality there were few places to hide. Awake, getting lost was a futile task. I knew what could be found behind each door. I knew which ones to open and which must be left closed.

Tonight, I am barefoot and wandering through this jigsaw house. This puzzle of orange daisy wallpaper, blue shag carpeting, and the fake marble countertops that peel back like stickers when I pick at the edges. I am barefoot and I will not wet the bed tonight. I will not make that dream trip down the dizzying, eagle-after-eagle-after-eagle wallpaper hallway to the bathroom only to wake up drenched in my own sour pee. It was the sound of the plastic mattress pad that woke me, reminded me that I must not do that ever again.

The sound of my feet across the kitchen floor makes me think of rain against glass. I concentrate on the way my heels, toes, heels, toes make rain in the midnight kitchen.

The door to Ma and Daddy's room is wide open, not locked shut, not locked tight with yelling voices behind. It is open like the inviting lid of a toy box, like the lid on my crayon box, and it is impossible not to look inside. Daddy looks like a big bear on the bed. He is spread out across the mattress and his back is so wide I could spread my whole body across it if I wanted to. The white bedspread with the pills I can't help but pluck off when I get sent here to nap or to cry is crumpled up at the foot of the bed. Daddy doesn't like any covers on his feet. Not even in wintertime.

I can feel the need to pee like a heart thudding softly in my stomach. I put my hands between my legs and push the nightie up tight, concentrating on the soft flannel on my naked skin. Eagle after eagle after eagle, and there is yellow light coming out from under the bathroom door.

"Ma," I whisper. "I gotta go. . . ." I hadn't worried that I might need to wait.

She doesn't answer me and I put my hands on the door, lean into the door and whisper, "Ma. I don't wanna pee my bed again. I got up so I wouldn't pee my bed."

Again, I can't hear anything inside. I push gently, knowing that if she's sitting on the toilet like last time, I'll get spanked. I'm certain that if I find her sitting at the edge of the toilet, leaning toward the roll of toilet paper that's teetering on the edge of the sink instead of on the roll where it is supposed to be, then there is bound to be trouble. But not more than if I wet my bed. Not more than if I wake up with my nightie soggy around my hips.

The door opens real slow, orange daisies orange daisies orange daisies and the yellow yellow glow of a bare bulb hanging still and bright in the center of the room. I think at first that Lily is only sleeping, sprawled across the floor like Daddy sprawled across the bed. Her nightie is yanked up under her arms, her face buried in the fuzzy orange bath mat. But I can hear her crying and Ma has got something in her hands, a tube that is connected to Lily's bottom, a bag of water at the end like the kinds you see on *All My Children* when someone's in the hospital. And Ma is kneeling next to her, her hair spilling like lemonade across one shoulder. She is pushing the tube into Lily, holding her butt to keep her still. But Lily doesn't scream, she only grabs handfuls of orange carpeting from the bath mat. I can see it between her fingers. *Hold still, baby. Hold still.*

I stand in the orange-daisy yellow, bare-bulb light of the midnight bathroom and stare at Ma's hands working quickly, making that tube disappear. And I know that whatever Ma is doing to Lily is worse than anything she might do to me if I wet the bed.

I must have made a sound, because Ma turns her head and sees me there, stands up so quick she bangs her head on the light bulb. "Shit," and it is swinging and the light is flashing off and on like when Daddy plays Monster in the living room at night (until Ma reminds him about the lightning). Then it goes completely dark and Ma is cussing softly. And then all I smell is the dark, awful smell of excrement. The terrible, earthy smell of when the dog next door gets loose and messes in the yard, the stink of the bathroom after Daddy on Sunday mornings. I feel my stomach turning and then I can't hold it anymore. The pee is hot on my leg. It runs all the way down one side and then pools underneath my foot.

I feel Ma's hands on my back pushing me out the door. *I'm giving Lily her medicine, Indie. Go back to bed.* And she is pushing me so hard that she must not even notice that I wet myself.

When I am back out in the hallway, the light goes on again under the crack in the door, and Ma is whispering to Lily. *It's okay, honey. You'll be better soon. Everything will be okay.*

In this particular dream, I cannot find the puzzle piece that explains what Ma was doing to Lily inside the orange daisy room in the middle of the night. So, instead I grab a dark jagged piece from the puzzle box and make it fit into that crack under the door so I don't have to see the bright light or hear my mother's apologies.

I GOT UP EARLY, just past six o'clock, but Rich had already left for work. Lily had squeezed fresh orange juice with oranges from the tree in the front yard. There were eggs Benedict with hollandaise sauce and fresh paprika sprinkled on top of perfectly round poached eggs. Freshly ground coffee with real cream.

"What time do you want to go to the hospital?" I asked.

"Rich said he'll take you when he comes home for lunch," Lily said, refilling my juice glass.

"You're not coming with me?"

"I really can't leave," she said. "I should stay here with Violet."

"Why doesn't Rich watch her?" I asked. I held my fork tightly and stared at Lily, who would not look at me.

She shook her head. "Besides, you'll just pick her up and bring her back here. The hospital's close. It'll only take a couple of minutes. Ma knows I'm not coming."

"Did you talk to her?" I asked, wondering how I could have

missed this conversation unless Lily was on the phone with Ma in the middle of the night.

"I called the hospital this morning to find out what time they were going to discharge her. They said she'd be ready at noon."

"I really wish you would come with me. I'm not sure I want to do this on my own."

"You won't be alone," Lily said, smiling. "Rich will go with you. Ma likes Rich, though I have no idea why."

I watched her to see if she might give in. The hard veneer of her expression did not change. She merely blinked her eyes quickly like she always does when she wants to dismiss something.

I poked the sharp tines of my fork into the resistant egg, and the yellow center ran thickly over the pink disk of Canadian bacon and perfectly toasted English muffin. But when I raised the forkful to my lips, I couldn't eat. The egg white made me nauseous and I set the fork back down.

"I'm really not hungry," I said.

"Fine," Lily said angrily and pulled the plate away from me.

Rich drove cautiously toward the hospital. With the windows rolled up to keep the hot air outside, I could smell his cologne. Like Lily's perfume, there was something terribly noxious about this scent. It was more masculine than Lily's, with a slight musk to it, but it was still pungent. I thought of the scent of pine in Peter's jacket.

Rich seemed hesitant to turn on the radio.

"Go ahead," I nodded when he motioned tentatively to the stereo. "I'm easy."

There are a million stations in Phoenix. At the cabin we get the college station, and if we put the antenna out the window we can sometimes pick up a couple of stations in Portland. Here there were too many choices. Rap music thudded violently under my feet, and then he switched quickly to something else. Country twang, and then a talk show. For five minutes we filled the empty space between us with the white noise of too many decisions. He shrugged finally and turned the stereo off.

"Lily woke me up last night," I said.

"Was she outside wrestling tumbleweeds again?"

"I don't think she's sleeping very well."

"She's not sleeping at all," he said, turning to me and frowning. "She's been battling those tumbleweeds for weeks, and every time we get a dust storm they roll back in. And when she's not up with the tumbleweeds she's taking showers. Three or four a night. I hear the water come on and I think, *She's already clean. What's she doing?*" He chuckled a little and then his voice grew soft, "She hasn't slept in our bed for months."

I pulled the visor down to shield my eyes.

"I know she's worried about Violet and now your mom," he said. "But she's not herself anymore. She's pissed off all the time. Everything I say sets her off. Like it's my fault or something."

"Like what's your fault?"

"I don't know. Violet being sick maybe. Her not being able to sleep." He shrugged his shoulders and smiled.

"That's ridiculous," I snorted.

"I really don't know what to do," he said. "She won't let me help. She hardly lets me near Violet. I try to go to the doctor's appointments with her, but she doesn't want me to come."

I opened my mouth in disbelief, remembering what Lily had said about him not taking her seriously.

"I know, it's crazy," he said apologetically.

I nodded, but didn't say anything my conversation with Lily. Somehow it seemed safer to agree with his confusion than compound it by telling him that Lily was a liar.

"How's the restaurant?" he asked, smiling and turning to look at me.

"Good," I said, grateful. "I've been making muffins."

We parked the car and walked through the thick, hot air to the hospital entrance. Inside, I found the elevator and looked at Rich, who seemed similarly uncomfortable here.

"You can stay down here in the lobby if you want," I said.

"You sure?" he asked, though I saw his shoulders relax, releasing the anxiety he must have felt.

I nodded.

When the elevator doors opened, I stepped out and held the door open for a doctor who was running down the corridor. He was dressed from head to toe in blue scrubs. His shoes were covered in what looked like shower caps. His face mask was like a bandana around his neck.

"Thanks," he smiled.

I had walked only a short distance down the corridor when I realized that I was on the wrong floor. I stopped in front of a big glass window and looked in at the newborns. I have never wanted to be a mother, but I have always been fascinated by babies. Especially new ones. I love their smell and the way their eyes dart from one color or shape or flash of movement to the next. I crossed my arms and peered at the rows and rows of incubators. And then suddenly my hand flew to my mouth.

In one incubator, a baby no larger than my own fist lay trembling. In the next incubator there was an infant whose skin was yellow with jaundice, its eyes sealed shut like a kitten's. These were not the healthy ones, not the rosy-cheeked ten pounders named Ashley and Joshua. These were the sick babies, the crack babies still shuddering from the impact of their mothers' violent wombs. These were the babies without names whose eyes were set wide apart from the liquor or heroin in their mother's blood. The ones who were missing fingers or toes. The ones who had had only enough nourishment to grow to the size of lemons inside their mother's reluctant bellies.

I pressed my hands against the glass and allowed my eyes to focus on the shuddering baby in the far corner. There were tubes going in and out of every orifice, a blue knit cap on its head. Compared to these babies, Violet looked like the picture of health. Her stuttering breath would go unnoticed inside these vibrating glass walls.

As a candy striper passed with a rolling cart filled with food trays, I felt a wave of nausea rush over me like the car sickness I felt as a child. Uncontrollable, completely overwhelming. I backed away from the glass and ran back down the hallway to the elevator. Inside, I stared at the numbers above the door so that I would not have to see the blood-splattered blue pajamas of another doctor, I counted the floors and tried not to remember the other times I'd been in the hospital.

The psychiatric ward didn't look much different from the neonatal ward. It was quiet here. Quiet and green. The walls were pale and moss-colored, and there were fake plants perched precariously on every counter. I walked past the solarium, looking for Ma's room, and a voice followed me. "Indie?"

I stopped and stepped back, peeking my head into the room, windows and plants filtering the Arizona sunshine. A large-screen TV and two blue couches. My mother set down a magazine and stood up.

She wasn't dressed yet. She was wearing a soft pink robe, similar to one I saw hanging on the back of Lily's bathroom door. Her hair was down, past her shoulders, blond with curly silver strands making it appear messier than it actually was. Her skin was pale, transparent, and stretched tightly across the sharp bones of her face and fingers.

"Ma," I said as if to confirm that she was, indeed, my mother. She smiled, the skin of her lips pulling back tightly against her teeth. She held out her arms then, gesturing for me to come closer.

"Ma, you look terrible."

"Thanks," she said bitterly.

"I thought you were being released today," I said. "I came to bring you back to Lily's. Rich is downstairs."

She looked absently out the window at the polluted Phoenix skyline and shrugged.

"Ma," I said, annoyed. "We came to bring you home."

"I think I should probably stay until they get the latest blood work back," she said. "I'm very ill."

"I know," I nodded. "But the doctors told Lily you could be released this afternoon."

"Maybe." She sighed and sat down on the couch. Her bare knee peeked out through the folds in the robe, sharp like a stick instead of a bone.

"Where's your doctor?" I asked.

"It's something in the house," she said softly. "Asbestos. I think your father put asbestos in the walls to poison me."

I felt my knees grow weak. I sat down across from her. I felt like I was looking at a child. She was thinner than Lily. Her hands were shaking.

"Where's your doctor, Ma?" I said again.

"He doesn't know a goddamn thing!" she said loudly, startling me. "They're all fucking quacks here. They tried to tell Lily I did this to myself. They tried to blame it on me."

Her eyes were big and wet, turning the same shade of blue as Lily's as they filled with tears.

"It's okay, Ma. You stay here and let me go find your doctor."

She looked out the window as an airplane flew overhead.

"Ma, promise me you won't go anywhere."

She didn't look at me but nodded slowly.

I left the solarium and went to the front desk. A nurse was talking softly on the phone. She was twirling a strand of hair that had come loose from the chipped white bobby pin that held her cap on.

"Excuse me," I said.

She raised her eyes and looked at me, irritated. She covered the phone with her hand. "Can I help you?"

"I need to find my mother's doctor. Her name is Judy Brown. She's in two-eighteen."

"That would be Dr. LaVesque in Toxicology," she said and uncovered the phone. She started whispering into the phone again.

"Excuse me, I need to know who her doctor is for *this* ward," I said.

"She's been released," the nurse said again, slapping her hand against the mouthpiece of the phone again.

"She has not been released. She is sitting in her robe in the room down the hall."

"The paperwork was signed this morning. She is under Dr. LaVesque's care as an outpatient."

I rode the elevator down to the lobby. When the doors opened, I was briefly tempted to walk out the front door and go straight to the airport. To leave Rich and Ma in the hospital. To get on the next plane back to Maine. Instead I walked to the lobby, where I found Rich reading a *Reader's Digest* and chewing the edges of a Styrofoam coffee cup.

"What's the matter?" he asked.

"Can you help me figure out what's going on?"

When he took my arm, I felt a lump growing thick in my

throat. "They're giving me the runaround, and Ma's still got her robe on."

He pulled me into him as if to shield me from something and muttered, "We'll get it all figured out. Don't worry. It's probably just a mix-up. These hospitals are so big they can hardly keep track of who's coming and who's going."

I closed my eyes to fight the sting of tears. But on the back of my eyes all I could see were my mother's long fingers reaching for me. The pink of her robe and the exposed bones that used to be her legs.

Ma was just confused. She had even signed the release papers, but she hadn't gotten dressed. Her doctor explained to Rich while I helped Ma pack her bag that her records were being transferred to the Mountainview hospital, and that she was to check in with the referred psychiatrist when she got there. The toxins were gone from her body now. Dialysis had replaced her poisoned blood with clean blood. They had flushed the poison out of her. The only lingering effects were the weakness of her joints and muscles. Fatigue.

Ma sat in the front seat of the car with Rich, and I stared at the back of her head all the way back to Lily's. I could see when she had stopped bleaching her hair; there was a good inch of silver roots at her part. Rich talked softly to Ma about Lily and Violet, about the heat, and about what Lily might be making for dinner. I watched the cars whizz by us on the freeway, wishing that Rich would get us home quicker, that I could get out of this crowded place that smelled vaguely of poison.

When we pulled onto Rich and Lily's street, I saw Lily standing on the front porch holding Violet. She was barefoot, and her hair was loose around her shoulders. Tangled. Her shoulders were shaking, her face was absolutely white, and the tracks of her tears were like fresh scars.

"Jesus," Rich said, pulling into the driveway and throwing open the car door.

Ma sat motionless in the front seat, and I stared out the tinted window at the strangely altered colors of this scene. At their blue hands and at Violet's blue face. At Lily, a strange blue Madonna, barefoot and trembling. Through the closed window, I watched Lily sobbing and Rich holding her shoulders. I watched him take Violet from her arms as Lily crumpled to the floor. Even when the ambulance pulled up in front of the house, I didn't open the car door. I just sat behind my mother and watched Lily's small mouth opening and closing, muttering silent explanations. *She stopped breathing. God, she stopped breathing.*

FROM MY ROOM, Lily's tap shoes on the piece of plywood Ma laid down on the kitchen floor sounded like rain. From my fever bed, where my head was thick and heavy, the rhythm of metal on wood could have been a special lullaby for me. When I closed my eyes and I could feel my heart beating behind my eyelids, I imagined the storm outside that was making this song. I imagined black clouds, thunder, and the tap-tap-tap of Lily's rain.

I came home from school because of the small welts on my stomach. Chicken pox. The childhood illness I had managed to avoid for so long, Ma assumed I must be immune. But by the time Daddy got me out of Mrs. Kinsey's reading class and into the car, I was itching all over and my skin was hot to the touch. He had to go back to the bar, but before he left he poured me a glass of orange juice and ginger ale and let three maraschino cherries sink to the bottom, leaving red trails behind.

Daddy took Benny with him to work, because the moment Benny saw Daddy carrying me into my room with a cold washcloth on my head, he started to cry. As Benny's voice trilled over Ma's head, piercing and strange, she seethed, "Benny, why don't you go with Daddy to work? Let Indie get some sleep." And Benny followed behind Daddy out the door. I watched him through my bedroom window, skipping behind, almost tripping over his own feet. He had forgotten all about my fever by then. And I was alone in my room, and Lily was making rain with her feet.

I drifted in and out of sleep. Outside it was not raining; it was a perfectly sunny May day, but the metal rain was insistent and I was confused. I covered my throbbing head with the heavy feather pillow and tried not to think about the red bumps all over my skin. About the way it felt like ants were crawling across my back.

I woke up terrified, and it was dark outside. When I sat up, I felt my blood moving from my head down into my shoulders and arms. The beating of rain was inside my brain. The ants had become bees and my skin was buzzing. I got out of bed and walked slowly to my door. I felt as though I might fall down at any moment, that the pull of the earth was somehow stronger for me.

It must be midnight, I thought. It was so quiet here. *Everyone must be sleeping.* I was thirsty and I hoped that my reluctant legs would carry me to the refrigerator for orange juice or a glass of milk. Slowly, I made my way to the kitchen. I was so cold I almost expected a puff of white steam to escape from me when I opened my mouth. I looked up at the clock over the stove. 5:00 A.M. It was morning and I didn't know where the night had gone. I was disoriented and my legs were buckling. Benny was sitting at the kitchen table with a large Tupperware bowl and a box of cereal. He looked like a giant leaning over that big bowl. His face was covered with Cocoa Puff dust and there was a triangle of milk on his T-shirt.

"Where is everybody?" I asked.

"Lily's got rocks," he said.

"What?"

He was using a ladle to eat the cereal.

"Ma says she has rocks."

"I don't know what you are talking about, Benny," I said. *"Ma!!!"*

"THEY'RE NOT HERE!" Benny hollered back.

My head was pounding in new rhythms of pain. I sat down next to Benny when the edges of my vision started to turn black and fuzzy, when everything started to hum.

"Where are they?" I asked.

"Lily got rocks and Mrs. Dexter took them to the hospital. Daddy's at the bar doing invention."

"Inventory?"

"Uh huh." He smiled and dipped the ladle into his bowl.

"Did Lily eat something bad?"

"No."

"Did she have a stomachache?" This was like some awful game of charades.

"Yes! And she hasn't gone poo for four days. She has rocks."

"She's constipated?"

"Backed up," Benny said, smiling from ear to ear.

Sun was starting to stream through the kitchen window, making a small beam of light on the table next to Benny. I laid my head down in the warm puddle of sun.

"You've got chickens?" he asked and laid his head down next to mine. His eyebrows were raised, concerned.

"Um hmm," I nodded.

"Don't worry. I told Ma I would take care of you," he said and stroked my arm with one of his thick fingers.

I fell asleep at the table. When I lifted my head, my neck was stiff and Benny was putting his bowl in the sink. The clock over the stove said 8:00. I went to the living room, turned on the TV and lay down on the couch under an old army blanket Ma had put over the back to hide a grape juice stain that Benny made. In and out of sleep again, I kept confusing the sitcom plots with the design of my dreams. Artificial laughter with the other sounds of the house. One game show turned into the next, all the colors of the prizes and the passionate kisses of the soap-opera actresses turned over and over like the spinning wheel on *The Price Is Right*. I remembered at noon that I should have been at school, and wondered briefly if Ma might be mad that I'd missed my bus.

By 1:00 Ma and Lily still weren't home. Benny was on the floor next to the couch with a jar of peanut butter, a knife, and a box of graham crackers. He took turns making one for me and then one for himself until my throat was thick.

It was Daddy who finally came home and carried me back to my bed. *Indie, honey, where's your Ma?* he asked, pulling the blanket up around me when I shivered. *How long has she been gone, sweetie?*

A long time, I said, my head pounding behind my eyes.

It was Daddy who poured the cold pink calamine lotion into the palm of his hand and then cooled every stinging welt with a careful drop. *Does it still itch, honey? Is it better now?* He waited until my eyes were so heavy I couldn't keep them open anymore. Until my skin stopped prickling.

And it was Daddy who took Benny into the bathroom and cleaned the peanut butter from his hair and face. *You're a good kid, Benny. You took good care of your sister.*

In my bed, the sheets were cool on my hot skin. In my room, the whole world was quiet.

The next time I woke up I heard the front door opening and Lily's feet pattering down the hall. Then I heard Ma's sighs and Daddy's fist coming down hard on the kitchen table.

"What were you thinking?" he said. "You left *Benny* here to take care of Indie? She's got a fever. Jesus, Judy."

"I was at the hospital with your *other* daughter, Ben. I couldn't exactly leave her on the kitchen floor holding onto her stomach, could I? Do you realize she hasn't gone to the bathroom in four days? I thought at first she was just holding it again, but then I thought it might be her kidneys, the way she was grabbing at her back. So I took her to the emergency room. Forgive *me*."

"I don't care if she hasn't gone to the bathroom in a *month*. You don't leave a goddamn sick kid at home alone." Daddy's voice was so deep it felt like it was inside me.

"Benny was here," Ma said.

"I was here," Benny said. "I took care of Indie's chickens."

"Benny, why don't you go play outside?" Daddy said. His voice lowered, the low steady beat of a drum. "Couldn't you have called me at the bar?"

"I didn't think you'd appreciate being disturbed," she said.

"What the hell is that supposed to mean?"

"You know *exactly* what that's supposed to mean."

"I don't know what you're getting at, but I do know one thing. There better have been something seriously wrong with Lily to justify you leaving Indie alone here with Benny all day."

"Well, if you'd *listen*, I'd tell you. I told Dr. Murray to do a urinalysis. She wouldn't go to the bathroom because she said it hurt to pee. I was afraid it might be kidney stones."

Stones, I thought. Benny said she had rocks. *Sticks and stones may break my bones, but games will never hurt me.* Was that how it went? I saw giant playing cards behind my eyes. A brand new dishwasher. A grand piano.

"Well, did he give her some antibiotics?" Daddy asked, sounding tired.

"He said the urinalysis turned up fine. But I'm pretty sure she's got a bladder infection. I talked him into writing up a prescription. And the reason why I was so late is because I had to go to the grocery store for some cranberry juice. It'll help her flush out her system."

"The doctor said there was nothing wrong?" Daddy said.

"The *doctor* doesn't know everything. The *doctor* isn't with her every day, is he?"

Their voices were starting to spin like the game show wheel inside my head.

"She was screaming," Ma yells. "It could have been her appendix, for Chrissakes."

I recollected the sounds of Lily's rain. Her tap shoes on the plywood stage. I didn't remember screaming; I only remembered the sound her feet made. *She's lying,* I thought. *Daddy, don't listen because she's making it all up.*

I covered my head with the pillow. Daddy's soft voice was like chocolate milk beneath the lemon–juice sour of Ma's insistence. I put the pillow over my good ear until their voices disappeared, until all I could hear was the thick calamine coolness of the cotton pillowcase and heavy feathers.

L ILY RODE WITH VIOLET in the ambulance, but she shook
her head when we offered to go with her. Violet was
breathing again. They just wanted to do some tests. She would call
from the hospital. To Ma, she whispered, *You just got home from the
hospital. Why don't you get some rest?* To Rich, she said, *Can you put
something together for dinner? Do you think you can manage that?*

Rich and I went inside, lit up cigarettes in Lily's pristine
kitchen, and poured ourselves gin and tonics in big glass mugs.
Ma stood on the porch long after the sirens had faded, holding
the door open, letting the hot air in and the cold air out. She was
wearing clothes I didn't recognize; it had been so long since I'd
seen her. Pale yellow cotton sweater, so thin I could see the bones
of her shoulders almost poking through.

"Ma," I said. "Come inside. Let's help Rich make dinner."

"I don't know about dinner, but I can make some mean scrambled eggs," Rich smiled.

Ma didn't move from the doorway.

"Breakfast sounds great," I said.

"When Benny was a baby," she said, turning to face me. Her long fingers were pressed against the door frame. "When I found him in his crib and he wasn't breathing, there was a second when I hesitated. A second when I panicked. But then my instincts kicked in. It didn't have anything to do with the mechanical things in the text books. When you have a child . . ."

The sound of Benny's name coming from Ma's mouth made me tremble. I stood closer to the open door so the warm air might rush over me and take away the chill.

"Come inside, Ma. Let me make you some tea," Rich said.

Ma reluctantly closed the door and came into the smoke-filled kitchen. She coughed softly, and Rich snubbed out his cigarette in a glass ashtray we had found at the bottom of a drawer. She sat down at the kitchen table next to me.

"It's something you don't understand until you have a child of your own," she said, squeezing my hand. I pulled away.

"Something a *mother* knows," she said, frowning at Rich.

Rich took a big swallow of his cocktail. I pulled another cigarette from the stale pack we'd found in the same drawer as the ashtray.

"Do you have any Sleepy Time?" Ma asked. "I haven't slept more than a couple of hours since I've been in the hospital."

"I think so," Rich said, opening a cupboard filled with the accoutrements of Violet's illness. Bottles and syringes. Rubber suction devices to keep her nasal passages clear. On the second shelf he pulled out the familiar green box with the bear in the rocking chair on the front. "Here we go."

The teakettle's whistle startled me. I'd forgotten that we'd put it on to boil as Rich and I prepared dinner. I jumped back from the toaster where I was making toast. I bumped into the stove, and the frying pan filled with scrambled eggs fell to the floor. The hot copper pot rested on my bare leg for a moment before I registered the pain.

"Oh God," I said and kicked my leg. Immediately a long thin line of blisters appeared on my calf.

"Oh shit, are you okay?" Rich asked, pulling the lever on the fridge. There was a cascade of ice and then he was holding an ice cube to the burn.

The ice melted against the heat of my skin, and then made it nicely numb.

Ma sat still at the table, dipping her tea bag in and out of the empty mug. The teakettle was whistling, insistent.

"It sounds like the train," she said.

A lump grew thick in my throat. I remembered the sound of the train near our house in Mountainview.

We were only able to salvage some of the eggs, and the bread ripped when I spread the cold butter on the toast, but it reminded me of the times when Daddy made breakfast for dinner for Benny and me. The times when Ma and Lily were away and it was just Benny, Daddy, and me. It reminded me.

Ma said she was tired and went to bed while we were loading the dishwasher. "Let me know when you hear from Lily," she said.

Rich and I drank several more cocktails.

The phone rang as I was rinsing out the sink. Rich looked at me and a fear so real it made my heart buzz flashed across his face. He wiped his hands on a soft pink dish towel and picked up the phone.

"Oh, Peter, hi. Yeah, hold on one second," he said and handed the phone to me. There were a few stray soap suds on the receiver.

"Hi," I said.

"Hi." His voice was deceptively close. It made me homesick to hear him talking about the ordinary things. A new employee.

The produce delivery girl's broken arm and a forgotten box of Roma tomatoes in the walk-in cooler. It made me lonesome to hear about the small breaks in his daily ritual. Of hard cider with Joe and Chuck at Finnegan's instead of going home. Of the new record he bought to fill the house with music, to drown out the sound of my absence.

"Things are a mess here," I said finally.

"Your mom?"

"No, she's fine. Violet's sick though. She's at the hospital. We're waiting for Lily to call."

"I should let you go then," Peter said.

"No," I said. "Just a couple more minutes. Tell me about the trees."

And while Rich finished up the dishes, I curled the phone cord into the other room and imagined red and gold and orange, fading now into early winter, to the sound of Peter's voice.

"Sleep tight," he said softly.

"You too."

The phone rang again as soon as I hung up the receiver. Rich's hand shot out and grabbed the phone from the wall. He stood motionless and quiet, listening to Lily on the other end of the line.

"Oh thank God. Good. Good." He nodded and turned to me, his face relaxing, his shoulders descending in relief. "Overnight? Okay. Do you need me to bring anything? You sure? Okay. Kiss her for me," he said and then quietly, "Love you." He hung up the phone.

"Is she okay?" I asked and wrung out the sponge.

"They're doing some tests. EKG, MRI. I don't know. It may not have been her asthma. It may have been a small seizure or something. One of the doctors suggested it might be epilepsy, but Lily seems okay. Calm at least."

"How are *you?*" I asked.

"Good," he smiled. "Relieved. Hungover, though, I think. That'll teach me to start drinking at noon."

I hugged him quickly, noting how soft he was compared to Ma and Lily.

"I'll go let Ma know," I said.

I walked up the stairs to the unused nursery where Ma was sleeping on a small daybed next to the window. The wooden crib that Peter and I had given Lily for her shower was in the corner. There were stuffed animals propped up inside, fresh out of their packages. Plastic eyes staring resolutely at the wooden bars of this cage. A mobile hovered motionless above. It smelled like baby powder and fresh plastic diapers. There was no indication that a child had been inside this room. The diaper pail was empty. The plastic infant bathtub had never been used. It reminded me of the time we went to look at the model version of this home before Lily and Rich were married. There were three models to choose from, each one decorated to look as though someone lived there. And the illusion was precise, convincing, until you tried to lift a plate from the place mat on the dining room table or remove a book from the bookshelf and found that everything was glued down. That the cereal boxes were empty and the television was made of cardboard.

I stood over her for a few moments before I reached for her shoulder, which was bare in her sleeveless nightgown.

"Ma," I said softly.

She rolled over and opened her eyes wide.

"It's okay, Ma. Lily and Violet are spending the night at the hospital, but everything's fine. They're doing some tests."

She sat up and smoothed her hair with the palm of her hand. "It was a seizure, wasn't it?"

"Maybe," I said. "What makes you think that?"

Ma put her fingers between the slats of the venetian blinds and peered out at the dark night. "Lily had seizures when she was little, too. Don't you remember?"

"It may just be her asthma," I said. "They just want to rule some things out. Get some sleep. Our bus leaves tomorrow at noon."

I left the room before she could argue. I couldn't stay in this house another night. I felt a new urgency to get this over with. I was afraid that if I spent one more night with Ma and Lily that I might be woken by voices I didn't want to hear. Lily cussing at tumbleweeds. Ma talking in her sleep. My own startled breath when I woke again and again from the same dream.

When I came down the stairs the next morning, Lily was pouring coffee, Rich had already left for work, and Ma was holding Violet at the kitchen table, a cloth diaper thrown over her shoulder, Violet's head resting against her chest.

"Good morning," Lily smiled brightly. Her cheeks were flushed pink, and the window over the sink was wide open. A cool gust of air blew in and rustled the pale curtains.

"You're home already?" I said, wiping the sleep from my eyes, wondering if the kitchen would be empty when I opened them again. But I wasn't seeing things. Ma was rubbing Violet's back in circular motions. The thick blue veins moving under her transparent skin like small rivers.

"It's fall," Lily said, motioning vaguely to the open window. "The heat finally broke. It's seventy degrees outside."

"How is Violet?" I asked.

"She's doing just fine. She had some of Gramma's homemade oatmeal this morning and some apple juice," Ma said, cooing at Violet whose eyes were fluttering against sleep. "Now she's taking a little nap after her breakfast."

"Did they figure out what happened?" I asked, staring at Violet in disbelief. Her cheeks, like Lily's, were flushed pink. It was as if someone had colored her in, brushed pink watercolors on her papery skin, dotted the centers of her eyes with pale blue drops of light.

"Not sure yet, but she's doing just wonderful today. And now Gramma's here to make sure it doesn't happen again, right Miss Violet?" Ma said, holding Violet away from her and looking into Violet's watercolor eyes.

"Have you got the shuttle schedule, Lily?" I asked.

"We need to talk about that," Ma said, lowering Violet back against her chest. "I'm not going back up to Mountainview quite yet."

"What?" I asked.

"Now don't freak out," Lily came in. "It's just that I could really use the help with Violet until they figure out what's going on, and Ma's afraid she'll get sick again if she goes back to the house."

"What?" I said again.

"I'm pretty certain it's something in the walls. Your cheap father could have used lead-based paint on all those walls. Put asbestos in. There could be radon in the basement. It's a deathtrap," Ma said, rocking Violet against her.

"What we were thinking is that you could go up there and get everything checked out," Lily said. "Make sure everything is fine before Ma goes back."

I stood staring at them both as they looked at me with identical expressions and identical eyes.

"I can't believe this," I muttered.

"Now Indie, it's the least you can do. Really. Do you want me to wind back up in the hospital?" Ma spoke softly so as not to wake Violet, but her voice was stern.

"Ma, they didn't find anything like that in your system. They

said it was rat poison, arsenic, for Chrissakes. Are you guys nuts?"
I was shaking, holding my coffee mug, trying not to spill the hot
coffee on my hands.

"It's something in the house, Indie. You didn't believe them,
did you? That I'd do this to myself?" Ma scowled at me, and then
starting talking to me as if I were a child. "Jesus. Can't you see
that's just their way of making more money? If they say I'm *crazy*,
then they can hook me up with some billion-dollar-an-hour psychiatrist friend of theirs up in Mountainview and convince my
entire family and maybe even me that I'm losing my marbles, and
for the rest of my life I spend all of my money and most of my
time hoping they'll cure me. It makes a hell of a lot more sense if
I spend my money getting the mess your father made of the house
cleaned up. That's the only *cure* I need."

I looked at Lily. She was leaning against the sink, one arm
crossed across her waist, the other hand holding a coffee cup.

"What do *you* think of this?" I asked Lily, furious.

"I think it's a good idea," she said, shrugging, revealing absolutely nothing. "Ma can stay here with me until you've made sure
the house is okay. Then she can go home, and you can go home,
too."

"*Wonderful,*" I seethed. "Of course, we won't worry about
what this so-called deathtrap will do to me."

"Indie, don't be ridiculous. Environmental toxicity is cumu-
lative. Spending a week in the house is not going to have the same
effect as thirty years, now is it?" Ma smiled.

"Fine," I said, setting my coffee cup on the counter and raising
my arms in defeat.

The shuttle to Mountainview was almost empty. I put my suitcase
under my seat and leaned my head against the window. Rich was
standing outside, waving sadly. I felt bad leaving him there with

Ma and Lily, but I couldn't have stayed another second in that house. I figured I would get to Mountainview, go through the motions of getting the house checked, and then go home. I didn't care about proving Ma wrong. She'd have some sort of explanation for anything the inspectors did or didn't find. As the bus pulled away from the curb and then onto the freeway, I was glad that I was making this trip alone. I might even be able to turn it into some sort of vacation. This time of year in Mountainview wasn't so different from Echo Hollow. The aspen leaves would be gold and there might be a dusting of snow up on the mountain. I could take long walks, maybe start writing something, visit some old friends. It wouldn't be so bad, going home.

The bulk of the trip from Phoenix to Mountainview is through the desert. Uneventful for the eye, and colorless. Paloverde, yuccas, and saguaros standing in clusters or alone. Cactus wrens swarming around flowers wilted and gone to seed. I know the desert is very much alive, even in autumn when everything appears dead. But through the window on the way to my childhood home, all I saw was a stationary landscape and all of the colors of *barren*.

Two

I HAD NOT BEEN to the Mountainview house in almost five years. The last time I was in Arizona I never left Phoenix. The last time I had been at my mother's house, it was Christmastime, and the whole house was covered in snow. It looked pretty, draped in a crystalline cloak of white. But now the front yard was naked. The grass was burned brown from late summer sun, and Ma seemed to have given up on landscaping. I could see where the row of river rocks used to be, but most of them were gone now and the remaining ones were strewn out of any sort of order. The small garden of herbs and flowers was nothing more than a vague recollection. The soil here is so full of clay it takes patience to make things grow. From the looks of it, Ma had finally completely lost hers.

I walked across the front yard and up the broken steps to the porch. It was cluttered with junk: broken furniture, cardboard boxes, and stacks of weathered newspapers tied into bundles with twine. I noticed that some of the furniture had price tags, white stickers stuck to bureau tops and chair seats with my mother's estimation of what they were worth in ballpoint pen. Yard-sale leftovers that nobody wanted. I opened the drawers of a bureau that I remembered being my father's. It was full of junk. Handkerchiefs, Chinese finger cuffs, coins, batteries, and crumpled receipts. She hadn't even bothered to empty it out. No wonder no one wanted it. My father's history in junk was in these drawers: mismatched socks he left behind, magic tricks, and bar napkins with disconnected phone numbers scrawled in his and others' handwriting. I shut the drawer and reached up to grab the key from the door frame where Ma said it would be. Nothing. I ran my finger across the top of the door, waiting for the key to jangle to the floor. But it wasn't there. *Goddamnit,* I thought.

I used to break in when I was in high school. I remembered the pounding sound of my heart after I had closed my boyfriends' car doors out on the main road and walked the quarter mile up our driveway, trying not to make a sound. I remembered the way my blood would thud dully in my ears as I slowed my pace at the front yard and walked quietly around to the back of the house where my window would be propped open with three quarters, just enough space for the paint stirrer I kept hidden in the bushes. Five years ago at Christmas I'd found both the quarters and the paint stirrer waiting for me expectantly, and it had made Peter laugh. Now I wasn't worried about making noise. There was no one to hear anymore. Our nearest neighbor was still a mile away.

The backyard was worse than the front. It looked like a junkyard, a playground for ghosts. The swing set Daddy had bought for us was still cemented down, but rusted. The swings were missing seats; rusty chains hung down crooked and loose. The slide was riddled with holes where rust had eaten away at the metal. The pink and blue paint was gone. There was more furniture in the backyard. The wooden headboard of my childhood bed, the decals I'd put there reflecting the sun. Propped up against the side of the house was our washing machine and a pile of chair legs. Benny's purple beanbag chair, its zipper rusted and broken. Beans spilled all over the ground. The couch that had been in the back-yard for all those years was gone, though, as if the wild sunflowers had finally completely strangled it. I imagined that if I dug deep enough, I might find soggy bits of green burlap upholstery in the dirt.

The dirt yard turned slowly into a field of dying sunflowers. A waist-high sea of fading, yellow miniature suns. You could drown in that ocean; this I knew. There was an undertow in this field. You had to be careful or it would pull you under.

I didn't know what I might find inside the house. I was almost afraid to pry open the window where my three quarters were still allowing midnight entry. The paint stirrer was gone, but I found a piece of wood that did the trick, and the window rose slowly until there was space enough for me to crawl inside.

My old room was empty. The bed frame that matched the headboard was nowhere to be found. The floor was darker where the bed used to be. The wallpaper was also darker where the headboard used to lean up against the wall. Each step I took ech-oed and resounded. It felt strange coming into the house this way. I felt like an intruder, moving in the backward way of thieves.

Remarkably, the main rooms of the house looked normal. The living room was tidy. The plants were drooping in the windows, but there were pillows propped up on the couch, the carpet was clean and bright, and the curtains were ones I didn't recognize. The refrigerator was full of food, though much of it had turned bad in the time that Ma had been in Phoenix. I emptied out the containers that looked suspicious and poured a chunky carton of milk down the drain. To anybody who might visit, this would look like any other single woman's house. A welcome mat for wiping the mud off your feet, ceramic figurines, and a clock with batteries that hadn't died. But when I went down the hall opening doors, every bedroom was empty. And in the room she shared with Daddy, the floor was scarred. I pictured her dragging the furniture, too heavy to lift, never minding the scraping of bureau legs on the wooden floor.

I closed all the doors to our empty rooms and went back to the kitchen, which at least resembled a normal home. When I picked up the phone to call Peter, I half expected that there wouldn't be a dial tone. That the receiver would be glued down.

"I made it," I said.

"Good," he said. He must have gotten the phone in the office; there was no noise behind him.

"Ma didn't come with me," I said.

"What? I thought that was the whole reason why you went."

"It's complicated. Ma's staying in Phoenix to help Lily with Violet, and I'm getting the house checked for lead and asbestos. Don't ask. I don't know how long it's going to take, but I plan to get out of here as soon as I can."

I thought about telling him about the furniture wasteland in the backyard, the empty rooms, and my father's drawer. But I couldn't figure out a way to talk about it that didn't sound ridiculous. And so instead, I said, "I miss you."

"Esmé wants to come here for Thanksgiving weekend, after dinner with my folks. Is that okay?" he asked.

"Sure," I said. "That would be great."

"She'll be so happy," he said. "She says all she wants to do is sit on the porch swing and read."

"Surprise, surprise," I laughed.

I stared out the kitchen window at the rusty swing set and thought of the swing that Peter had built for us.

"Well, I've got to decide what Joe's going to make for entrées tonight," Peter said.

I didn't want him to hang up. I held on to the phone and listened to him breathing.

"You okay?" he asked.

"Yeah," I nodded, hoping the motion of my head might convince us both that I was telling the truth. "I'm fine."

After we hung up I went into the living room. This room looked nothing like it did when I was growing up. The black-and-white TV with the aluminum foil–wrapped antenna had been replaced with a wide-screen TV inside a pressed-wood entertainment center. The walls were papered in a yellow and blue instead of the eagles of my childhood.

I felt something like hunger deep in my stomach, and decided to go into town to get some groceries. The car keys, unlike the house keys, were where Ma had said they would be. I got a sweater out of my suitcase and went out to the garage. It was getting chilly; heavy clouds had moved across the peaks of the mountain. Some days you wouldn't even know there were mountains looming over this town for all the clouds. These looked like snow clouds. Maybe it would snow in town soon, too.

Ma's car wouldn't turn over. I sat patiently so as not to flood the tank, and then tried again. The engine roared to life and the stereo was turned on full blast. Talk radio. Doctor Somebody condescending to a weepy-sounding man. I turned the stereo off and let the engine warm up. The car, like the living room and kitchen, was immaculate. The ashtray was clean, the upholstery and floor mats looked recently vacuumed, and it smelled vaguely of artificial pine.

I backed out of the garage and turned around in the driveway. Our driveway winds downhill for a quarter of a mile before the turn onto the main road into town. In the rearview mirror the snow clouds had completely enclosed the peaks. It was like a magician's trick. Making mountains disappear.

It's only a couple of miles into town; the car hadn't even warmed up when I pulled into what used to be the Foodmart parking lot in almost the exact spot where I'd been struck all those years ago. I had marked this place in my mind, remembering even after all this time. Of course, the Foodmart was bought out years ago by Smith's, whose neon sign glowed eerily in the prematurely dark afternoon. But the way the giant oak's shadow fell across this space at this time of day was like a compass. Even with the newly paved lot, I knew how far away the cart I was in was from the doors to the store. I knew how far away Ma had been from me.

Inside, I got a cart and started to fill it with groceries. I didn't plan on staying long, but I also didn't plan to starve. If it did snow and I couldn't get into town, I certainly didn't want to be stuck in that house without food. It had happened to us once; we'd been stranded and hungry before.

A Navajo woman wearing a traditional dark velvet dress and rows of turquoise beads laced around her neck was ahead of me in line. She was reading a *National Enquirer,* and the child in the baby seat of the shopping cart was restless. He twisted and turned, trying to reach for something, anything, from the candy rack. His face contorted with frustration when his small hands wouldn't reach. His large black eyes grew wet, and I felt the storm that was about to burst. Then, without moving her eyes from the newspaper, the woman reached out her hand and touched his cheek, halting the tear that was about to fall. She shook her head gently, *no,* and his bottom lip quivered.

I had to write a check for the food, but they wouldn't take an out-of-state check without a guarantee card. *Listen,* I wanted to say. *I'm from here. This is where I grew up. You might not know this, but I was struck by lightning in your parking lot.* As if this might entitle me somehow. But instead, I reached into my wallet for a credit card I'd promised myself I wouldn't use and paid for the groceries. I wasn't a local anymore. I hadn't been since I was seventeen.

In the parking lot, the Indian woman was unloading her shopping cart into the back of her pickup truck. Her long braid swung like a rope when she picked the little boy up out of the cart and put him inside the cab of the truck. It was almost twilight now, dark and cold, and the growing wind rustled the handles of her plastic bags. As I unloaded my groceries into the backseat, I watched her. Her engine wouldn't start. She tried three times before I opened up Ma's trunk to look for jumper cables. Nothing. Not even a spare tire.

I ran across the parking lot anyway and knocked on her window. She looked startled, but then she rolled the window down.

"If you have cables, I can give you a jump," I said.

"Nah, that's okay. She'll start soon enough."

"You sure?" I asked.

She nodded and stared straight ahead. The little boy was sitting quietly in the front seat, sucking on the ear of a worn purple Barney.

"It's really no problem," I said, hoping she would take my offer.

She pumped the gas pedal a couple of times and then turned the key. The engine trembled and then turned over. She smiled and turned to me.

"Good, good," I said as she rolled up the window.

As I walked back to Ma's car I felt embarrassed. I crossed my arms against the cold and got into the car.

By the time I pulled into Ma's driveway, it was completely dark. It took two trips to get the groceries into the house. Inside it was quiet. I turned on all of the lights except for the ones in the bedrooms and turned on the radio on the kitchen counter. No stations were coming in, though; it was too windy. I could almost taste the snow in the air. To fill the silence, I turned the TV on really low, and let the voices keep me company as I got dinner ready.

I'd gotten some Chinese food from the deli. Little cardboard cartons with greasy noodles and batter-dipped chicken inside. They weren't warm anymore, so I filled a plate and put it in the microwave. The plate spun around and around, the noodles crackled and hissed, and then I used oven mitts to carry the hot plate into the living room. Ma would kill me. Little plastic containers with hot mustard and bright pink sweet and sour sauce threatened stains on the upholstery. But Ma wasn't here, and I was hungry. And the living room was the only place in the house that felt even remotely cozy.

I sat down on the couch. It was stiff. Too stiff. I set the plate on the coffee table and stood up. I pulled the cushions off one by one. There was no bed hidden inside the couch. And there were no beds in the bedrooms. I wondered if my mother, like Lily, was no longer sleeping. And I wondered where I would lie down tonight. I ate two platefuls of food until my lips were slick, my stomach was full, and there was a small monument made of white cardboard on the kitchen counter. Then I lay down on the unforgiving couch and waited for snow to fall.

NOVEMBER 3, 1999. Mountainview, Arizona. *No witnesses have been located concerning the living conditions of Judy Brown, 55, a thirty-year resident of Mountainview. Neighbors would have made complaints, had she any. However, the nearest neighbor, one John Dexter, has "not been up that way since her boy died" when his wife, Eleanor, "brought the family there a pot roast." Complaints were filed not by neighbors, but by her daughter, Miranda (Indie) Brown, who returned to the residence after nearly five years of remaining safely away. Indie ap-*

parently sat down in the backyard shortly after her arrival, reading a newspaper from early July 1978. Staring out at a sunflower skyline, Indie shouted out at the trees. The newspaper was yellowed and fragile with time, and the words crumbled in her hands.

I WALKED CAREFULLY around the back of the house to find Benny. He discovered this hiding space by accident one day, but now he used it every time we played hide-n-seek or whenever he just needed a place to hide. So I knew now without seeking that he was under the porch, lying flat on his belly where I wouldn't even put my hand for fear of what might live there. What might appear to anyone else as cowardice (this slithering on the ground and under the broken latticework of our house to get away) actually showed incredible bravery.

"Benny," I said. "Come out. It's over."

He didn't answer.

"Benny, you can come out now. Daddy went to work."

I could see Benny through the lattice. His face was in his hands.

Ma came around the corner then, still wearing her nightie. She was holding Lily on her hip, even though Lily's feet nearly touched the ground. She and Daddy had been fighting about the Miss Desert Flower contest again. This time Daddy gave in. He was tired. I could see it in the way he finally just shrugged and threw up his hands. He didn't even bother slamming the car door this time.

"Where's your brother?" she asked, looking around the backyard. Then she saw the soles of his dirty sneakers. His feet were as big as Daddy's now. Bigger even.

"Benny," she said, leaning down as far as she could with the extra weight of Lily.

I bent down too, sticking my head near the opening where he had crawled, and whispered, "I'll take you down to the creek if you come out."

His feet moved and then he was shimmying backward out from under the porch. When he stood up, he was covered with red clay. It would take Ma an hour to get it off of him, and it wouldn't ever come all the way out of his clothes.

"We're going swimmin'?" he asked, probably forgetting why he'd gone under there to begin with.

"Sure," I said. "Go inside and get your swim trunks."

"We're going swimmin'," he was clapping his hands together and hopping up and down on one leg. "I gotta get my new trunks. I gotta find my new swim trunks."

Benny hopped awkwardly through the back door into the house. He'd grown almost five inches since the summer before. He didn't know what to do with all that height.

"Indie," my mother reprimanded.

"What?" I asked, imitating her annoyed tone of voice.

"He needs to learn to mind without bribing him."

"I was going anyway," I said. "It's hot."

Ma could fight with Daddy, scream and slam doors and throw things until she was almost blue, and then suddenly allow this certain peace to descend upon her. You never knew when the yelling would stop, but when it did, her voice went gentle. From bitter to smooth warm milk within seconds. And today she'd won, and she was happy.

"Okay. Be back in a couple of hours," she smiled, rocking back and forth with Lily still on her hip.

I grabbed my backpack and Benny found his trunks, which were still soggy from the last time we went to the creek. I made him put them in an old bread bag to keep them from getting my stuff all wet. I had suggested that he put them on and let them dry while we walked, but there was no arguing with Benny. He did things his own way, even if it didn't make too much sense to the rest of us.

"Did you see that?" he asked just after I accidentally let the screen door slam shut behind me.

"Indie!" my mother screeched. Her transformation from calm to hysterical was just as quick as the reverse.

"Sorry, Ma!" I hollered back and followed Benny's gesture to the front yard.

"It was a giant mouse!" he said, looking quickly from me to a spot on the grass.

"Are you sure?"

He nodded and pointed again. "It was brown and it ran under the porch. It looked like that mouse we found in the dryer. 'Member? 'Member the one that was dead inside the dryer and got rolled up in Daddy's T-shirt? 'Member, Indie?"

"That was just a field mouse. It was probably a squirrel." I shifted the heavy backpack so that the weight of it was even across my shoulders. "Let's go." I took his hand and tugged gently. His large hand closed over mine and he resisted my pull.

"It was a giant mouse," he insisted, staring sadly at the front lawn. "I'm gonna go under that porch again and find him."

"Okay, Benny," I nodded. "We'll look for it when we get back. But let's go so we can get a good spot by the creek."

"It was brown and it had squinty eyes."

"Okay, Benny. We'll look for it later. Come on."

His grip loosened on my hand, and he followed behind me, tripping as he turned his head back to look for the mouse.

To get to the creek from our house without crossing the train tracks you had to go all the way out to Depot Street and then go under the overpass to get to Highway 79. It was a lot quicker to go the back way, though, through the field behind our house, through the woods, and then across the tracks to the highway. Of course, we always pretended that we were going the long way, and then when I was pretty sure Ma was preoccupied with something else, we would edge along the side of the garage and make a run for the woods. It was hard with Benny because he made so much noise. But he was learning to be quiet. If I had taught him anything it was how to make Ma think he was doing exactly what she wanted him to do.

Today, Benny was distracted by the so-called giant mouse, so I had to remind him to squat down and walk like a duck under the kitchen window so Ma wouldn't see our heads bobbing along. He finally stopped looking for the mouse and quietly followed me to the garage, where we crawled through the waist-high grass in the field and then ran to the woods.

"I didn't make a single sound," Benny said when we got to the tree I'd designated as the safety zone, where he could talk. "Not even a breathing sound."

"I know Benny, you did great," I said. I was out of breath. It was hard to run with my backpack on.

"I almost made a breathing sound when I stubbed my toe on that rock, but I held it inside," he said, pointing to his chest. "Deep down."

"I didn't hear you at all," I said and pulled the backpack off. My shoulders ached.

"Did you bring my new swim trunks?" Benny asked, tugging at his earlobe.

"Benny, you saw me put the bag inside the backpack."

"Can I see them?"

"No," I said, pulling the backpack back on.

"You brought them inside that bread bag because they were wet. Right, Indie?"

"Shhh," I said. "Let's go."

I loved the walk through the woods to the tracks. The Ponderosa pines smelled so sweet in the summertime, like butterscotch, some people said. The ground was completely covered with their spiny needles. I could have lived my whole life here, surrounded by the giant trees. It was cool and dark and quiet.

Daddy was the kind of person who didn't like the woods. He wasn't happy unless he was somewhere with a lot of noise and people. When he bought the bar from a friend and moved all of us to Mountainview from California, he'd never been anywhere in Arizona except for Phoenix. He didn't know that up here there was almost nothing but woods. Of course, like Daddy always said, wherever there are people, there will be bars. And if a bar was open, there would always be someone who needed a drink. There was always somebody to talk to at Rusty's, always some story to hear. Daddy didn't even mind if he'd heard a story a thousand times. He'd rest his elbows on the smooth, polished wood of the bar and listen to Simon telling tired old Vietnam stories, or Nancy talking about the way her boyfriend used to make her the prettiest Indian jewelry before he got his fingers cut off in the factory. And how now all he did was smoke weed and watch basketball on TV. Daddy wouldn't trade the sound of Johnny Cash on the jukebox and the music of the cue ball clacking against the other balls on the smooth green felt of the pool table for anything. I loved it too, but sometimes all that noise got my tongue confused. The sounds of the bar tasted like cigarette smoke and sour lemons. I could only take the bitter olive of Nancy's sadness and the sickly sweet maraschino cherry of Sheila's flirting before I longed for the forest.

Benny liked the woods too, but only during the day. He wouldn't even go near the edge of the forest at night. But now he was skipping and tripping over his big feet through the maze of trunks and branches. He was happy here. He almost never cried in the woods.

After not too long, the woods opened up again to Highway 79, which ran all the way down into the canyon. But to get to the road, you had to cross the tracks. It wasn't as safe here as it was in town, where there were flashing lights and wooden arms that descended to protect you every time a train went by. Out here, you needed to put your ear to the ground and listen because it was easy to confuse the sound of the train with the sound of your own breaths or the wind whistling through the tops of the trees.

"Benny, come here," I said and motioned for him to join me as I knelt down to the ground.

We had done this before. He lay down on the ground, pressing his ear against the cool gravel near the tracks, and squeezed his eyes shut.

"I don't hear nothin'," he said, opening his eyes. "It's safe."

I raised my eyebrows at him. "Are you sure?" I could feel the train through the thin soles of my flip-flops.

"You check, Indie," he said. "I don't know, maybe I heard somethin'."

"No," I said. "I trust you." I started to stand.

"Stop," he said. "Just a minute. Let me try again."

I smiled.

"I hear it, I hear it!" he squealed. "It's coming!"

"Good, Benny," I said. "Looks like you just saved my life."

"I just about saved your life," he said. "Phew."

"Let's move back," I said, pulling him back away from the tracks.

Within seconds the train approached us; the bright yellow light on the front could have been the sun. Benny yelled into the scream of the train, trying to match its noise with his own. When the caboose rolled past he waved frantically to the conductor, who looked startled to the see such a tall boy grinning and jumping and screaming. He returned the gesture and Benny kept waving until the train was gone and the ground was still and soundless again. Only then did he tentatively step across the trembling tracks to the other side.

I don't like to swim. That's not why I liked to go to the creek. Benny was the swimmer in our family. Swimming was the one thing he was truly good at. In the water he could have been any other fourteen-year-old boy. In the water everything else just floated away.

We went to our usual spot, hoping that tourists hadn't already discovered it. Weekends were always a little risky, and there was nothing worse than tourists spreading out their godawful beach towels on the smooth gray rocks that were rightfully ours. Nothing worse than some old lady with frosted hair spilling her suntan oil in the clean water. Sometimes the rainbows of oil would last for days after the tourists had already gone home.

We crawled down through the woods and across the wobbly bridge to Benny's favorite place. There were no people here. It was only the end of May. Too early in the year for tourists, I guess.

Benny pulled off his cutoffs, grabbed the orange bread bag with his mildewy suit inside, and went behind a tree to change. When he came back out the other side, he disappeared into the creek. I sat down on my favorite rock. It was only inches from the water; when the creek was high, the running water would sometimes splash over the rock, touching me with its wet fingers. If I lay on my back it felt almost as if I were swimming. This was the closest I ever came to going in.

But there was no time to dream-swim today. Inside the backpack I had the books I'd been carrying around for a month. One was a high school geometry textbook I bought at the school library book sale. The other was Ma's Sears catalog. I would have torn out the page instead of lugging that thing around, but I was afraid she would have noticed. Ma knew the catalog like the lines in the palms of her hands. The pages were dog-eared and worn. Pink ruffly party dresses. Shiny white buckled shoes. I knew that she wanted these things for Lily, but that we didn't have the money. These dresses were the blueprints for the patterns she pieced together to the make the homemade versions we *could* afford. And to me, the dress that hung from a curtain rod in my parents' bedroom looked just as good as any in this catalog, but I'd watched her hold the catalog up to the dress she made and shake her head.

"It's pretty, Ma," I said.

"Chintzy fabric," she said, shaking her head. "It'll fall apart after one wash. And the flowers are plastic. The ones in the catalogue are silk. Hopefully, the judges won't be able to tell the difference from so far away."

"Why don't you buy the one in the catalog then?" I asked.

"Ask your father," she said, turning to face me. Her face was pinched tight, cinched into small pleats like the skirt of Lily's new dress.

I was careful not to let the water splash on the pages of the catalog. I'd dropped one of my own books in the creek once and couldn't get the pages to lay flat again after it had dried in the sun.

On page 454, past the party dresses and maternity bras and Barbie accessories, were the few pages of sporting goods. A free-standing basketball hoop. A bowling machine with tiny pins on strings. And two different styles of pool cues. The one I wanted had the biggest picture. *Spalding personalized 2-piece pool cue. 57" maple shaft with inlaid blue, black, and white rings. Brass to brass joint. Nylon sleeve included. 2 lbs. $29.99.* Ever since the catalog arrived in the mail I had been eyeing that stick. The pages opened up to this almost as quickly as they opened up to the frilly dresses and shoes of my mother's fantasy.

At night I imagined walking into Rusty's, carrying that beautiful bag. I imagined sitting down at one of the booths near the pool tables and screwing the two pieces together while all the other tournament contestants watched. I imagined the way the smooth wood would feel in my hands. Not like the warped sticks that hung in the rack on the wall. You had to aim just a little off the mark to make a shot with those cues. When you rolled them across the smooth felt, they wobbled. But the Spalding personalized two-piece pool cue wouldn't wobble a bit. And the tip was probably perfectly rounded. No chips or dings at all. I had twenty-three dollars saved. I was hoping Daddy might splurge for my birthday, but I doubted it. Plus, there would be shipping and handling charges. Two pounds. To get it here on time for the tournament would cost me a fortune. There was also the matter of getting Daddy to let me enter. But now, with him agreeing to let Lily and Ma go to Phoenix for the pageant, I figured he'd have to let me play. It only cost $5.00 to enter.

I ran my finger across the glossy picture and then closed the catalog. I could see Benny just beneath the surface of the water, silent and graceful. He could hold his breath for hours, it seemed. It used to make me panic a little, but now I didn't worry about him anymore. He was smart in the water.

The geometry books were to help me with some of the trick shots that Little Ike had been teaching me. Little Ike was my size. He offered to teach me how to shoot because he knew better than anyone else that there were special skills needed to play pool when you were only four-foot-six. Plus, he was the only one who didn't seem to mind playing with a kid. Some of the older guys pretended that I wasn't even there, especially when I was playing really well. One time I played against an older guy and beat him in one turn. After he broke, he didn't even get a chance to shoot again. He kept slamming his hand down on Daddy's pool table and checking the pockets like he might find some trap doors or magnets inside that sucked all the balls in. People didn't like being shown up by a kid, and certainly not by a girl. I was polite, though. Little Ike also taught me how to be a good sport. *Always shake hands before the game starts and after it's over. Always say, "Good game."* I remember the guy's hand was big and sweaty. Up close I could smell motor oil on him. Motor oil and beer.

Ike said, "It's all geometry. You study your geometry, and you'll be a great pool player. It's probably the only math you'll ever use in real life. Except for maybe adding up your winnings." I stared at the drawings of an isosceles triangle and then lined up some stones to try to the make sense of geometry.

"Benny," I said into the water as I shoved the catalog and textbooks back inside my backpack.

Benny would stay in the water until his skin was wrinkled up like a prune if there was nobody there to stop him. He ignored me the first few times I called for him to get out of the water. Finally, he came out of the creek and walked over to where I was gathering up our things. I handed him a towel, which he wrapped around his shoulders like a cape.

Underneath the towel he slithered out of his stinky swim trunks and handed them to me.

"They stink," I said, pinching my nose.

"Do not," he said, shaking his head, burying his nose in the trunks. His towel dropped to the ground.

"Get dressed," I said, embarrassed by his nakedness, hoping that there were no tourists at the lookout above.

"Why?"

"Put your clothes on, Benny," I said, starting to get nervous. I peered up toward the lookout, shielding my eyes from the sun.

"No!" he yelled and skipped from one rock to the next, dangling the swim trunks from one of his long, thin fingers.

"Benny," I said. "Please."

"Make me, make me . . ." he sang. His thin white body reflected in the rippled surface of the water. His skin was covered with goose bumps.

I heard leaves rustling above me. When I looked up I saw people in brightly colored shorts and T-shirts hiking above.

"Benny, if you don't put your clothes on I am going to leave," I said. And then I turned and started walking up the hill. I shouldn't have threatened him. I knew even as I struggled through the brush that I shouldn't even pretend to leave him. But my stomach turned as I imagined the hikers looking down and seeing my brother, my retarded brother, naked on the rocks, playing keep-away with a pair of stinky swim trunks. I knew I shouldn't do this, but I kept moving up the embankment.

When I finally turned around, I saw Benny lying on the ground near the stream. His shorts were around his ankles, and both of his knees were bleeding. His body shook as he quietly sobbed, and I felt like I might throw up. I ran back down the bank and sat down next to him on the ground. Silently, I helped him pull the clean shorts up over his cold white bottom and poured handfuls of cool creek water on the fresh cuts in his knees.

"I'm sorry," I said. "I didn't mean for you to get hurt."

"I saved your life," Benny said, tugging on his earlobe. "You would have gotten runned over by the train. But I listened and I made you wait."

"I know, Benny. I'm sorry."

"The train would have killed you and you would be dead like the mouse in the dryer," he sobbed.

"I'm sorry," I said. I rolled up his swim trunks and stuffed them back into the bread bag. Benny's crying subsided and I helped him up. He inspected his new cuts.

"I'll put some Bactine on them back at the house," I said.

"I'm gonna find that giant mouse under the porch when we get back."

"Okay," I said, grateful that he wasn't mad at me anymore for leaving him naked at the edge of the water. The nice thing about Benny was that he would forgive just about anything. The one thing he didn't do was *forget*. There was nothing wrong with Benny's memory, nothing at all.

"It was bigger than a squirrel even," he said. "Bigger than a cat."

I FELL ASLEEP ON THE COUCH with the TV on, and woke at 4:00 A.M. to snow on the screen and snow falling softly outside. I leaned my head against the window and wondered if it was snowing in Maine. It was early, too early, and it was likely that the snowflakes, like stars, would be gone by morning. I must have fallen asleep sitting up, because when I woke up later my neck and shoulders were stiff. Outside, there was no evidence of snow. The sun was warm on my face and I could hear water dripping from the eaves.

I wouldn't be able to the call the radon and asbestos people for a couple days. I'd already tried every number in the Yellow Pages, and no one had any open appointments until Monday. I thought I might go into town again. Maybe go to Rusty's to visit Rosey. She was still working there the last time I came to visit. She was there when Daddy bought the bar and later when he left it. I suspected she'd be there until the building itself crumbled.

Outside, the air was crisp and bright. I brought my coffee onto

the front porch and sat down on a wooden box. The magic hand-
kerchief had been lifted from the mountains, revealing two snow-
dusted peaks jutting into the too-blue sky like monoliths. I
breathed the cold air until my lungs felt almost numb. When I
exhaled, a puff of smoke escaped from my lips. This was my favorite time of year when I was a kid. I loved the way autumn
teetered on the edge of winter, how it could be a hot Indian
summer one day and the next morning you could make angels
just by breathing. In Maine, there was more warning. The leaves
announced the beginning and end of fall. The air was bitter long
before snow fell.

As I blew across my coffee cup, the phone rang. I opened the
screen door and went into the kitchen to answer it.

"Hello?"

"Hi, Indie, it's Rich."

"Hey." I was glad it wasn't Lily or Ma. "What's up?"

"I'm just checking on you," he said. "Making sure you're
okay."

"I'm fine," I said. "It's a little creepy up here, though. Did you
know Ma emptied out all the bedrooms? There's a shitload of
furniture in the backyard and on the porch. I think she was trying
to sell it."

"Hmmm," he said. It was quiet behind him.

"Where are you?" I asked.

"I'm here. Judy and Lily just took Violet to the doctor. They're
taking some chest X rays."

"Still no answers, huh?"

"Indie, your mother was talking about Lily having a history of
seizures. Do you remember that?"

"Lily was always sick," I said. "I can barely keep track of all of
her health problems."

"See, that's news to me. I mean, Lily never gets sick now.

113

Never. And this is the first time I'd ever heard *anything* about seizures. Even when Violet first got sick and the doctors were going through our medical histories, I don't remember her saying anything about seizures. And now, I don't know, it just seems . . ."

"Maybe Ma's exaggerating," I shrugged. "She's been known to do that."

"It's not her that I'm worried about. I know what to expect from her," Rich sighed. "It's just that Lily is going along with it. All of a sudden she has this whole history of epilepsy or some other thing she's never even mentioned before. It doesn't make any sense."

I sat down at the kitchen table and sipped my coffee. It was cold and bitter.

"I wouldn't worry too much. If it's something that might help the doctors figure out what's wrong with Violet, I guess that's all that matters."

"I guess," Rich said, sounding remotely defeated. "I'm just not making that connection. Violet stopped breathing. She wasn't convulsing; she was completely limp. You saw her. I can't even figure out why they'd be testing for epilepsy. I'm worried that the doctors might be wasting their time chasing after some crazy notion your mother came up with instead of figuring out what actually happened to her."

"What do you mean?" I asked, dumping the cold coffee into the sink.

"I mean why she stopped breathing."

"Maybe you should talk to Violet's doctor," I said. "Maybe something's just getting lost in translation."

"Maybe," he said. He was quiet and then he said softly, "You know, I really was calling to see how *you* are."

"Ready to go back to Maine," I laughed.

"Are you really going to have those people come check the house?"

"I suppose. Who knows? Maybe they'll find tanks of toxic waste in the basement," I said.

"Rat poison in the water?" Rich laughed.

"You just need to remember the family you're dealing with sometimes," I said. "We operate on an entirely different logic than most."

I drove Ma's car into town and parked in the lot across the tracks from Rusty's. Just as I was about to cross the tracks, the red lights started to flash, the arm descended, and the train whistled in the distance. I stood back from the tracks and waited for the train to come, covered my ears with my hands as it passed, and stared through the blinking spaces between the cars to the other side.

Instead of going straight into Rusty's I walked across the street to the smoke shop for a paper. It smelled like pipe tobacco and chocolate inside. Heady and sweet. The woodstove in the center of the store was hot. I stood next to it while I waited in line. I pulled a handful of change out of my coat pocket and put it on the counter. I grabbed three nickel candies from a bin and un-wrapped one while the girl behind the counter scooped my change and pocket lint into her palm.

I tucked the newspaper underneath my arm and walked across the street to Rusty's. I stood staring at the smoked glass for several moments before I finally opened the heavy door. As my eyes adjusted to the darkness, my heart sank. It had changed. Not so much that it looked like a different place, but enough that it felt off-kilter. Wrong. The booths along one wall had been removed. Now there were high round tables with bar stools situated around them like red vinyl petals on a flower. The wood-burned plaque that said NO SNIVELING was gone from behind the bar. The elk and deer heads that had hung on the walls like quiet friends had been replaced with ugly paintings of abstract landscapes and buildings. Oceans in unbelievable squares of green and blue. Triangular cathedrals without doors. I was happy to see that the mahogany bar Daddy had polished to impossible smoothness remained the central fixture in the room, and the mirrors behind the bar were the same beveled ones of my childhood. The jukebox that Benny loved was still there, but all the songs were different. And when I peered through the doorway where saloon-style doors used to hang, my heart sank. In the room where the extra pool table had always been, the uprooted booths and elk heads lay in heaps. Boxes and a broken cigarette machine.

I thought I might be the only one in the bar until a man came out of the bathroom and sat down several stools away from me at the end of the bar. He nodded at me. Then the bartender came through the swinging doors from the kitchen, retying her apron.

"Hey," she said. Her voice was raspy, disconnected from her pretty face. Black hair pulled back into a messy ponytail, a widow's peak breaking the smooth white expanse of her forehead. "What can I get you?"

"Bourbon?" I said, more like a question than a request.

"Sure thing." She smiled and spun around to the bottles. I watched her thin wrists as she handed me my drink. There were snakes tattooed around each of them.

"Thanks," I smiled, and wished I'd ordered a beer.

She turned around to the sink where the soapy water was so greasy the bubbles were almost gone. Her shirt lifted when she bent over, revealing her back. Her spine was bony. Her skin almost transparent. I took one sip of the bourbon and felt sick.

"Excuse me," I said.

"Yeah?" she said turning around.

"Does Rosey Jimenez work here still?"

"I don't know. I just got this job two days ago. Is she a bartender?"

"No, she used to work in the kitchen," I said, my heart dropping. "Back when my dad owned this place."

"Sorry," she shrugged. "Maybe come back in tomorrow."

"Sure," I said, feeling defensive and angry that the fact that my father had owned this bar didn't seem to register, or count to her for that matter.

I left the bar and thought about trying to look Rosey up in the phone book at the phone booth outside the bar, but instead I sat in the car in the parking lot until the sun started to make my eyes ache, and then I drove to the nearest car wash and paid for the full cycle. There was something safe and familiar about this. Something pacifying about the whirring of water and the soapy circles against the glass. Inside this car, inside this car wash, nothing had changed.

INDIE, I TOLD YOU fifteen times to put your laundry in your drawers. If I wash one more clean shirt because it wound up on the floor instead of in your dresser, I swear I'll stop doing the laundry."

Ma was standing at the kitchen table, spray-painting Lily's tap shoes silver. One had started to dry and was stuck to the newspaper she'd put underneath.

"Shit," she mumbled, peeling the paper off the side of the shoe. All that had been on Ma's mind since Daddy gave in was the Miss Desert Flower contest. From the second she sealed the envelope with the entry form and the glossy black-and-white picture of Lily inside, the only thing she'd been concerned about was getting ready for Phoenix. She even cut back her hours at the nursing home so that she could get Lily ready. There were sequins to sew onto bodysuits and tap shoes to spray-paint. She hadn't even noticed that I'd been going to visit Daddy at the bar after school every day instead of coming straight home. But now here she was, losing her patience again. Maybe she could clip it to the cuffs of her jacket like Benny's mittens. Hang it around her neck on a string like my house key.

"Indie? The laundry?"

I wasn't thinking about laundry. I was thinking about the Spalding personalized two-piece pool cue.

"Now," Ma said and started to pull the chair I was sitting in away from the kitchen table.

"In a minute," I said. I was counting the change I'd been saving. My red plastic piggy bank was lying on its side on the table, the rubber plug removed from its stomach so I could get at the disappointing stash inside.

"I *said* now," she said and pulled harder on the chair. I felt the chair legs scraping across the linoleum.

"Ma . . ."

"GET UP!" she hollered. She kept yanking, and the chair tilted backward. I tried to hold on to the edge of the table, but the Formica was slippery. Suddenly, I lost my balance entirely and I was falling backward. My head hit the floor and bounced a bit. The pain was dull in the back of my head. Dull and insistent when I scrambled to my feet.

"I wasn't doin' nothin', Ma!" I screamed and ran past her out the front door. She caught the back of my shirt and held me still on the front steps.

Benny was sitting on the garage roof, which he could get to by crawling on top of Daddy's dead truck. He was wearing the plastic Batman cape he'd gotten for Halloween the year before. Lily was all the way across the front yard, twirling her baton. She wasn't wearing the new red, white, and blue costume though. Ma had already sealed that in a plastic bag inside her suitcase so that Lily wouldn't lose any more sequins in the grass before they got to Phoenix. Lily caught the baton behind her back and then laid it gently down. She raised her arms over her head and then threw her body forward, rising up into a perfect handstand. Her bare feet were pointed straight up toward the sky, her skinny legs squeezed tightly together. She walked quickly on her hands across the yard to the steps, and she didn't hesitate for even a second before she started to climb the stairs, still walking on her hands.

"Let me *go*," I seethed and pulled gently away from Ma. My head was aching, thick and steady. But I didn't run across the front yard. It would have been dangerous to get in Lily's way. A lot more dangerous than ignoring a pile of clean laundry on my bed.

Soon, Lily had arrived at the last step, where she let her body bend forward until her feet reached the top landing and she pulled herself back up, arms raised. Her face was red, but she was smiling. She looked toward my mother and my mother nodded, her expression serious. Lily nodded back in that strange silent language of theirs, and then dismounted. A flawless and light front aerial off of the top of the stairs, landing gently on the ground in a split.

My mother let go of me and applauded. She was smiling so wide that her lips almost disappeared, her lipstick smearing across her front teeth. I pulled away from her and walked into the driveway. I could feel the bump growing on the back of my head where I had fallen. There was a funny taste in the back of my throat, and I thought for a minute it might be blood. The side of my tongue was sore from where my teeth had come down on it when I fell.

But now Ma had forgotten all about me. She'd probably even forgotten about the laundry. On the roof, Benny clapped his hands wildly and shouted.

"Good pumpkin," Ma said, swatting Lily's bottom. "Now go in and get cleaned up. Your knees are grass-stained."

Ma looked at me, standing in my bare feet in the driveway,

and shook her head. There was nothing but disappointment in the way she scrunched her eyebrows up.

Benny crawled down off the roof and ran over to hug Lily. He squeezed her so tightly her feet came off the ground. She let out a small squeak like a rubber toy.

"Can I go see Daddy?" I asked. Each word made the pounding worse. I could feel my heartbeat in each rhythmic thud at my temples.

"I want those clothes put away first. And Benny, you stay here."

"I'm hungry," he said. "I want onion rings. I like the onion rings at the bar. Rosey makes mine without the onions. I hate onions. But she takes the onions out for me. One time I ate an onion and my head swelled up. Remember that?"

"I remember," Ma said, annoyed.

"Onion rings, onion rings," Benny said, running up Lily's steps, the Batman cape flying behind him.

"Be careful," my mother said as Benny reached the top and prepared to jump.

"*Onion rings!*" he screamed and leapt from the stairs to the ground, landing in his own version of a split.

"Jesus Christ," my mother said. "Indie, will you bring him to your father for some onion rings?"

At Rusty's, Benny liked to sit at the bar. From one of the shiny red stools he could look through the smoky glass out at the people going by on Depot Street. He could also talk to Rosey through the window to the kitchen, and the jukebox was within reach. Once, for Benny's birthday, Daddy gave him a whole roll of quarters from the safe and he played his favorite songs until all the quarters were gone and everyone in the entire bar was about ready to go crazy with listening to the theme from *Rocky* and "The Year of the Cat" over and over again. Daddy knew now just to give him enough quarters to keep him occupied until his onion rings or french fries or tacos were ready.

"Hi Daddy," Benny hollered.

Daddy was standing on a ladder dusting off the antlers of Zeus, the only animal Daddy ever killed. What most people didn't know was that he hit him with our Nova, not with a shotgun. He was driving, not hunting, when he and Zeus had their confrontation. Eddie Grand drove his pickup truck out to where Zeus and the Nova lay intertwined in a crazy embrace of metal and fur, brought him straight to the taxidermist, and had Zeus's head mounted on a solid piece of oak. Daddy never lied about how Zeus came to his final resting place on the wall just above the good liquor. But he certainly didn't discourage Eddie's stories either.

"Benny, can you give me a hand here?" he asked and stepped down from the ladder.

"Can I have a quarter?"

"After you give me a hand." Daddy grinned and handed Benny the dust rag. "I need you to go find the Pledge in the kitchen and bring me back a clean rag to wipe down the bar with. Ask Rosey to help you."

"And then she'll give me those onion rings without the onions, right? Because my head swelled up that one time she forgot to take the onions out."

"You'll have to take that one up with Rosey," Daddy said and folded up the stepladder.

"Hi Daddy," I said. My head was still pounding dully.

"How's my little Indian Princess?" Daddy asked, winking at me. That was Daddy's nickname for me. There wasn't an ounce of Navajo or Hopi in me, but when he called me that I felt like I really *was* an Indian princess. Like I might find out that my mother wasn't my real mother at all. That Daddy had once been married to a beautiful Indian lady who died when I was born. When Ma was ignoring me or yelling at me or forgetting to pick me up again at school, I dreamed that my real mother wasn't from California but from here. That she was the real reason why Daddy moved us all back to Arizona. It wasn't too hard to pretend, either. In the summertime my skin turned the same color as coffee, the same color as Laura Yazzi's from my class. Sometimes I looked for my Indian mother in the mirror.

"Does your mother know you're here?" Daddy asked.

"Yes," I said, raising my eyebrows.

Daddy raised his eyebrows too and then wiggled his ears. This was *our* special language. It made me giggle.

Little Ike was sitting at the bar finishing up an order of Rosey's enchiladas. I sat down next to him and spun around on the stool. I could feel the blood whirring behind my eyes.

"Hi Ike," I said.

"Hey Indie. You wanna shoot some pool?" he asked, wiping enchilada sauce from the corners of his mouth.

"Sure," I said.

"What time's your mother want you home?" Daddy asked.

"Who knows?" I shrugged.

"Well, then we've got plenty of time," Ike smiled. Ike's voice was like a kid's; everything about him was small. He lived in the trailer park on the south side of the tracks near the Sacred Heart. He said that because he was a little person, his house was more like a castle than a trailer. That the world was a pretty big and exciting place when you were under five feet tall.

Benny came out from the kitchen with a red plastic basket filled to the rim with onion-less onion rings in one hand and a rusty can of Pledge in the other. His face was twisted in concentration. Rosey followed behind with a dust rag.

"There's not gonna be a thing left to that bar if you keep on polishing it. All that rubbing is gonna wear down the wood," she said, handing Daddy the cloth.

"See your reflection in it, though. That way all my customers can see how drunk they look before they go home. This bar has saved a few marriages the way I figure it," he said.

Ike slapped his little hand on the bar and chuckled. He pulled his snuff can out of his pocket, grabbed a matchbook from the wooden bowl of Rusty's matchbooks at the edge of the bar, and yanked a match out. He carefully scooped a bit of the snuff from the can onto the match and then snorted.

Benny sat spinning on the stool closest to the jukebox, stuffing the crispy onion rings into his face as fast as he could.

"You feeding that kid?" Rosey asked, wiping her hands on her apron. "You'd think he never ate nothing at home."

"I'm a growing boy," Benny mumbled, his mouth full.

"Grow much more and I won't be able to afford to feed you," Daddy said and sprayed the long section of the bar that no one was sitting at. The whole room smelled like lemons.

"Can I have a quarter?" Benny asked.

Ike jumped down off the barstool and reached into the front pocket of his little-boy Levis. He pulled out two quarters and laid one in the palm of Benny's outstretched hand. He kissed the other quarter and held it up to the light. "For luck against Minnesota Skinny here."

I smiled, but my head was still pounding.

Benny picked a song, and Sheila came out of the kitchen. She was retying the red canvas apron around her waist, careful to make sure she wasn't covering up her belly button. Her *navel*, she would say. That black hole of a belly button was the key to her tips, she said. And halter tops were God's greatest gift to waitresses. I don't think it was her navel that the customers were looking at, though.

She wiggled her hips while Andy Gibb's soft voice crooned. She didn't know the words, but she sang along anyway. Sheila had been working at Rusty's since January. She was Eddie's cousin. She was eighteen, only six years older than me, but I couldn't imagine how in six short years I might metamorphose into that. I couldn't imagine that a halter top would ever have anything to halt on *my* chest.

Ike racked the balls and I found the best cue leaning against one of the booths. I couldn't wait until I had enough money to buy the Spalding cue. I chalked up my hands on the pyramid of white chalk by the men's-room door and then waited until Ike was happy with his rack. You never break while your opponent is still standing on the other side of the table. Ike had a friend who got knocked out cold because someone didn't wait. The thirteen ball hit him square between the eyes before he dropped. When I leaned over to shoot, it felt as though I'd been hit it the back of the head with a cue ball instead of by our kitchen floor.

I hated to break. I didn't have the same sort of power as a regular-size person. But Ike had taught me exactly how to use the strength I did have, and how to set the cue ball just off to the right or the left of center. I didn't get any balls in, but it was a good break. The balls weren't all bunched up together like they sometimes were when I broke.

Ike was the best pool player in the whole bar. He'd been playing on these tables since before Daddy even owned Rusty's. But the thing I liked about Ike was that he never let me win. He played against me just like he played against Simon or Eddie.

Ike sank four balls and then missed the fifth. "I'm not going to do you any favors letting you have the easy shots," he said, leaving me nothing to shoot at.

"Come on, Ike," I said.

The way to win at pool is the same way that you win a chess

game. You have to set things up, to be able to look ahead, to see what will happen to the balls after you make the first shot. There are some people, like Ike, who plan the whole game out before they even shoot.

I had solids, the little ones, and Ike had me surrounded. Finally, I saw how I could probably get the two ball in the corner pocket if I squeaked it by the eight ball. One slip, though, and the eight ball would go flying into the side pocket. It was risky, but I didn't have too much of a choice. I recited my little voodoo-Hail-Mary-birthday-wish in my head and shot. Once you see it, you need to shoot. *Go with your gut, and follow through.* The ball went right past the eight ball and down the table to the pocket. It looked like it might not go in, but then it rolled softly into the corner.

"Sweet!" Sheila's voice was pure Red Dye #2 and cherry-flavored.

"Thanks," I said, and tried to concentrate on my next shot. I stared at the table, and all the colors and balls started to make me feel dizzy. Almost carsick. Benny put his quarter in and selected 5050, the theme from *Rocky*. The music pounded in my ears, and I leaned over to make a shot and couldn't see the balls anymore. The edges were fuzzy, and my ears were filling with heat and liquid and pounding.

"Indie?" I heard Daddy's voice swimming to me.

"Go get some ice." Rosey's hand felt warm and soft on my shoulder. The other one swam through my tangled hair, touching the place where bone had met linoleum. "There's blood in her hair."

They helped me to sit down at one of the booths, and Benny sat across from me.

"That is some terrible bump. What happened?" Rosey was rubbing my back in small motions, circular and soft. I could have stayed like that forever, with my head down on the cool table and Rosey's hands on my back.

"You got an egg on your head?" Benny asked.

I nodded and felt the ice numbing the bump. Daddy brought me a glass of ginger ale with a straw. I sipped and felt the bubbles making the edges sharp again.

"What happened?" Daddy asked.

I thought about the red piggy bank, about the pool cue I wanted, about Ma and Lily being gone for a whole week. I remembered the way my skin felt on the cold linoleum and the smell of silver spray paint and the sparkle of sequins. I thought about what would happen if I told Daddy what Ma did. About the way Ma's voice would sometimes explode in the night after Daddy came home. About the way their voices rolled like thunder under the floor, through the crack under my door, and into my bed as I lay trying to sleep.

"I fell out of the swing," I said. "I went too high." And I could see myself for a moment in the backyard, swinging on the metal swing set we got from the catalog. I saw the way the mountain peaks magically appeared as I rose above the tree line. I felt the pinch of metal chains on my fingers and felt gravel in my knees.

"Why didn't you tell anybody?" Rosey asked. "You could have a concussion."

I shrugged my shoulders. "It's just an egg. I've had plenty of eggs before." I could keep the thunder quiet tonight. I could hush the rumbles with my words.

I DON'T KNOW WHAT I expected. I guess I imagined that they'd be wearing rubber suits, masks. I imagined them being enclosed in yellow. But the man from the environmental toxicology testing firm looked like he could have been a cable man, a meter reader, or someone who might dig a hole in the backyard for a pool. He pulled up into the driveway in a pickup truck and came up to the door. I could hear him wiping his feet on Ma's bristly green doormat before he knocked.

I opened the door and he said, "I'm here to the get some soil and water samples?"

"Come in," I said.

"The radon guy will be here later this afternoon, but I can do some checks for asbestos and take some X rays of your walls."

I tried to picture what he might see inside these walls, what cancers might be lurking underneath the paint and paper.

"X rays?" I asked, motioning for him to the come into the kitchen.

"For lead," he said.

"Oh."

He walked to the sink and turned the tap. Water rushed into the sink. "Does your water come from a well?" he asked.

"No," I said.

"Well then, I'll just take some soil samples."

"No, you better take some of the water anyway." If I left out one check, Ma would never come back and I'd be stuck here. "Better safe than sorry."

"Sure thing," he smiled. "Can't be too cautious. I'll just be a couple of hours. Then we'll send the samples to our lab. We should know in a couple of days what your problem here is. I'd like to suggest the long-term radon test over the next ninety days or so, though. That'll give us a better reading."

"No, no," I said. "I'm not going to be here for that long." The mere thought of staying inside this house for the next three months made me feel dizzy.

"Don't you live here?"

"No. It's my mom's place. I'm getting it tested for her."

"Well, in that case, when Kirk gets here just let him know you want the short-term test. He'll need to get into your basement to put the charcoal canisters down there. In a couple of days we should be able to get a reading. It won't be quite so accurate as a long-term test, but if you're in a hurry . . ."

"That sounds fine. What time will he be here?" I asked. "I need to run some errands."

"Probably around two or three. You want me to lock up when I go?"

"That'll be great. Help yourself to the coffee, and the door locks when you shut it," I said. I knew Ma would have a fit if she knew I was leaving a stranger in the house, but the less time I spent there the better.

"And how do you get to your basement?" he asked. "I can look for asbestos down there."

"There's a bulkhead in the backyard," I said, pointing through the kitchen window. "It's not a full basement, just sort of a root cellar."

Rosey's address was on the east side of town. She and her family used to live down near the creek in a big house, but after José died and her children left home, she must not have needed so much space anymore. Ma had been invited to José's funeral, but she didn't go. It was Daddy who called me to tell me. He drove all the way out from California to attend, though he said it would have been worth it just to have some of Rosey's tamales. The Jiminez family's roots went deep in Mountainview; nearly three hundred people went to the funeral.

I turned onto her street and found her house among the identical square adobe cottages like Legos in a row. I parked the car across the street and walked slowly to her front door. I probably should have called, but for some reason I felt nervous, as if I might not go through with it unless I were standing right at her front door.

She had a small porch that was still decorated for Halloween: plastic bags of leaves with jack-o'-lantern faces, witch decals in the window, and a string of papery ghosts. A cat stared out at me from the windowsill. Its mouth opened and closed in a cry. As I was about to knock, a dog started to bark and I jumped. It yelped as if it were being strangled, and I worried for a moment that it might appear and attack my legs.

"Shhh," a voice said, and Rosey's face peeked through the curtains above the cat. Her eyes stared at me blankly for a moment; then she smiled, and I could hear her scurrying to unlock the door.

"Indie!" she cried, throwing open the door and reaching up to hug me. She was so little, her head pressed into my chest. She pulled away from me but continued to hold my elbows. "Aren't you a pretty site for these tired eyes! Come in, come in. I just made some menudo."

I followed her into the tiny house. It smelled wonderful; the air was thick and spicy. Green chiles and cilantro. I could hear the pot bubbling on the stove.

"What are you doing home?" she asked, motioning for me to sit on the love seat next to the window.

"Ma's been sick," I said.

"Oh no, your poor mama," Rosey said. "Is she in the hospital?"

"No, no," I said, petting the calico cat as it crept cautiously across the back of the sofa behind me. "She's in Phoenix with Lily. She'll be coming back up here soon."

"So much traveling isn't good for a sick woman," Rosey said, shaking her head. "You tell her when she gets home to call me and I will bring her my tamales."

"I will," I laughed. The cat settled next to me and began to purr.

"My tamales are good medicine."

Ma would never call Rosey. Ma almost never went into Rusty's. For the longest time Rosey and Sheila and any of the other waitresses could have been the same woman for all Ma was concerned. It wasn't until Benny died that she finally met the woman who fed us and made sure the bumps on our heads were taken care of.

"I went to Rusty's to find you yesterday," I said. "How long ago did you leave?"

"Oh my goodness, over a year now. New owners changed the menu. Not so much Mexican food anymore. Besides, they took Zeus down. How could I work without Zeus?" she laughed. "I was going to find something else, and then José passed on, and . . ."

"I'm sorry," I said. "About José. Was he sick for a long time?"

"Oh no. It came suddenly. A heart attack. He just came back from swimming in the creek with my granddaughters, my *nietas*. Took a sip of lemonade and fell down. No pain. That's all. He was an old man."

"I wish I could have come home for his funeral," I said, and reached for her hand.

"Your Daddy was here, that's enough. I don't need you coming from three thousand miles away for a funeral." She stood up and clapped her hands together. "Now, we eat some menudo."

I followed her into her kitchen and watched her as she ladled bowls full of the strange soup. She was wearing a floral housedress and an apron. She seemed to have shrunk a little, as if the stories she told me when I was little were true—that when women grow old they become smaller and smaller until they turn into mice and scurry away. I imagined her black hair now turned silver becoming whiskers. Her wrinkled skin turning gray and soft. The tip of her nose turning pink.

I never would have eaten half of the things that Rosey served at the bar if I'd known what they were, so Daddy had a policy of *eat before you ask*. And usually, by the time I finished eating, I didn't care anymore what had been put into the pot.

We ate quietly. The chimes on a clock in the living room announced the half hour like the chimes of church bells.

"How is your Peter?" she asked, reaching across the table and squeezing my arm.

I smiled. Peter and Rosey had met only once in all these years, but she had liked him. Everyone always likes Peter. She had even given him her special recipe for *pan dulce*. For weeks after that Peter perfected his yellow and pink frostings, offered them to me like small treasures stolen from some other place and time.

"You still being stubborn?" she asked.

"What?"

"No wedding? No babies?"

"No wedding. No babies," I smiled.

She frowned. "Who will take care of Indie when she gets old then? When she gets sick? Look at all you do for your mama. What would your mama do without you?"

"I guess I'll worry about that when I get old and sick," I said, trying to laugh. But the menudo turned from liquid to a rock in my stomach.

"Your face is full of worry already," she said. She reached for my empty bowl and went back to the pot on the stove.

"No more," I said. "I'm stuffed."

"You have a worried face," she said, shaking her head. "Just a little more and then you tell me what you are worried about."

I knew better than to turn away her offer. I even helped myself to another warm flour tortilla.

"I used to the make them homemade, but now they sell them at the Smith's down there where the Foodmart used to be. I know it's lazy, but they taste almost as good as mine," she said, dipping her tortilla into the soup.

"They're good," I nodded.

"Is it your mama that worries you?"

"No," I said. "She'll be fine. She always is."

"You're still mad at her," Rosey said, shaking her head. "Since you were a little girl. I can see it in your face. It's making lines by your eyes, all that anger."

"I'm not mad. I'm just irritated. You know?" I tried not to think about the way my eyes looked tired, had looked tired for so long I couldn't remember my old face anymore. "I came all the way here and now I'm at the house by myself, waiting for her to come home. She doesn't *need* me."

"Sometimes it's better not to be needed," Rosy said. "If somebody always needs you, you never get anything done."

I chuckled, relieved, and dipped my tortilla into the soup, swirling it around and around the last piece of tripe.

"That's not it though," she said. "You think you can fool me by changing directions like that." She shook her finger at me and then reached across the table and touched my face. "Always talking around things, this one. Never get to the point. That's your way, no?" She pointed to the motions I was making in my bowl. "Always talking in circles instead of getting to the meat."

Later, when the radon man came up from the cellar and handed me the box he'd found stuck in a crevice in the dirt wall, I thought about what she'd said. *Always talking around things. Never get to the point.*

I sat down at the kitchen table after he'd left and stared at the box. It was unopened, from a medical supply company in Phoenix, addressed to the nursing home where Ma used to work. The postmark was more than twenty years old. When I peeled back the packing tape and let the hundreds of packaged syringes spill onto the Formica tabletop, I considered her words. *Always talking in circles.* But what she didn't understand is that sometimes the center lacks clarity, and it's easier and less painful to move along the periphery. And besides, circumnavigation is sometimes the only way to return to where you started.

*T*HE NEEDLE DREAM BEGINS *with the sound of doors softly closing. Imperceptible, if I were to press my hand against my good ear. But my hands are at my sides, and I am stubborn, and I am standing at the foot of my bed listening to the doors closing.*

Through the night window, I see the shadows of animals in the backyard. I see the outlines of thieves. They are hiding in the cushions of the old couch, behind sunflowers, illuminated only vaguely by the bright star sky. The only thing that separates me from the backyard jungle junkyard is the pane of glass and splintered window frame. And the only thing that separates me from the other terrible thing is this sound of closing doors.

Tonight, Lily made dying sounds in her sleep. She could have been one of those animals from the yard, growling and hissing. A coyote or a wolf. Through my wall, I could hear Ma hushing her to sleep. I could hear the motion of her hands making circles on Lily's skin. A water glass being set on the nightstand. The creak of a window and a small breeze blowing across her forehead. With my ear pressed against the wall so hard I could almost fall through into the other room, I could hear Ma shh-shhing her. Singing, *It's okay, baby. Mama's here. It's going to be just fine.* I pressed my ear so hard I could feel my heart beating in the wall. And for a moment, I thought they might be able to hear too. I fell asleep on my knees to the sound of my heart in the walls and Ma's lullabies to Lily.

But now, I am standing at the foot of my bed. Still but trembling. My heart has escaped from the walls and found itself quickening in my chest. But this time I have memorized the maze of this house. I have written its paths on the back of my eyes. I know the intricacies of corridor and door, corridor and door. I know where the wallpaper has faded from my pressing my ear against these walls to hear what's happening on the other side. And knowing this, it's easy to find them.

I do not open the doors anymore. This disrupts the dream, turns the bare bulb light off and on. Off and on, rendering them the same. Ma's hands no different than Lily's. Their hair flowing together in one stream. No tributaries, only this one continuous river. I do not open doors anymore. I don't need to, because there are cracks in the woodwork of this old house. I have traced their paths with my fingers, written maps, and imagined labyrinths. I am the cartographer of these slivers. And now, I find the largest one, the most dangerous one, and look inside.

At first there is only the orange paper daisies. Yellow sink and tub and floor. But soon my eyes register their bodies. Lily curled on the floor, holding her stomach. Ma kneeling next to her, touching her hair. *You'll feel better soon, honey. Be a good girl and let me give you your medicine. All the best girls let their mommies take care of them. Are you my best girl?* And then I turn away from the sliver, and press my ear against the cool wood. I hear the crackle of paper, it could be candy wrapper plastic, a Crackerjack prize inside. But when I look again, I can see through the sliver that it is a needle. I know this ritual of vaccination. The bruised arms raised against mumps and tuberculosis and tetanus. But Ma is not a doctor. Not even a real nurse. And the orange daisy room is not the clinic, where even the ceilings are blue. Lily knows now not to cry. And unlike me, she's not even afraid anymore of the needle, hovering in Ma's hand like a hummingbird. She doesn't even tremble until later, after Ma has gone back to sleep.

She doesn't cry until later, when the sun moves through my curtains like hot fingers. She doesn't make a sound on the other side of my wall until the morning birds beat their wings and release their voices in the trees. She doesn't scream until all of the sounds of morning (Benny singing, coffee brewing, Ma and Daddy arguing) have reached their crescendo. Until after the poison Ma put in her starts to make her bleed.

N OVEMBER 8, 1999. Mountainview, Arizona. *Indie Brown is grappling with new evidence in the case against her mother, Judy Brown, also of Mountainview. Reportedly a number of telling items were discovered yesterday in the cellar of their Mountainview home. The items were recovered by an environmental consultant who was testing the house for radon. No radon was detected. Instead he found a twenty-year-old box hidden in the cellar like so many cobwebs or lost toys. This new evidence may or may not support Miss Brown's suspicions that her mother and sister, Lily Hughes of Phoenix, are in fact withholding evidence of unspeakable crimes. Further, X rays of the walls of the home indicate the presence of something transparent and neglected. It is unclear the nature of this finding, but if you knock gently on the walls, you can hear something rattle. If you press your ear firmly, you can almost hear it breathe.*

I went to my mother's bureau. She had dragged the heavy oak bureau from her bedroom as far as the hallway. It wasn't even pushed flush with the wall; she must have gotten tired and just left it there. I searched through her drawers frantically, looking for whatever it might be that would help me make the phone call to Phoenix. Something that would help me ask Ma the questions for which I already knew her answers. *Did you hurt Lily? Did you make it all up?* But there was nothing revealing inside her bureau drawers. I unfolded every T-shirt. Unrolled every pair of stockings and socks. I walked down the hallway to the bathroom and opened all of the drawers, looking for answers in the blond hairs still wound around hairbrush bristles. Inside the prescription bottles with pills like candy. In the pale blue powder compact, where I saw only a small circle of my own face staring back at me.

I went back outside and stood staring at the remnants of my family's history. The junkyard of dreams. I walked through the labyrinth of remaining furniture, opening drawers and cupboard doors, looking. And then I began to move the puzzle pieces, rearrange them. Trying to put together our lost history with furniture left out in the rain. I propped the back door open with a metal folding chair and started to drag the furniture back inside. Although according to the thermometer hanging crookedly on a tree near the porch it was only forty degrees, I took off Ma's sweater and worked in my T-shirt. I turned the heat off in the house and left the front and back doors open. I dragged the bureaus and beds, the vanities and the desk I used to write at when I was a child back into the house. I pushed the old washing machine into the garage and set it next to the new one. I filled the empty rooms one by one with our old things, with the furniture, the wooden skeletons of our lives.

For hours, I struggled to rebuild the bed frames, to remember the layouts of each room. I worked until my hands and back and legs were tired from lifting and repairing broken pieces. My neck was sticky with sweat, and outside the sky was turning pink and orange as I finally dragged an old mattress into Benny's room and positioned it on the metal frame. My heart thudded dully in my temples and chest as I lay down. The precarious bed creaked and sagged with the weight of my body. But I wasn't afraid of it collapsing. I wasn't worried that the pieces might all fall apart again. Because for now, everything was intact.

Outside, the sunset faded into the royal blue of night. Through Benny's window, the back porch light glowed strangely on the backyard. I couldn't see them, but I knew that all the sunflowers were dying. The snow had frozen them at first in hard yellow smiles, but now they were curling into themselves, folding over, genuflecting. When I blinked and opened my eyes, I half expected that the landscape through this window might change. But the desolate yard, now empty of furniture, remained the same.

I stared at the ceiling until the room was completely dark. Until I could count the forgotten glow-in-the-dark stars still stuck there, holding the afternoon sun. Benny didn't understand the night sky, the rules of the planets or the order of constellations. In Benny's sky, the sun revolved around the moon, and the stars spelled out the letters of his name.

Exhausted, I fell into a sleep so deep it was undisturbed by dreams.

In the morning, I opened up the front door for some fresh air and turned the heat up to eighty degrees to the combat the cold. I could hear the furnace struggling to warm the house. I was also starving, feeling as though I might faint if I didn't eat right away. The syringes lay spilled across the kitchen table like the contents of a piñata.

A cat wandered into the kitchen while I was making macaroni and cheese and would not leave.

"Scoot," I said. "Whose are you anyway?"

The cat was black and white, a crooked black mustache underneath her small pink nose. I put her outside, closed the door, and tried to forget about her as I stirred the orange powder and milk and margarine into the pot of hot pasta. But she stood outside the front door, crying, begging to come in.

"Fine," I said. "But I don't have anything to give you, you know."

She peered up at me and her tail made figure eights. Her mouth opened and she cried. I could see her ribs through her fur. I could also see that her breasts were pink and full. She had kittens somewhere.

"Damn it," I said and opened the cupboard to look for something to feed her. I found a can of tuna, and though I knew this probably wasn't good for her, I drained the oil out of the can and used a fork to flake half of the tuna into a bowl.

"There. Are you happy now?"

She ate the tuna and then asked for more. I gave in, and soon she had cleaned her paws and curled up on the couch as if this were her home. I thought about Jessica, hunting in the woods behind the cabin at home, disappearing for days at a time and coming home with dead birds and moles for us as souvenirs. She didn't like to spend time with Peter and me unless it was on her terms. She rarely purred, making it seem that we were privy to a special moment on those rare occasions when her body would shudder and rumble under our cautious fingers. But this funny black-and-white cat began purring even before I touched her stomach, which she rolled over and exposed like a gift.

"You like it here?" I asked. "I suppose you've moved right in?"

She purred loudly and I sat next to her with a fork and my saucepan of macaroni and cheese. I ate until the pan was empty

save for the thick orange sauce on the sides. Peter would kill me
if he knew that I was eating this way. His breakfasts were always
made of something warm and healthy. Homemade oatmeal with
plump raisins and slivers of apples we picked in the neighbors'
orchards. Buckwheat pancakes like sponges filled with warm maple syrup. Peter took time and care with making meals. He took
the greatest pleasure in all the small details. Chuck Moony called
him Martha Stewart, but Peter didn't seem to mind. He always
made sure there were pinecones in wooden bowls around the
house. That the Thanksgiving turkey was one he had first picked
out and then shot with his own rifle. Each log that made the walls
of our house was carefully inspected for character and flaws. Each
photo and picture thoughtfully chosen before hung. I missed him.
But I couldn't bring myself to call him. That would mean ex-
plaining things.

The cat purred and stretched so that I would continue petting
her.

"Where are your babies?" I asked.

She closed her eyes and rubbed her face with her paw.

"Where did you leave them?" I asked.

But she only lay there, waiting for more affection.

"Fine, I'm going to go take a look around. I'll let you know
when I find them. Okay?"

I walked outside, shivering in the cold morning air. I looked
under the back porch and then wandered over to the old shed
where Daddy used to keep the lawn mower and his tools. It was
the slightly open door that told me where to look, and sure
enough, behind the rusty lawn chairs and boxes of old magazines,
I found a pile of kittens, squirming and crying. I reached down
to touch them, and could feel the warmth of their bodies before
my fingers even reached their fur. There were five of them. A

pretty big litter. They were mostly black and white, but there was one gray one. Something inside ached. While the others leaned into my fingers, searching with closed eyes for milk, the gray one was still. I touched its small chest and pushed gently. And then tears began to run down my face in surprisingly hot streams. My skin was cold, cold, but my tears seared into my cheeks like small bolts of fire.

I turned around and the cat was standing in the shed doorway, staring at me.

"Get in there, won't you?" I screamed at the cat. The kittens kept crying. "Jesus Christ."

I picked up the dead kitten and held it under her nose. "What were you thinking? What on earth were you thinking leaving them here?" I felt my whole body rocking, my shoulders rising and falling as I sobbed.

I grabbed a spade from a shelf in the shed and carried the kitten in my palm to the back yard. I laid its body down and started to dig a hole. But the ground was reluctant to yield, even to the sharp spade. I stabbed at the ground and flicked the cold clay-filled soil until there was space enough to put its body inside. Afterward, I filled the hole and wiped my tears with the sleeve of Ma's sweater. I looked toward the mountains, which were covered with snow.

Rich," I whispered into the receiver that night.

"Indie!" he said loudly. This meant that Ma and Lily were close. I hadn't realized until now that we had been conspiring. I could hear Ma's voice in the background, cooing at Violet. Lily was asking Ma to clip some fresh basil.

My hands were sweaty on the receiver.

"Rich, I'm worried about Violet," I said.

"She's doing okay. Your Ma's doing well too. She and Lily are making lasagna. Judy even went to the gourmet Italian place for their homemade sausages. The spicy kind."

"Rich, you need to talk to the doctors. And you need to watch Violet." I stared at the pile of needles on the table in front of me.

"Here, let me take you in the other room. I'm getting some static."

.I imagined him stepping away from the kitchen into the hallway. Maybe walking past the living room and sitting down on the bottom steps. I could almost see him resting his elbows on his knees, his chest falling in a sigh.

"I'm going to take Violet away," Rich said softly.

"What?"

"I don't mean to put you in the middle of this, but I'm afraid that if I don't say something to someone that they'll think I'm the crazy one." His voice was shaking, wavering as if balancing on a tightwire.

"Rich, what did the doctors say?" I asked, my heart dipping and rising again.

"They're getting ready to call Child Protective Services. They have suspicions that Lily made her stop breathing. That she *smothered* her, for God's sake. Did you know this wasn't the first time that she's supposedly stopped breathing? They're saying that Lily's called *five* times." He sighed. "Five times, Indie. While I was at work. While I was back East this summer. She never even told me."

Sweat broke out across my forehead.

"But there's no way to prove it. Someone would actually have to catch her. But they're certain. They say they've seen it before. Some fucking syndrome. *Munchausen* something or other. *By proxy,* I think. It's like a goddamn talk show. They showed me profiles, they had books on it."

"Maybe they're wrong," I said. I felt guilty, caught. As if this were my lie. As if there were something precious to protect. I'd seen *plenty* of talk shows, weekday afternoons after I'd lost my job. I'd seen the jerky black-and-white surveillance videos of women smothering their children, putting poison in their IVs. I'd also watched the outraged women with pink sweaters and wet-mascara eyes who'd been accused. Who'd been blamed. The ones whose children had been really ill. The ones whose children sometimes died. I put my hands on my knees, hiding old scars. "She could really be sick. What would happen then?"

"And all of those ridiculous tests came up negative. She has asthma. That's it."

I leaned my head down on the table, let my cheek press against the hard cool tabletop.

"Lily has no idea that I've been to the hospital. Indie, I feel like I'm out of my mind."

"What are you going to do?"

"I'm going to leave. With Violet. I have to."

I could hear Lily's voice in the room with him. *Did the tests come back on the house yet?*

My throat was thick. "Tell her I'm still waiting. That I should know in a couple of days," I said.

She'll know in a couple of days, he said.

"When?" I asked.

"Soon," he said and then louder. "Dinner will be ready soon. I'd better go. I'll give Ma and Lily your love."

I stared out the kitchen window after the phone went dead in my hands. I closed my eyes and stared through the other window I had etched there for this very purpose. Here was a landscape distorted by the plastic walls of an oxygen tent. Distorted by words and gestures, by bodies and voices confused. Lily's hands, like Ma's hands, making circles on Violet's stomach. Lily's voice like Ma's voice whispering secrets into Violet's small ears. And Lily's breath, like Ma's breath, bringing Violet back again and again.

JUNE 1, 1964. Los Angeles, California. *A blue room. A mobile of impossible butterfly wings. I wasn't born yet when Benny stopped breathing. He got tangled up in his blanket, and he was blue. Ma said it took her almost twenty minutes to get him breathing again. That if she hadn't been trained in CPR, he was sure to have died. That she breathed her own life into him, and that it was her breath that brought him back. Benny would have died. But she breathed her own life into him. She breathed her own life. In this story, in every story, she's always the hero.*

I USED TO BELIEVE that the lightning chose me. That it sought me out. That its touch was not an accident at all, but something devised by the sky. Maybe this made the reality of my mother disappearing into the Foodmart less painful. Maybe it helped to blur the sharp edges of the picture of her in her polka-dot dress with Lily on her hip. Maybe it just helped explain something I didn't have words for then, and still don't now. This I know: It allowed me to forgive the sky, when I couldn't forgive my mother.

Sometimes, I still imagine that it was not an accident at all. That had my mother taken the time to roll the shopping cart back into the store with her instead of walking away, her white pumps clicking against the pavement, then I might not have been privy to the same truths. And if the monsoons had already passed and I had simply sat there until she returned, bringing me a coloring book or a candy bar, then I might not have known how to be careful in our house. Sometimes I think that the lightning was a gift. That the light's invisible hands offered me the cold heat of understanding. Every now and then, I make an offering to the sky, express my gratitude with arms outstretched under rain or snow or sun. *Here I am at nineteen: far away from home. July in the mountains. The Birches Hotel looks like a paper cutout castle in the misty afternoon. I imagine that when the rain comes, it will dissolve into the clear blue lake below. Like paper or sugar or sand.* The help is not supposed to go inside the castle, except through the employee entrance in the rear. Not supposed to swim in this water. And certainly not supposed to walk barefoot toward the forbidden golf course, still wearing the uniform that smells of starch. But still, I walk with purpose across the parking lot where someone is carving a swan from a giant block of ice. I walk past the girls' dormitory where I am living with two other college girls in a room that is smaller than my bedroom in Mountainview. Where there is one phone in the hallway that sometimes goes dead before you are done talking. We really are alone here. All around us are mountains and lakes. The nearest town is almost ten miles away, and none of us have cars.

I take my hair down from its tight ponytail and let it fall down my back. Loose and warm on my bare arms. I step carefully onto the manicured lawn. I am tentative because I fear that the green may be deceiving. It could be soft crushed velvet or emerald shards that would cut the tender bottoms of my feet.

Because of the sky, the men in their plaid pants and bright yellow shirts are all inside the clubhouse, drinking thick liquor in fishbowl glasses, arguing with their candy-colored wives. The golf course is empty except for the carts, which could be carriages for ghosts today in the thick mist. I step around one of the empty carts and raise my face to the sky. I try to conjure a storm just by wishing.

I can't remember why I came here except that it meant I would not have to go home the first summer after my freshman year. I didn't expect that it would be like this. The brochures only showed the castle and the lake nestled in the mountains like a fairytale place. They didn't mention that we would be stuffed into small, hot rooms, or that we would be fed the leftover food we served in the chandeliered dining room.

But as I walk across the dewy grass and the air is thick with electricity, this feels like freedom. Ma tried to the convince me to come home. She was lonely now without Daddy. I knew the familiar acid taste of her pleas in the back of my throat, so I held the phone to my bad ear, and her voice was only a muffled hum arriving weak and pathetic after traveling through the tunnel of too many years.

I walk across the impossibly green rolling hills of dreams. I can barely see in front of me for all the haze. The rain comes slowly this time, beading up on my hair and skin. It tastes green. When the thunder rolls under my feet and through the thick white air, I am not afraid. I have an agreement with the sky. An understanding. *This is freedom,* I think, *spinning barefoot on someone else's playground.* And I trust the sky, because I can't trust anything else.

THE NEXT MORNING, I awoke feeling purposeful. I walked outside to the shed, wearing my nightgown and a pair of boots I found in the garage. They were probably Daddy's, they were so big. The mother cat was lying defeated on her back, the four remaining kittens purring and burrowing into her. When she realized I was there, she opened her eyes and lifted her head.

"I brought you some food," I said. I'd gone to the grocery store and bought several cans of the same kind of cat food I bought for Jessica and a plastic food and water bowl.

I set the bowl down near her, and she struggled to free herself from the hungry kittens. She managed to get away from them and they squeaked and crawled on top of one another, looking for her nipples. She ate until the bowl was empty, drank the water almost as quickly.

"I'll bring you some more later," I said when she looked up at me. "Now feed your babies."

When I called the animal shelter they said I could bring her and the kittens by in the afternoon. They assured me that they'd be able to find homes for all of them, that they wouldn't be separated until after the babies were weaned. I figured I'd stop by to say good-bye to Rosey on my way and then come back and get a taxi to the bus station. The buses ran twice a day to Phoenix. If I took the five o'clock, I'd make it to the airport in plenty of time to catch a red-eye flight.

I couldn't wait for the lab tests to come back on the house. I already knew what they would say anyway. I couldn't stand another night of sleeping on my mother's couch, being awakened by the train every hour when it shook the house. I couldn't bear another morning in that kitchen, eating macaroni and cheese out of the pot, or another moment staring at our old things. I missed the café. I missed the cabin. I missed Peter.

When I called to tell him I was coming home, he knew not to ask about Ma. He must have heard the explanations in my voice as I sat staring out the kitchen window at the field of dead sunflowers. He only said, "Good. Joe will be fine here alone. I'll be at the airport at six." And then, when the lump in my throat grew so large I was afraid I might choke, he whispered, "I love you, you know."

I felt almost happy as I gathered my things from around the house. I picked up my socks and T-shirts, put all of my dirty clothes in the washing machine in the garage. There is nothing worse than bringing home a suitcase of dirty clothes. I finished the orange juice and milk. Took everything else that might go bad out of the fridge. I decided to leave the furniture in the rooms, though; let Ma deal with it when she got home. I didn't want to the expend another ounce of my energy moving things around this house. I left the box of syringes on the table for Ma to find. The open lid was like an open closet door, spilling her secrets, and I didn't care anymore.

When the laundry was done, I went outside to gather up the mama cat and her kittens. Most of them were sleeping, and the mother was cleaning herself. I set down the cardboard box lined with an old blanket and put my hands on my hips. "I know you're not going to like this. But I haven't got much of a choice." And then I reached down and started to lift the sleeping kittens by the scruffs of their necks and set them gently in the box. The mother stopped licking her paws herself and looked at me. "Relax," I said. "You're coming too." And she barely resisted when I lifted her up, feeling the sharp angles of her ribs, and set her inside. She only walked around in circles until she settled down, her belly exposed and ready for when they woke up.

I carried the box carefully out of the shed, afraid to disturb them any more than I already had. I heard the phone ringing as I closed the shed door. "Shit," I said. I set the box down and ran into the house. Ma didn't have an answering machine, and I thought it might be Peter calling to get my flight information.

"Hello?" I said, out of breath.

"Indie, it's Rich."

My heart thudded loudly.

"Hey," I said.

"Indie, I don't know how to the tell you this." Silence. "Christ."

"Oh God," I said. "Is it Violet?" I was conscious of my breaths. My heart was pounding so loudly, I could feel it in my temples and throat and chest. "Rich, what happened?"

"It's your ma. Something terrible. God, I don't know how to say this."

"Ma?" I asked. "What's wrong with *Ma?*"

"It happened this morning when she went to the Safeway to get some formula for Violet. She took my car. She must not have been paying attention. She went right through a red light."

"I don't understand," I said, bending over, my stomach feeling tight and sick.

"She couldn't have felt anything. The other car, it was one of those new SUVs. The impact of it . . ." Rich's voice was soft, fading. "Are you okay? Please say something."

"She just got out of the hospital. She's *fine*."

"Indie, there was an accident." Rich's voice was far away. It felt like snow, falling softly. Like a bird's wings, it was so gentle.

"She ran a red light."

NOVEMBER 10, 1999. Phoenix, Arizona. *My mother pulls out of the Safeway parking lot into traffic. It is Wednesday, and everyone is headed somewhere. It is hot outside, and she has the air conditioning on so high, it is tickling the small hairs on her arms. Maybe she is listening to the radio. Tapping her fingers on the steering wheel with the rhythm of the music, or simply with impatience. There is a case of formula for Violet on the seat next to her. She is stuck in traffic only a few blocks from Rich and Lily's house. She peers into the rearview mirror to check her hair. There is one curly silver hair that will not lay flat. She runs her hand gently across the top of her head, smoothing. She touches her pale pink lips. Opens her mouth just a little. She is only looking for lipstick on her teeth when the light turns green. And then she is moving again, with all of the other cars, a weekday, early morning parade. The station wagon in front of her is full of children, two of them are looking at her, making faces. The boy sticks up his middle finger, flipping her off. Brats. The light ahead turns red, and the station wagon comes to an abrupt stop. She steps on the brake and Rich's car lurches forward, the case of formula almost falling to the floor. Irritated, she makes a face at the child who is still looking at her through the station wagon's rear window. The light turns green, and she is moving again, and she is impatient now to get back to the house. She leans over to adjust the case of formula, which has slipped forward. It is heavy, and it takes a couple of pushes to get it back on the seat. When she looks up again, the station wagon is farther ahead of her now, already through the light, but the child is still pressed to the glass, sticking his fat pink finger up at her in an easy gesture. She feels her skin grow hot, and she steps on the gas. But before she can decipher the meaning of yellow turning red, it is too late. Before she can remember the word for* stop, *the color for* wait, *the sound of* accident *the station wagon has turned right. Before any of this registers, the only color she sees is the blue of her knuckles and of the metal as it comes through her door. And then it is over. Just like that.*

THREE

IT BEGAN SNOWING that night. The temperature dropped down to twenty degrees and clouds moved across the mountains like a dark woolen coat. I stood outside after Rich called and watched them moving, covering the peaks' shoulders. Enclosing them. The sky turned an impossible shade of violet before it grew black, and my fingers were almost numb with the cold. I had turned off all the lights in the house, and the blackness was absolute. The snow clouds swallowed the stars, and *moon* meant nothing other than a faint memory of something bright and white. It was so dark I could have had my eyes closed. I could have been asleep instead of standing in my mother's backyard.

Peter was on his way, flying for the first time in years, so that he could be with me by morning. *Here he is in the midnight airport: buying a plane ticket and a magazine he knows he won't be able to read. Sitting in the bar near the gate, digging in his pockets for stray dollars to pay for the beer. Smiling at the waitress who is distracted, tired.* Airports are the loneliest places to be at midnight.

Ma's body had already been sent to the crematorium. I couldn't imagine what kind of place that might be. When I tried to picture the building, all I could conjure was a shopping plaza in Phoenix. *Target, Bank of America, Safeway, Crematorium.* I pictured neon-lit aisles and cashiers in aprons. Gumball machines that dispensed ashes when you put in a quarter and turned the knob. Fake tattoos or Superballs.

It started snowing that night. In a year it is easy to forget how cold winter is. Seasonal amnesia is the only way to survive in climates like this. It is almost impossible to remember the realities of winter when the sun is shining and the sky is bright. I turned on the back porch light and made my way to the shed, where I had left the kittens when the phone rang. They were crying and trying to stay warm. I carried the box into the house and set it next to the couch. I found another blanket and offered it to the mother cat, who would not look at me. I lay down on my stomach on the couch, my head resting on one of Ma's stiff pillows, watching them wriggle and squirm.

Peter said Chuck Moony would watch Jessica and the house. That he and Leigh would stay there to keep an eye on things while he was gone. He said that Joe could take care of the restaurant, that everything would be fine. But I knew that he was only thinking about getting on the airplane. That he wasn't talking about the things that wouldn't be fine. Remembering the time we almost fell from the sky is easier than remembering cold. It's the kind of recollection that lives in your knees instead of inside your bones. When you think *plane crash,* there is something tangible. It is easier to the imagine than *freezing* or *numb.*

Ma would be cremated wearing one of Lily's dresses. She hadn't brought any dresses with her to the Phoenix. Nothing appropriate. It struck me as almost funny that Ma would be cremated in someone else's clothing. She bought all of her clothes from catalogs because she didn't like the idea that other people had been inside the clothes that hung on the racks at stores.

The mama cat was cleaning the kittens one by one, moving her tongue across their small warm bodies until their fur shined. Indiscriminately, as if each of them were the same. Outside it was snowing. The snowflakes were so big they could have been white petals from a cold flower instead of snow. I reached down and touched the mama cat's head. She looked up at me, annoyed, and I moved my hand out of the box.

Peter would close his eyes when the plane started to taxi down the runway. He would lean his head back against the headrest, put his hands on the tops of his thighs. When the plane roared and accelerated, he would pull the seatbelt so tight it would cut into his stomach so he could concentrate on this pain instead of the possibility of falling.

When I'd asked how Lily was, Rich said, *Not well. She's not doing so well at all.*

Outside it was snowing cold white petals. And they didn't melt when they touched the ground, because the ground wasn't warm. The earth was frozen and unyielding. The hole I'd dug to bury the kitten in was shallow. I couldn't dig deep enough into the reluctant earth for a proper hole. I tried to give the mama cat some more food and water, but she didn't seem strong enough to crawl out of the box. *Please,* I pleaded. *You need to eat.* But she just lay there, and the kittens sucked, sucked, sucked on her red nipples.

When the wheels lifted and the plane rose off the ground, Peter's heart might dive a little. It might plunge in preparation for the falling of the body. He would not smile at the flight attendant in her nylon stockings and navy blue when her eyes scanned across the other midnight passengers. And she wouldn't notice anyway. Fear to her was simply an expression on every third or fourth face.

I wondered about the bones. About what happens to the bones

after the fire. Did they burn too? Did they crumble? Did they resist when the body fell away, an insistent skeletal shadow until the last moment?

The vents blew hot air across the room, but there were cold pockets that you could fall into if you weren't careful. I walked barefoot and stupid into one when I went to make some tea. I stood for a moment in this cold space and it felt like I had no fingers or toes. In the other room, I could hear the kittens suckling, sucking.

Peter would feign sleep. He might pull the plastic shade, lean his head against the window, and pretend that he was only dreaming. But each bump in the sky would startle his eyes open. Each cough, each laugh, each bell of ice ringing inside someone's plastic cup would make him remember where he was tonight. And even when the plane landed, he would not trust the ground beneath his feet.

I thought about the bones. When I thought about Ma's death, I only saw the purple swirl of a borrowed dress, and bones crumbling like snow.

In the living room, I pulled the kittens off the mother. It was like unsnapping a dress. I lifted the cat onto my lap and forced her eyes open wide with my fingers. *What is the matter with you? Do you want to die?* And then I cradled her in my arms, my hair wet with tears and stuck in my mouth. *I'm sorry. Come on, please let me feed you.* And outside, the falling snow made everything white.

When I heard the taxi door close and saw Peter walking up the driveway, my head started to buzz. It was like seeing a ghost in work boots and jeans. Even far away his posture was as familiar as my own hands. I went outside without bothering to put on a jacket. I ran down the driveway, my feet pounding against the cold ground until I was inside the warm circle of his arms. We stood there for a few minutes, staring at my mother's house.

"You'll catch pneumonia. Let's get you inside, okay?"

I nodded and we started to walk back up the driveway. His jacket smelled like the woods at home, like he'd carried a bit of the forest with him. I leaned into him, allowed his arm to curl around my shoulder, and breathed the woodfire smell of him. He opened the door and we went into the kitchen.

"Brrr," he said. "What is it Chuck says? Colder than a witch's tit?"

"No, that's the right way to the say it. He says, 'Colder than a *widget's* tit.' "

"Well, it's nice and warm in here," he said, and took off his jacket. He draped it over the back of one of the kitchen chairs and sat down.

The first winter we spent in our cabin, we didn't know a thing about keeping warm. The apartments we had lived in when we were first together were always equipped with clanking, hissing radiators. The first morning I woke up in the middle of the night and there were crystals of ice forming on Peter's beard. We learned quickly how to keep a fire stoked. How to treat the woodstove like a hungry infant in need of middle-of-the-night feedings. We learned the pricelessness of a down comforter and thermal underwear.

"You want some coffee?" I asked. "Ma doesn't have a coffeepot, but I bought some instant."

He looked at me blankly for a second at the mention of Ma. "Please," he said.

I turned on the stove and watched the coils glow red underneath the teakettle. I concentrated on the jar of instant coffee, on the label peeling away from the glass, on the sparkling crystals inside.

"The house looks different from what I remember," Peter said.

"I had to the bring half of the furniture back inside the house from the front porch and the backyard," I said.

"Why was the furniture out there?"

I shrugged my shoulders.

I pulled the water off the burner before it whistled. I poured the water over the coffee and stirred each cup until the crystals turned the water a muddy brown, and then remembered there wasn't any milk; I'd finished it when I was getting ready to go home. Before Rich called.

"There's no milk," I said, my hands shaking. I turned around and looked at Peter, feeling helpless. Apologetic.

His cheeks were speckled with coarse black hairs, an unshaven shadow. His black hair was messy, his cheeks still blushed pink from the chill.

"It's okay," he said. "Really." He reached for the coffee cup and my shoulders started to the shake.

"I'm not used to this," I said.

"I know." He nodded and took the coffee cup from me. He set it on the table and reached for my hand, pulled me into his lap, and touched the top of my head.

"I'm not sad," I said, my chest heaving. "Why don't I feel sad?"

He didn't answer; he only pulled me in closer to him. He touched my eyelids with his fingers and pressed my good ear into his soft sweater. And for a few moments, he gave me complete silence and darkness, with only the fading scent of pine to remind me that I was alive.

Because there was no food in Ma's cupboards, we drove into town that night to get some pizza. It was nice to sit in the passenger's seat again. To not worry about hidden spots of ice or an elk appearing in our headlights. It was a bright night. The clouds had cleared and the sky was littered with stars, suspended like shining marionettes.

We decided to go to Anthony's, the place just north of the tracks, the one with wooden booths scarred with graffiti and wall-paper that looked like bookshelves. There were pool tables in the back and they served the pizza with bowls of ranch dressing for dipping. In high school my girlfriends and I could get served beer there. There was a guy who worked there who would give us paper Coke cups filled with Budweiser instead of soda. We'd get drunk in the back room and play video games with the tokens he slipped us with our change.

Peter parked the car next to the train station and helped me tie the wool scarf tightly around my neck. I felt like a mummy.

"I swear, you're going to get sick unless you bundle up," he said.

I breathed the smell of wool for a second and then pulled the scarf down, uncovering my mouth. "What about you?" I said, motioning to his bare neck and mittenless hands.

"I've got a natural scarf," he said, rubbing his scruffy chin and neck.

"Are you growing a beard again this winter?"

"Depends," he said. "Will you still kiss me?"

"I suppose," I said. I actually liked it when Peter let his beard grow. It wasn't prickly like you'd imagine.

"Kiss me now?" he asked, leaning toward me.

I kissed him and felt everything grow weak and warm. Peter still has the ability to make me feel the way I used to feel when we first met. Most people wouldn't believe it. Fourteen years is a long time to share a life. And there are times, of course, when one of us grows bored or annoyed. What used to be butterflies may now be something less striking than the orange and black of a monarch. Something more common and predictable, a loping gray moth with slow beating wings. But its wings still flicker.

We were greeted by a blast of hot air when we opened the door to the pizza place. The music coming from the jukebox was loud, the rhythm steady underneath our feet. It was busy inside. There were groups of high school kids huddled inside the wooden booths. Little kids crawling across the big wooden tables reaching for another piece of pizza.

"Same as usual?" he asked.

"Mmm hmm," I nodded, distracted by a couple in the far corner. The girl was probably only fifteen or sixteen. The boy looked older. They were sitting on the same side of a booth. His arm was stretched across the back of the seat. She was crying softly, and he was staring straight ahead. Her face was blotchy with tears. She could have been inside her bedroom instead of a pizza place full of people. She was fiddling with a pair of pink mittens and crying. A bent silver pizza pan with two remaining slices was on the table in front of them. He reached across her and grabbed a napkin from the dispenser. He handed it to her absently and kept staring ahead as she blew her nose. Finally, he stood up and started to walk toward the door. She stood up and followed behind him. When he turned around, he shook his head *no*. I watched her shoulders tremble and then she sat back down in the booth alone. He walked briskly past Peter and me, hands shoved into his pockets and head lowered. The girl looked helplessly after him, wiping at her eyes with the crisp white napkin. It made my heart ache.

We brought the pitcher of beer and the plastic tumblers to a table in the pool room. We sat down in a booth and Peter filled both glasses, carefully tilting them as he poured so there wasn't too much foam.

"Thanks," I said and sipped at mine.

He nodded and reached across the table for my hand.

"You got a dollar?"

"Sure," I said, reaching into my pocket and finding a couple of wrinkled bills. I'd found a whole stash of loose change and small bills hidden in a Tupperware bowl in Ma's kitchen.

"I'll be back. I'm gonna pick something on the jukebox." He motioned to the glowing jukebox in the other room. It was too quiet here without music.

We were the only ones in the back room except for a couple of bikers. Their bikes were parked outside the window so they could see them. One of them was smoking clove cigarettes, and the room smelled strangely like the minestrone Joe made at the restaurant. They were talking softly, their bandannaed heads leaning close across the table. One of them was stroking his long gray beard. Probably a couple of guys on their way through to California or stopping on their way to the Grand Canyon. There were a lot of people who came and went through Mountainview. Not a lot of people who stayed, though.

Peter came back in behind the waitress who was carrying our pizza. "Hamburger, onions, and extra cheese?" she asked.

"Thanks," Peter said, startling her. She turned around and handed it to him. He winked at her and she blushed.

"I'll be back with the ranch," she smiled.

"Indie's famous cheeseburger pizza," Peter said, setting the pizza down.

"I haven't had one of these in a long time." I smiled. "I wish they made them at Lotus." Lotus Pizza is our local pizza place in Echo Hollow. It is sort of a trendy college hangout. Pizzas with white or wheat crust. Pesto, artichoke hearts, goat cheese. I prefer the standard greasy variety they serve at Anthony's.

The songs Peter had picked were what we call our sappy songs, nostalgic songs (for us, anyway) that are guaranteed to be on almost any jukebox in any pizza place or bar in the country. The rep-

ertoire of sappy songs has grown over the years, but there is something comforting in knowing that for a dollar you can transcend
space and time.

I ate and ate until my stomach ached. We ordered another
pitcher and were laughing about something Chuck Moony had
said when one of the biker guys came up and asked us to play
pool.

"What do you think?" Peter asked, squeezing my knee under
the table.

"Sure," I smiled. It had been a long time since I'd had a cheeseburger pizza, but it had been even longer since I'd played pool.

"Rack 'em up." He smiled. His voice sounded like a crumpled
brown paper bag.

I racked the balls carefully and Peter selected a cue from the
rack on the wall.

When it was my turn, the guy who had been smoking cloves
said, "You're not some sort of shark, are you?" As if that were
impossible.

I shrugged my shoulders and flirted, just a little. Then I shot.
My hands and eyes had not forgotten. When I was still working
at the paper, I used to meet Peter and Joe at Finnegan's Wake to
play once or twice a week. I made four balls in, and the bigger
guy snorted.

We won the first game and lost the second. The two guys
bought us another pitcher of beer and I was starting to feel a little
drunk. It felt nice, though, to have Peter's hand on the small of
my back. Two bikers transformed into gentle bears. I think this is
what Daddy loved about Rusty's so much. Where else would you
see a couple like Peter and I yukking it up with a couple of guys
whose lives were stored in the back compartments of their Harleys?

When the waitress came in and told us they were trying to close up, I felt a little anxious.

"I don't want to go back there," I said to Peter as we put on our jackets.

"You want to get a room across the street?" he asked. "We can do that, you know."

"The Montenegro?"

The Montenegro was the oldest hotel in Mountainview. I'd never stayed there, but I'd snuck upstairs from the hotel bar once to use the restroom when the line downstairs was too long. The lobby was red-velvety and chandeliered. The wallpaper in the stairwell was faded, as were the chaise longues. The rooms were named after the stars who had stayed there. Their names were engraved in copper plaques on the doors. BING CROSBY. FRANK SINATRA. AUDREY HEPBURN. Peter and I were given keys to the BETTY GRABLE suite. I'd asked for Frank Sinatra's room, but it was occupied. I couldn't remember what Betty Grable looked like.

Peter led me by my hand up the winding stairs to our room. We didn't have any bags for the eager bellboy, but Peter tipped him anyway.

The Betty Grable room was small but cozy. There was a marble fireplace and a big oak bed elaborately carved and impossibly high. I climbed up the built-in steps, lay down, and stared at the ceiling. Peter was inspecting the velvet curtains, peering through them at the street below. He wandered into the bathroom and turned on the light.

"Was it expensive?" I asked.

"It was worth it. Come look at the bathtub," he said.

I got up and poked my head in. In the middle of the room was one of those deep clawfoot tubs. The feet were ornate and gold.

The fixtures were all gaudy; the frame around the mirror looked like it belonged in Versailles instead of inside the Montenegro. I stared at my face, half expecting that Betty Grable might be looking back at me.

"You want to take a bath?" Peter asked, stepping into the empty tub. The edges came up past his knees.

I nodded. I hadn't showered in a couple of days. The water pressure in Ma's shower was weak, and the few showers I'd taken left me feeling as if I were still covered with a slight film of soap. Now my hair felt heavy and in need of washing.

While Peter turned on the water and started a fire in the fireplace, I took off all of my clothes. I looked at the autographed picture of Betty Grable hanging above the bed, at her antiquated hourglass figure, and touched my stomach, noticing that the softness of my belly was gone. When I was with Peter my appetite was healthy. Without him, I ate sporadically: a whole box of macaroni and cheese or nothing at all.

"It's ready," Peter said finally. It had taken almost twenty minutes for the tub to fill up.

He was already inside the bathtub, up to his neck in steamy water. He'd propped the window open so we could look down at the street.

In the tub, I ran my fingers across the familiar rivers of the scars on Peter's legs. I sat with my back to his chest, and let his arms and legs close around me. I let the hot water close around me. I let the ghost of Betty Grable, whoever she was, close around me, and forgot for a while about going home.

"I could reserve the room for the rest of the week," he whispered after we had crawled under the covers.

He didn't want to be in that house either, and something about that made me feel angry. Just for a moment. But instead of answering him, I only pretended that I'd already fallen asleep.

ILY'S PICTURE WAS IN the newspaper. Ma bought ten copies at the Foodmart. She cut out the article from one of the copies and stuck it to the refrigerator. The photo was of Lily wearing the Stars and Stripes costume with the white vinyl boots that zipped up, standing with one leg on the ground and the other bent at the knee and raised as if she were marching. She was holding her baton over her head and smiling. Ma had taken the picture herself before Lily got sick. For the first whole day of summer vacation, Ma had sat at the kitchen table with Daddy's big electric typewriter. Benny and I weren't allowed in the kitchen—even to get a bowl of cereal or something to drink. She wanted to get it to the newspaper before Lily got out of the hospital, and that meant she had to deliver it to the *Mountainview Tribune*'s office by five o'clock. From my room, I could hear her pounding at the keys and Daddy saying, "Judy, it's *electric*. You don't have to pound so hard." From the doorway, I could see the strained expression on her face. Her shoulders hunched over like they were when she was sewing. All day, she sat there throwing away draft after draft of the article into the wastebasket by the sink. By the time she finished, she'd gone through a whole box of typing paper. But finally I heard the pounding stop, and she was holding the finished article up, reading it aloud to Daddy.

JUNE 15, 1978. LILY BROWN, BEAUTY PAGEANT HOPEFUL, SERIOUSLY ILL. Mountainview, Arizona. *Lily Brown, a local elementary school student and contestant in the upcoming Miss Desert Flower contest, was recently hospitalized. Though a diagnosis has not yet been made, the Brown family remains hopeful that she will recover soon and be able to attend the pageant in Phoenix next week. The doctors are also optimistic. Though this is Lily Brown's first pageant, she is not nervous at all. From her hospital room, she said, "I just want to meet the other girls and have fun. It doesn't matter if I win or lose." Lily is also goodnatured about her illness. "The doctors and nurses here are very nice." The family requests that any gifts or cards be sent to the hospital, in care of Lily's mother, Mrs. Judy Brown.*

Lily was home from the hospital by the time the newspaper came out. There was something wrong with her stomach, Ma said. She would be on medication for a long time. But they would still be leaving for the pageant next week. Ma was a nurse; Lily would be just fine.

I didn't have a birthday party. Ma said that taking care of Lily and keeping Benny out of her hair was enough stress without a bunch of sixth-grade girls to boot. I reminded her that the school year was done, and I was technically a *seventh* grader now. She said she didn't care if I was a senior in high school. I would have a family party and that would have to be enough. *You want your sister to get better, don't you?* she'd asked me. *Aren't you being a little selfish?* And so I gave in. Daddy said he'd take me and Benny out for pizza after I got my presents.

Ma got my cake at the Foodmart. It was white with blue flowers on it. I would rather have had chocolate, but she said they were all out of chocolate and that white cake would have to do. I sat at the kitchen table with the cake glowing in front of me, twelve small flames and only one wish. I thought about the Spalding personalized two-piece pool cue from the catalog. I had been dropping hints for a whole month. I even left the catalog open on the table once, hoping they might notice that I'd circled the picture with a red pen. Daddy had even hinted the last time I was at the bar playing pool with Ike that he bet I'd play like a pro if I had a decent cue. He'd even winked at me.

But when Ma brought my presents into the kitchen, there were only three small packages on the table. And none of them matched the dimensions described in the catalog.

I unwrapped the present from Benny first. It was wrapped in tissue paper, with a Christmas bow stuck on the front. Inside was a God's-eye made from two crossed sticks and about a hundred different colors of yarn.

"I made it at school." He smiled. "It's a gawdzeye. Here, you can wear it." He grabbed it from my hands and helped me loop the circle of yarn over my head. It hung against my chest, the bark on the sticks scratchy against my skin.

"I love it, Benny. Thank you," I said, kissing him on the cheek.

"I made it at school. Miss Carsey said mine was the prettiest. I used all of the rainbow colors. Even black." He reached for it and pressed it into my chest. "It's called a gawdzeye."

"I want to give mine," Lily said. She was sitting at the table with us for the first time since she got home. She'd been propped up on the couch in the living room for days, pale and sleepy. She handed me a package that Ma had obviously wrapped for her. I carefully undid the tape and pulled out a package of barrettes. There were four barrettes on the cardboard card. Each had a row of tiny rhinestones.

"Lily picked those out herself. Aren't they pretty, Indie?" Ma said, taking the barrettes from me and holding them up to the light.

"They're nice, but I'm getting my hair cut anyway," I said.

Lily's bottom lip quivered, but I couldn't stop. "You can't really wear barrettes with short hair."

"Indie," Ma said, her voice stern. "They're lovely, Lily. And you are so thoughtful. She didn't have to do anything, you know. She's been in the hospital, for Chrissakes."

I grabbed for the last present and tore it open. It didn't even matter that it was the pair of jeans I'd been begging for since my best friend, Starry, came to school wearing a pair just like them. Because it wasn't the Spalding personalized pool cue, and the cake was white instead of chocolate, and because as hard as I wished I never got what I really wanted.

"Thanks," I said and balled up the wrapping paper.

"You are the single most ungrateful child I have ever seen," Ma said, low and steady.

I could see Daddy getting ready to stand up and walk away. He always ran away when Ma started. He always ran away and left me to deal with her. For once, I wanted to be the one to escape.

"Thank you," I said, staring back at her, my voice rising. *"I love it. I love everything. It's exactly what I wanted."*

"Where are *you* going?" she said then, turning to Daddy, who was tying his shoes.

"Why do *you* care?" I asked.

"Indie, if you don't shut your mouth this very second, I'm going to . . ."

"What?" I screamed, standing up, throwing the jeans on the floor. "Wreck my birthday?"

"That is enough," she said and stood up.

Daddy was standing near the front door, his hand on the knob. Benny had crawled underneath the table. I looked at Daddy, pleading with my eyes for him to stay. Maybe it was because he hadn't left yet. Maybe it was because it was my birthday. But Ma only said, "I thought you were going to get pizza." Then she picked Lily up and carried her into the living room.

Benny crawled out from under the table at the sound of *pizza* and Daddy said, "Come on, then. Let's get a move on."

At the pizza place, I kept waiting for Daddy to disappear, to pretend he had to go to the bathroom or to the car only to come back with the pool cue wrapped in purple paper. But he never left the table except when Benny dropped his pizza on his lap and burned himself.

RICH WAS CARRYING VIOLET in a front carrier. Lily followed behind him, pale and even thinner than she'd seemed in Phoenix. They walked up the driveway like some strange army. Purposeful and certain. Peter squeezed my hand before he opened the door and let them in. Outside the sun was shining so brightly, it was almost deceiving. The thermometer read thirty-five degrees. For some reason it struck me as funny that we were only a couple of degrees from freezing. As if thirty-five degrees in November was only *cold*.

"Look at *this* little one," Peter said, cooing at Violet, who was remarkably bright-eyed and smiling. Her cheeks were flushed pink, not with a fever today but with the chill of the air. Peter shook Rich's hand and reached for Lily.

Lily has always adored Peter. From the first time I brought him home, when Lily was still in high school, he had her won over. She'd curled her hair and worn blue eyeliner that day. Her favorite sweater. I remember feeling so proud of him, so happy when she pulled me aside and said, *He's awesome, Indie. I want one too.* I remember she'd been wearing Bonnie Bell strawberry lip gloss.

"Let me get your coat, Lily," Peter said, helping her off with her jacket. She struggled to get her arms out of the big pink parka. "Much better," he said and hugged her. I watched her close her eyes and let herself be lost for a moment.

"Hey, Windiana," Rich said, hugging me. His hair was combed neatly and his eyes were bright and open like Violet's.

Peter helped Rich take off the baby carrier and took Violet into his arms. He loves babies. They terrify me, but Peter is at ease with small and fragile things. Rich sat down at the kitchen table and let Peter walk around the kitchen, talking softly to Violet, who peered up at him with curiosity.

Lily stood by the refrigerator, looking at Ma's handwriting on the dry-erase board. *Eggs. Milk. Dry mustard. Potatoes.* I hadn't been able to bring myself to erase her grocery list yet.

"Come see the kittens," I said because I didn't know what else to say.

"Okay." She smiled, turning away from the fridge, and followed me into the living room.

Inside the box, the mama cat was awake and licking her paws. She was healthier now. Her ribs were still prominent beneath her fur, but she was less lethargic. She would get out of the box when she heard the can opener. She was beginning to understand her own hunger as well as her kittens'.

"Oh, look," Lily said, kneeling down. She slipped off her shoes and sat cross-legged on the carpet, peering into the box. "Can I pick one up?"

"Sure," I said and sat down on the couch. But when she reached into the box, I felt my shoulders tense. "Be careful. Pick it up by the scruff of its neck."

"I know how to pick up a kitten," Lily said, annoyed, and

pulled the black one with the white ears and feet off of the mother. It cried out a little, and she cradled it in her palm.

"Look," I said. "Her eyes are open." Until today, all of their eyes had been sealed shut. Now the kitten in Lily's hand looked up at both of us with a milky blue intensity.

"Did you name them?" Lily asked.

"No. I wasn't even going to the keep them. I was on my way to the pound when . . ." I stopped.

Lily looked down at the kitten and blinked hard.

"Any ideas?" I asked. "For names?"

"No," she said and set the kitten gently back in the box.

I could hear Rich and Peter's voices in the kitchen, deep and soft. It reminded me vaguely of the sound of basketball on TV at night when Lily and I were small. Daddy would curl up on the couch, leaving enough room for me or Lily or Benny to curl up beside him. We took turns, but I always seemed to wind up there on basketball nights. In the crook of his arm, with my good ear pressed against his chest, I could never make out what the announcer was saying, but the sound was unlike any other. Comforting and safe. It tasted like warm tomato soup and grilled cheese sandwiches on days home sick from school.

"How was the trip up?" I asked.

Lily was pulling on a loose thread on her sweater.

"Fine," she said. "Violet slept the whole way."

"She looks good," I said.

Lily looked up at me, reminding me of the kitten; her eyes were a similar milky blue. I had no idea if Rich had said anything to Lily yet, about the doctors. About taking Violet away. Lily pulled on the loose thread. Her nails were freshly painted, like they'd been dipped in raspberry sherbet. The color of summertime.

We sat there in silence, a quiet too awkward and uncomfortable for sisters.

"What kind of memorial service do you think we should have?" I asked softly. "I mean, we have to plan this soon. I was thinking of something small. Just us, family. Daddy says he wants to come too. I called him last night, and he says he wants to come be with us."

"She knew," Lily said, staring at the yellow piece of yarn between her fingers. "She knew the light was red."

I sat back and rested my head against the back of the couch.

"Someone saw her accelerate. Someone on the street." She had unraveled at least an inch of the bottom edge of her sweater.

I closed my eyes and listened to the sound of Peter and Rich in the kitchen. The familiarity of Peter's shuffle across the kitchen linoleum. A soda can opening. Rich lighting a cigarette. I listened to the cats squirming inside the cardboard box. To the sound of my own breaths, steady and slow.

"She wanted to die," she said. "And we didn't listen to her."

I didn't want to talk about this right now. I didn't want to hear Lily's imagined version of this story.

"It wasn't an accident," she whispered.

I sat up straight and squeezed my hands together. My heart was beating hard in my chest. A hammer against my insides.

"She made a lot of things happen, Lily. To you. To me. To Benny. But this was an accident. If it wasn't, it would mean she actually gave a shit. That she felt bad. And you know as well as I do that she never felt bad for what she did. Never."

Lily's fingers were tangled in yellow wool. When she looked up at me again, her face had changed. Here eyes were intent, clear.

"Rich is leaving me." Her voice could have belonged to someone else. It was deep and strong. With my eyes closed, it could have been someone else sitting on the floor in an unraveled sweater. It could have been Ma. "I'm sure you know. He's accusing me of terrible things."

"Stop," I said.

"You don't understand," she said, her voice breaking a little. "It's not true. Whatever it is he told you."

"I said *stop it*."

Lily looked at me, opening her mouth to say something more, but no sound came out.

Peter and Rich came into the room then. Peter was holding Violet, beaming as if he'd never seen fingers so small before. Never smelled the faint sweet milky scent of a baby's breath. Violet reached for his new beard and touched it hesitantly. Peter smiled and let her fingers explore the dimples hidden beneath, play with his nose and ears. Rich was carrying a tray full of Peter's homemade chocolate croissants still hot from the oven. Peter had gotten up at dawn to make them. Next to the croissants was a bowl of fresh fruit: three different colors of grapes, slivers of mango, and circles of sweet mandarin oranges.

"Just something I whipped up," Rich laughed, setting our breakfast down on the coffee table. He grabbed a croissant and motioned to Peter, "I hope you don't do this for her every day. It'll spoil her. Hell, you've already spoiled me. I'm about ready to the hop on a plane to Maine." He took a bite of the croissant. "If you won't marry him, Indie, I will."

I felt my skin grow warm. Peter and I didn't talk about marriage. We had an understanding about these sorts of things. We had respect for each other's fears.

I looked at Lily, who had gotten up and gone to the window. She was clutching a ceramic doll from the knickknack shelf over the TV. She was staring blankly out at the front yard. I turned to Rich and he shrugged his shoulders.

"Lily and I were just talking about a memorial service," I said. "I think it should be small. Just family."

"At her church?" Rich asked. "Does she have a church?"

"We're Catholic," I said. Though *Catholic* meant little more to me now than Christmas carols and a nativity scene lit up with colored lights. Easter Sunday dresses and white shiny shoes.

"Where will you spread the ashes?" Peter asked, cradling Violet, kissing her forehead.

Lily set the figurine on the windowsill and crossed her arms.

"She has a plot," Rich said. "It's all taken care of. But they have to wait until spring. The ground, it's too cold now."

"Do you remember the time Benny got stuck under the porch?" Lily asked softly.

I felt my throat grow thick. Rich set his croissant down.

She kept staring out the window. "Ma was making cupcakes for him to bring to school for his birthday. He wanted green frosting and jelly beans." Lily laughed softly. "She put food coloring in the frosting until it was the right color. Then she sent him outside to play while they cooked, because he kept opening up the oven door to peek. But when they were ready she couldn't find him anywhere. We looked for him up on the garage roof and in the field. Finally, we heard him crying underneath the porch. He'd gone too far and he was stuck. Remember?"

Lily turned to face us. Rich was staring at his feet, and Peter was stroking Violet's hair. I felt sick.

"So Ma crawled underneath the porch and got him. She took off her shoes and crawled under there and helped him. It took almost an hour to get him loose. When she finally got him out, he had scratches all over his legs and a big bump on his head, so she let him eat his birthday cupcakes early. He ate so many he got a stomachache. She had to make a whole other batch so he would have enough for his class the next day."

I stared at Lily, standing by the window with a string of yarn falling from her waist all the way to the floor.

"She was afraid of dark places, but she went under there and got him. Don't you remember that?" she demanded, not looking at me but at Rich, who would not look back.

THE HOUSE FELT STRANGE after Ma and Lily left. After Ma had filled the blue train case with makeup and hair spray and bobby pins, stuffed the matching suitcase with child-size nylon stockings and Lily's costumes. After the car and trailer with the stairs for Lily's Stars and Stripes routine pulled out of the driveway, the house felt quiet, as if it were the middle of the night and everyone was sleeping, instead of a bright sunshiny Saturday in June.

Benny didn't know what to make of Ma and Lily leaving. He stood quietly at the front door, waving to Lily, whose pink palms were pressed to the back window, until we couldn't see the car or the stairs anymore. Even then, he didn't seem to know what to think of their absence.

Daddy was sitting at the kitchen table eating a glazed donut, reading the newspaper.

"How would you like to have a party tonight?" he asked without moving his eyes from the newspaper.

Benny turned away from the window. "A party?"

"Sure." Daddy smiled. "We can set up the barbecue in the backyard, invite some friends over," he said, folding the newspaper and setting it on the table next to the now-empty box of donuts. "What do you say?"

"I'm gonna have five hamburgers," Benny said. "On sesame seed buns. Oh, oh, oh, can we get those red chips, Daddy?"

"Barbecue chips?" Daddy smiled. "I suppose we could do that. Maybe get some watermelon?"

"Who will come?" I asked.

"Whoever you want to come."

"Can I have Starry over? Can she spend the night?" Starry was my new best friend. She and her parents lived in an A-frame about a mile down the road. I hadn't invited her over yet; I didn't usually like to have friends over.

"I only like hamburgers," Benny said. "I hate hotdogs. They smell like feet."

"Let me make a few phone calls, and we'll see what we can do," Daddy said. His eyes were bright.

That afternoon, Eddie Grand came by with a bunch of lawn chairs and a portable record player. Benny and I set the chairs up in the backyard and helped Daddy clean off his records. They were dusty because he almost never played them. When Daddy and Eddie left to go to the store to get charcoal and hamburger meat and Benny's chips, I called Starry. When I didn't get an answer, I remembered that she and her parents were visiting her grandmother in Las Vegas for the weekend. I hung up the phone and tried to think of someone else I could call, but no one seemed as fun as Starry. Starry knew just about everything, it seemed: how to shuffle cards with one hand, how to make her hair feather like two dove's wings at the sides of her head, how to do the Hustle.

Eddie's cousin, Sheila, who worked at the bar with Daddy, showed up while I was looking for an extension cord to plug into Eddie's record player.

"Hi Benny," Sheila said. She was standing in the doorway, holding a grocery bag.

"Hi Sheila!" Benny said, jumping up and down, clapping his hands. "Did you bring me hamburgers?"

"I brought you plates, sweetie. And plastic spoons and knives and napkins. Didn't your Daddy pick up hamburger?" She set the bag down on the table and tugged at her shorts. They were cutoffs, worn perfectly with white strings hanging down all around her shiny legs. Starry said you should put baby oil on your legs to make them look like that, but we never had baby oil in our house.

"Daddy and Eddie are at the Foodmart," I said.

Sheila smiled. "Hi, Indie."

"Hi," I said.

"Wanna see the records we got?" Benny asked, tugging at Sheila's elbow. She was four years older than Benny, but Benny towered over her.

"I'd love to," she said and followed him outside to the back porch where we had set up the record player. "You got any Bee Gees?"

While Sheila kneeled down by the box of records and flipped through them, looking for Andy Gibb, I emptied the bag she had brought. Underneath the paper plates and utensils was a pack of menthol cigarettes and a small blue box. I pulled both boxes out and then realized that I was holding a box of Tampax. I quickly put them back in the bottom of the bag and went outside.

"Found it!" She smiled, holding up the *Saturday Night Fever* record. I didn't know what the movie was about (I wasn't allowed to go when it came to the theater) but I'd seen it advertised on

TV and my bus driver played the soundtrack on our bus every morning on my way to school. Plus, Sheila always picked songs from this record on the jukebox at Rusty's.

"Here's the extension cord," I said.

"Thank you," Sheila said and plugged it into the record player.

"My dad really doesn't like it when people mess with his records," I said.

"I'll be careful." She put the record back in its sleeve and put her hands on her hips. "Your dad says you are going to be in the pool tournament next weekend. He's telling everybody you're a shoo-in."

I felt myself blushing. "I don't know," I said. "There's a lot of people better than me."

"Well, the way he talks about you, you'd think you were some sort of pro." Sheila's hair was curled like one of Charlie's Angels. She had blue eye shadow on and sparkly lipstick.

"You wanna see my room?" I asked.

Standing in the doorway of my room, I tried to the imagine how it might look through Sheila's eyes. My bedspread was white with rainbow stripes. When you put the two pillows together they made a full rainbow. I didn't have a lot of stuff on my walls, but around the edges of my bureau mirror, I had stuck the tiny class pictures of all of my friends. It looked like there were more than there actually were because I'd been putting them there since kindergarten. If you looked closely, you could see that there were really only four or five people. I had Lily's pictures and Benny's, too.

There was a stuffed alligator that I won at the county fair the year before on my bed, but for the most part, I didn't like stuffed animals. I collected board games, though, and I had a bookcase stuffed full of them. I played by myself most of the time because

Benny didn't have a lot of patience for games. It wasn't so bad. I would write the colors or the names of the two playing pieces on two pieces of paper. Then I would fold them over and shuffle them, picking one and setting it aside. Then I played for both sides. Afterward, I would read the name on the piece of paper that I had picked to the see if I had "won" or not. It wasn't as fun as playing with another person, but it worked okay.

"Where's this?" Sheila asked. She put one knee on my bed and leaned to look at the framed picture that hung over my headboard.

"California," I said. "That's where we lived when I was born."

The picture was a black-and-white photo of Benny and me at the ocean. He was five and I was three. He was big even then, strong enough to pick me up. He was standing behind me, lifting me up under my arms. In the picture, we were both soaking wet and my shovel and sand bucket were in front of us. Behind us was the ocean. I didn't know who took the picture. I didn't even remember it being taken. But I liked the way Benny was smiling. I looked pretty happy, too.

"I don't have any brothers or sisters," Sheila said. "I guess Eddie's kind of like a brother, though."

I nodded and then I heard the front door opening and Eddie's voice in the kitchen.

Sheila straightened her shorts again and said, "They're back."

In the kitchen Daddy was unloading grocery bags full of hamburgers and buns and charcoal. He handed me a pack of my favorite gum, Big Red, and winked at me.

"Hi guys," Sheila smiled. "Indie was just showing me her room."

"Benny, can you give me a hand here?" Daddy said, opening the fridge and handing him the hamburger.

"Who's running the bar?" Eddie asked.

"Rosey and Nancy," Daddy said. "They'll call if they need me."

"Hey, sharkie," Eddie said, wiggling his handlebar mustache at me. "Your Pa says he's gonna let you enter the tournament next week."

I nodded.

"Can I put on some music?" Sheila asked, touching Daddy's sleeve.

I felt drunk with food and sun and stolen sips of beer by the time the food was ready, but Daddy and Eddie and Sheila were drunker. Benny had been following behind them all afternoon, picking up their beer cans. He saw something on TV about a guy who built an entire house out of pop cans, and his wheels were spinning. When Daddy wasn't looking I snuck a few sips of beer out of the empties. Sheila had a habit of leaving her cans half full.

Now Sheila was lying on the old couch in the backyard, twirling one of her curls that had gone astray. Weeds were still growing up around the couch. I sat down in a lawn chair next to her, adjusting it so that it leaned back at the perfect angle. She was smoking a cigarette lazily, leaning her head back and blowing the smoke out of her mouth and nose. She was wearing earrings made of small brown feathers and beads.

Daddy and Eddie were shooting darts at a dartboard they had hung on a tree.

"You want a puff?" Sheila asked.

I nodded and looked around to make sure no one was watching.

She handed me the cigarette and I held it between my fingers like I'd seen her do. Nervously, I put the end, ringed with her lipstick, in my mouth. It was kind of soggy and tasted like ashtrays smelled, only mintier.

"Now breathe in," she said seriously.

I breathed in and my whole chest filled with smoke. Smoke went up my nose and into my eyes. I didn't want to make any noise, so I tried to swallow my cough. Sheila was laughing so hard, it made Daddy and Eddie look. Benny, who had been piling up the empties in the field, stood up. I was coughing and dizzy, but I'd never felt happier. It was the same feeling I got when I was playing pool with Little Ike. The eight-ball shot that wins the game.

"Jesus, Sheila," Daddy said, coming over and taking the cigarette out of my hand. "She's only twelve."

"I started smoking when *I* was twelve," she said.

"That's not the only thing she started early," Eddie said.

Sheila giggled and Daddy smiled. I wasn't sure if I was off the hook or not until Daddy reached for Sheila's hand and said, "You like this music so much, let's dance."

Sheila stood up and walked with Daddy over to where there was an empty space and they started to dance to the *Saturday Night Fever* record. Daddy was spinning her around just like the commercials I'd seen for the movie. All the spinning made me dizzy. I had to close my eyes to keep from getting sick.

"Watch this!" Daddy said, pulling away from her. He crossed his arms in front of him and jumped down onto his knees. He jumped back up and did it again. Benny clapped his hands wildly. I could still smell the smoke on my hands. The next time Daddy went down on his knees he cried out.

"Shit," he said.

"Are you okay?" Sheila gasped and knelt down next to him.

"I think I broke my goddamn kneecap," Daddy said.

"You want an ambulance, Travolta?" Eddie said, crushing a beer can.

"No, just get me over to the couch," Daddy said and draped

his arm over Sheila's shoulder. She stooped a little with the weight of him, but they made it over to the couch and Daddy plopped down.

"Now I need another drink," Daddy said. "Indie, honey, could you grab Daddy a beer and a bag of frozen vegetables for my knee?"

"Are you okay?" I asked, suddenly feeling really dizzy. I didn't know if it was the beer or the cigarette.

"I'll be fine. Just grab me something cold to put on this. And something cold to drink."

When I came out of the kitchen with a bag of frozen peas and a beer, Daddy was lying on the couch and Sheila was perched on the armrest behind his head. Her long, shiny legs were stretched out in front of her, and when she leaned over to the flick the ash of her cigarette in the ashtray I could see straight down her top.

"Oopsey," she said, setting her cigarette down and reaching behind her head to the retie her halter top. She flipped her hair back and made a big show of tying the strings.

I handed Daddy the beer and Sheila grabbed the peas from me. When she laid them on Daddy's knee, her hand stayed there, pressing them against his black-and-blue kneecap. I watched her big turquoise ring resting on Daddy's knee. I watched Daddy close his eyes when he sipped his beer. I watched them when the sun sank behind the peaks, when Eddie fell asleep in the lawn chair, and when Benny's tin can house fell over. I watched and waited for something else or something more until Sheila finally stood up and said she had to get home. The house was strange after Lily and Ma left. This I knew: The rules were different with Ma gone.

After Eddie and Sheila left and Benny fell asleep, Daddy was still lying on the couch. His knee was so swollen and purple it didn't look like a knee anymore. I was picking up all of the cigarette butts and greasy paper plates and corn cobs, putting them in one of the trash bags we usually used for pine needles.

"C'mere, sweetie," Daddy smiled and motioned for me to sit next to him.

I set the bag down and went to him.

"Did you have fun, honey?" His words all melted together. "Did you have a good time?"

I nodded and smiled. He closed his eyes and winced a little when he made room for me to sit down.

"Sheila really likes you." He smiled. "She told me."

When he kissed my forehead I could smell beer on his breath.

"You okay, Daddy?" I asked.

He nodded. "Indie, you know. It could be like this all the time. We could go away. We could . . ."

My heart started to beat so hard I thought he might be able to hear it. I waited for him to finish. But he only leaned his head back and closed his eyes again, then finally his breath grew deeper and he fell asleep. And I thought for a minute about running away with Daddy. About packing up the car in the middle of the night and driving away and never looking back. But when I thought about the way that Benny had stood on the porch waving good-bye to Ma and Lily, I felt sick to my stomach and tears pooled up in my eyes, and I knew that when Daddy went, he'd have to go alone.

As Rusty's Daddy sat at the bar like any other customer. Outside it was snowing again. Lightly, like dust instead of snow. It was twilight, the strange spot of time when the people who had been sitting at the bar since breakfast had left but before the nightly crowd had arrived. Daddy and I were alone. Though everything had changed, it looked more familiar now than it had the other day when I came looking for Rosey. The hazy neon of twilight and beer signs. The halogen glow of street lamps outside. The way the red light from the Budweiser sign twisted and turned inside Daddy's glass. This was something I could hold onto.

"This is weird, huh?" I asked.

Daddy shrugged his shoulders.

"I can't believe they got rid of the pool tables," I said. "I mean, it just feels like something's missing."

Daddy turned to me. He hadn't changed that much since I'd seen him last, but there was something older about him. Deeper lines by his eyes, maybe. Something more relaxed and knowing in them.

"You play much anymore?"

"Not really," I said. "Every now and then." I thought about how different it was at Finnegan's Wake. Lots of college kids. Playing pool at Finnegan's was more of a mating ritual than anything else. Boys with puffed up chests trying to impress the girls. Girls with too much perfume leaning seductively over the tables, using the sticks as flirtatious props.

Daddy set his empty pint glass on the bar and wiped at his mustache with the back of his hand.

"I got a postcard from Ike's wife a few years back," Daddy said. "He died in his sleep one night. She and their kids moved down to Phoenix after that."

"He did?" I said, feeling my chest tighten.

Daddy nodded.

The last time I'd been back to Mountainview, Ike had been at Rusty's. But then again, so had Rosey.

"I went to see the Rosey the other day," I said. "We ate menudo."

Daddy smiled. "That's what's really missing here. I would give everything in my wallet right now for some of her enchiladas."

"She's coming to the service," I said. "I think it's just an excuse to the bring us food. She already dropped off a whole pan of tamales."

Outside I could hear the piercing whistle of the 5:05 train. A passenger train. When I looked out the window I could see two stories of faces peering out through small windows glowing yellow inside. The floor beneath my feet trembled as it passed. Daddy stared into his empty beer.

The bartender came over. "Another one?" he asked, throwing

a damp dishrag across his shoulder. Daddy looked at me and my empty beer. I shook my head.

"Nah. I think we're done," he said, pulling his wallet out of his pocket. It was the same one he'd had when I was young. Brown leather with the embossed face of an Indian. Benny had given it to him for Christmas one year. He picked it out at the store near Rusty's where they fixed saddles. Benny liked the store because of the rows and rows of cowboy boots. A whole spectrum of leather. Behind glass were silver spurs and belt buckles. Belts hung like leather ribbons along one whole wall. Now the Indian's face had faded.

"Thanks, Daddy."

"Let's go for a walk," he said. "I'm not ready to go back yet."

We went across the street to the smoke shop so Daddy could buy some cigarettes. He grabbed a handful of Bit-O-Honeys from a plastic bin and handed me three of them. I untwisted the wrapper as we walked out into the snow again and popped the candy into my mouth.

Daddy put his hands in his pocket and stared at his feet as we walked down the brightly lit street. Every little shop had its Christmas displays even though it wasn't even Thanksgiving for another two weeks. White lights were strung like electric teardrops from all the bare branches of the trees.

"Do you ever miss it here?" I asked.

"Sometimes," he said. "Mostly this time of year. In California it's easy to forget what season it is. Christmas isn't much different than the Fourth of July."

We walked away from Depot Street, away from the traffic and noise and lights, toward the library. The snow was falling more heavily now, landing in large white puffs on Daddy's shoulders and hair. I could feel my own hair becoming heavier with the weight of snow.

The old stone library used to be a mental institution, back when Mountainview was first settled. Then it became the courthouse and jail. About fifty years ago, they took all the bars off the windows and lined the walls with shelves. It's a beautiful building. There are stone fireplaces and soft couches to sit on inside. It's hard to imagine people being locked up in there. Tonight, it was dark, only the faint glow of a few lights shining inside. We stopped when we got to the little wooden bridge that arced over the dry gully. In the spring it would become a stream.

Daddy sat down on the bridge, dangling his legs over the edge. I sat down next to him and shivered. He lit a cigarette and I breathed in the familiar scent of his smoke. In the silence I knew he was trying to figure out the best way to talk about Ma. He flicked the cigarette down below us before he'd finished it and put his hand over mine. The thick silver Hopi ring he always wore was cold against my skin.

"I'm okay," I said. "I'm really okay. And I think Lily will be okay too."

"Indie," he said, seeming relieved that I'd pierced the balloon of quiet around us. "You never knew your grandma."

I shook my head.

"She was a horrible woman."

I laughed, but his expression was serious.

"She was bad to your ma. She never really cared much about her, it seemed. It didn't matter what she did. Good or bad. It's like she was more of a nuisance than a kid."

Ma never talked about her parents. I always assumed she'd emerged full-grown. The notion of *before* never entered my mind.

"When I met her, she could barely lift her head up, she was so shy."

"Yeah?"

"Scared of the world. But those were good times, Indie. She

and I would ride—I had some piece-of-crap Duster—down to the beach. Did I ever tell you about the place where you could get shrimp tacos for a dime? A lot less expensive then. Filthy little taco stand on the boardwalk. And she had this way of making me feel like I was the only person in the whole world. Like I was some sort of king or something. Hmm. She never wanted to go back home. Sometimes we'd just drive for hours so she wouldn't have to go back to her house. 'Course, her ma probably never even noticed she was gone. I remember, she'd always get sand in the car. She'd never remember to shake out her sandals before we left. Funny. I didn't mind so much then. The little things, you know?"

Daddy sighed. " 'Course, things change. People change. Damn, places change. Rusty's, even . . . after all those years of slinging drinks and stopping fights. After all the conversations, it's gone. Like I imagined it."

I nodded and felt something inside my throat swelling.

"Daddy," I said. "Can I ask you something?"

He looked at me and squeezed my hand.

"You didn't leave because of Sheila," I said. My voice felt like a small bird, trapped inside my chest. Its wings beating in my throat. Scared. "You left because of what Ma was doing, didn't you? To Lily?"

Daddy took my hand and put it inside his coat pocket with his hand. I looked at him, but he would not look at me. I concentrated on the lines around his eyes. Like wings.

"I made mistakes," he said, still squeezing my hand. "All different kinds of them."

Snow fell across our laps, into our hair, making everything damp. But inside the warmth of his pocket, my hand, at least, was safe.

. . .

Daddy stayed on the outskirts of town at the new Super 8. Rich had reserved a room for himself and Lily and Violet too, but Lily said she wanted to stay at Ma's. I put sheets on the bare mattress in Ma's room, and while Peter took a walk and Lily took a bath, I helped Rich set up the portable crib they'd brought for Violet.

As I smoothed the sheets across Ma and Daddy's old bed, Rich struggled with the crib. Violet lay sleeping in her car seat next to him on the floor.

"I hate this thing," Rich said. "I can't wait until she's old enough for a bed."

"You didn't have a problem arranging for the service?" I asked.

"No, the priest was doing two funerals already. He's squeezing us in between the two. It will be short, I imagine."

"Thank you for taking care of everything," I said, and fluffed one of Ma's old feather pillows.

"There," Rich said, the crib popping open.

"Did you bring her oxygen?" I asked.

Rich looked up at me blankly. Down the hall I could hear Lily's bath water running.

"I mean, does she need it still?"

Rich lifted her out of the car seat and held her against his chest.

"I'm sorry," I said, feeling my face grow warm. "It's just that everything is so strange. Everything's turned upside down. Things I thought were true aren't. Things I thought weren't are. I'm sorry."

Rich laid Violet down in the crib and stroked her hair. Violet snorted a little and then her face grew soft and quiet again.

Rich looked up at me and said, "The night before everything with your mom happened, I was getting ready to leave. I had all

195

of Violet's things packed. I had the car loaded up with my stuff. I had maps in the glove box, highlighted maps, like this was just some sort of family vacation. I'd made reservations at three different hotels. I'd talked to my brother in Boston. About working for him. And the whole time, Lily was sitting at the kitchen table. Your mother was upstairs, sound asleep. And Lily was just sitting there looking at me like I was the one who was crazy."

Down the hallway, I heard the water shut off and the splashing sounds of Lily stepping into the shallow tub. I imagined her, frail and small, lowering her body into the steaming water.

Rich's voice grew softer. "And for a few minutes, I thought, *Maybe it's me. Maybe I'm nuts.* And I imagined what would happen if Violet stopped breathing while we were in some hotel somewhere. *What would I do?*"

Rich lowered his head. "And then I looked at her, sitting at the kitchen table, wringing her hands. And I knew that she was thinking the same thing. What would happen if she stopped breathing?"

"I don't understand," I said, shaking my head.

"She believes it, Indie. She really believes that Violet's sick."

Down the hall, Lily lay still in the water. I imagined her closing her eyes and lying down, allowing her ears to fill with the warm, soapy water. Holding her breath and letting the water enclose her. I imagined she might be thinking, *This is what it feels like. To stop breathing.*

"And then I unpacked everything. I carried in my suitcase and put everything away. I put Violet's clothes back in her bureau. I put the box of diapers back in the closet. I put Violet back in her crib," Rich said, touching Violet's closed eyelids. "I couldn't do it."

I heard Lily rising from the water, the sound of her bare wet feet slapping against the cold linoleum floor.

"When the police called about your mom, it was like a sign. And when I told Lily, she just looked at me as if to say, *I told you. I told you so.*"

"But that was an accident," I said. "Violet, this stuff with Violet, is Lily's fault."

He lowered his head.

"What will you do?" I asked.

"I don't know," Rich said. He turned his head when he heard the bathroom door open. "I have no idea."

I heard Lily's feet padding into the kitchen. Rich leaned into the crib and kissed the top of Violet's head. After a while I heard the teakettle whistle but Lily didn't remove it from the burner. It just kept whistling, the pitch escalating to a scream.

I KNEW THAT DADDY wasn't coming home.

The night smelled like firecrackers. Like burnt grass and singed fingers. Ma and Lily were in Vegas shopping for a tap costume for the Miss Pre-teen America pageant. Daddy was at the bar, and I was home by myself, watching fireworks on TV. But through the open window I could smell the aftermath of someone's barbecue and Roman candles.

I knew that he wasn't coming home, the same way I could feel the train in my bones a good half an hour before the tracks rumbled and the whistle screamed. I was learning how to predict departures.

Daddy called like he always did now that I didn't have Benny to keep me company anymore when Ma and Lily were gone. When he called, I stretched the phone cord all the way out the front door and sat down on the porch. The air smelled burnt. Extinguished.

In the background, I could hear the bar sounds. The clanking of glasses and rumbling of men's voices. I could hear Rosey in the kitchen. The sound of hot oil, fat crackling, and the hiss. I could hear the jukebox and Sheila's breath over Daddy's shoulder.

"Is it Indie?" she asked. "Are you calling home?"

"Hey baby," he said, like he always said.

"Hi Daddy."

"Did you go to Starry's to see the fireworks?"

"Uh-huh," I lied. "We hiked up the hill behind her house and watched from there."

I closed my eyes and felt the cold air, sleeping bag over my shoulder, saw the shiny black of Starry's hair at night. I felt the grass under my feet, damp and tickling my ankles. I felt my head resting against my balled up sweater, saw the stars and thumbnail moon overhead. When I squeezed my eyes shut tight enough, I could see an explosion of colored lights.

"Good. I'm glad you didn't stay at home," he said.

Behind him, I could hear plates of enchiladas chiming against the polished wood of the bar. I could hear the creaking sound of vinyl seats and the weight of someone new.

"Listen, honey," Daddy said, his voice softer than a July moon, more gentle on my tongue than a spoonful of night. "You know I love you." And the light filled my entire mouth, glowed and warmed my throat.

"I know," I said.

In the background I heard the bar noises. I could hear the balls cracking against each other, rolling, and sinking into pockets. The jukebox and Sheila's breath.

"Hold on a second," he said as a train passed.

On the back of my eyes, fireworks became the bright light of the train illuminating the tracks ahead of it in the darkness. When the sound faded, I opened my eyes and stared out at our empty driveway. I felt the summer air like a warm breath on my shoulders. Smelled the burnt sky.

Then, he said softly, "I'll see you when you get up in the morning."

"Daddy?" I asked. "Will you wake me up when you get home?"

But as he was about to answer, the train had already traveled from downtown to the tracks just past the woods by our house, and I couldn't hear him above the piercing whistle.

I knew that Daddy wasn't coming home.

Outside, the smell of fireworks faded. I sat on the porch until there was no evidence that the sky had ever been filled with color. I got up and kicked rocks from the driveway into the side of the house, watching how the sharp stones chipped away at the paint. I leaned down and looked into the darkness underneath the front porch, half expecting to see Benny hiding behind the lattice. But there was only the smell of earth and darkness.

Inside, I turned off the TV, went to Lily's room, and opened up her closet. I found one of the costumes she had outgrown and brought it out to the living room. From a drawer in the kitchen, I got a pair of scissors and sat down on the couch.

The rhinestones came off easier than the sequins; they were glued instead of sewn. I pulled and cut and twisted until the costume was just a shell, a skin-colored husk with little pieces of thread sticking out. In front of me on the coffee table was a pile of colored lights. The Fourth of July sky in my fingers when I scooped them into my palms and carried them to the backyard and threw them into the night.

Later, I lay in my bed, not sleeping, only counting the hours until he didn't come home. And with my eyes closed, the sounds of the night trains that passed marking time stopped sounding like trains at all. The rumble of the tracks turned into thunder, and whistles became cries. Became Sheila's laughter and the sound of Daddy's tires squealing out of the driveway one last time.

A FTER THE CEREMONY, we went back to the house and Rosey was waiting there for us with enchiladas. I had given her
a key and told her to make herself at home. The kitchen was warm
and smelled wonderfully familiar. This could have been a holiday,
a celebration, instead of what it really was.

Peter looked funny dressed up. I had only seen him wear a suit
once or twice in almost fifteen years: once at the Birches' employee ball and once when Chuck and Leigh got married. Most
of the time he wore jeans and T-shirts. Most of his clothes were
worn soft at the elbows and knees. Crusty with bread dough or
tree sap. There weren't many places in Echo Hollow that required
formal attire. He'd borrowed this suit from Chuck Moony, who
has been to a lot of funerals, but Chuck is about three inches
shorter than Peter, so it was a little small on him. He kept tugging
at the sleeves throughout the service. As soon as we got back to
Ma's house he went into the bedroom to change. Rich, on the
other hand, looked comfortable in his suit. In the morning before

we left for the church I had found him standing in the living room at the ironing board, spraying his white shirt with starch, steam coming in small bursts from Ma's iron. He might have stayed inside the safety of that stiff suit all day if Violet hadn't spit up formula on his shoulder.

"I think I'm getting a migraine," Lily said. She looked at Rich, her eyes asking for something. "I need to go lie down."

But Rich only shifted Violet to his other shoulder and wiped at her mouth with a clean cloth diaper.

Defeated, she went into Ma's room and slammed the door. I went to the kitchen to help Rosey.

"Hola," Rosey said. She was bent over, leaning into the oven to remove the now-steaming pan of enchiladas. *"Ay, que bonita,"* she said, gesturing to the dress I'd taken straight from the rack to the register at the store at the mall without even trying it on. It was nothing I would ever wear again. Black polyester with a shiny black belt around the waist. I would probably throw it away rather than packing it with my things when Peter and I finally went home.

"Thanks," I said. "You need some help?"

"No, no, no," she said. "You sit down."

I knew better than to argue with Rosey, so I sat down at the kitchen table and opened up Rich's pack of cigarettes. There were only a couple left, so I closed it and shoved it aside.

"Go ahead," Rich said. He was standing in the doorway, rocking Violet gently in his arms. "I've got another pack in the car."

"Thanks," I said and pulled one out of the pack. I only smoke on special occasions. I wondered briefly if this constituted a "special" occasion. I opened the door to the backyard a crack and stood by the open door, blowing my smoke outside.

"I picked up a platter of deli meats at Smith's, some pop and some liquor," Rosey said. She pulled off a pair of Ma's oven mitts and set them on the table. "I didn't know what everybody around here drinks, so I bought vodka and whiskey. I like, personally, the whiskey, but I don't know about everybody else."

"Where is it?" I asked.

"In that grocery bag." Rosey pointed to a bag on the counter.

"You want a drink?" I asked. "Rich?" But he had gone into the living room with Peter.

"*Si, si,*" she said. "Put a little Coke in there too."

I tossed the cigarette onto the cold ground outside; it sizzled when the burning end hit the damp grass. I grabbed a handful of ice from the freezer and filled two tumblers, pouring the thick whiskey over the ice, adding Coke as an afterthought. I handed Rosey the cocktail and motioned for her to sit down next to me.

"Your Daddy looked handsome in his suit." She smiled. "Nice to see him again."

I nodded. Daddy, like Peter, felt silly in a suit and was stopping at his motel room to change before he came back to the house.

"California seems to like your Daddy," she said.

I nodded again. When Daddy first left with Sheila all those years ago, he bought a bar somewhere just south of LA. He sold it a couple of years later when he and Sheila broke up. Since then he'd been living in San Diego; he owned a bar in Pacific Beach. Peter and I had gone there once. It catered mostly to bikers. Outside the bar on any given day the parking spaces were filled with Harleys, twenty or thirty of them in a row, each more elaborate and ornate than the next. Sitting at the open window that faced the beach, when a group of bikers left it looked and sounded like a flock of strange birds taking off. California *did* like Daddy. I suppose it always had. I wondered if he ever thought about what would have happened if he'd never met Ma and come to Arizona.

"The service was nice, no?" Rosey asked, finishing her drink quickly and setting the cup full of ice on the table. "That new priest is a *niño*, a baby, huh? Mama's milk still on his breath."

"He wore *sandals*," I said.

The priest at the Catholic church was young. He wore Birkenstocks with thick wool socks. Because there was a funeral scheduled right after Ma's he kept checking his watch throughout the service. The flowers from the last funeral hadn't been removed yet, so the church was filled with the strange heady scent of yellow roses. It felt somehow wrong to see yellow roses in November; contrary. I had to keep looking out the stained-glass windows at the dusting of snow on the ground to remind myself that it was almost winter. Maybe this is what Daddy meant about it being hard in California to know what time of year it was. And because the roses were leftover, I felt vaguely guilty that Ma's funeral was decorated with borrowed flowers. The priest had a tickle in his throat, too, and had to stop several times to cough. Each pause made me more and more uncomfortable. Daddy sat between Lily and me. Rich and Peter were on either side. Rosey sat alone in the back. Ma's doctor showed up, as did her hairdresser, and the boy she hired every winter to shovel her driveway. This, like the borrowed roses, is what made me sad. It wasn't that Ma was gone, but the glaring evidence of how alone she was in this world. *Everybody leaves her,* Lily had said. *Daddy left her, you left her. I'm the only one who stayed. I'm the only one. . . . She's lost everything. She lost Benny and then she lost everybody else.* Lily was the only one who cried, and somehow watching the tears rolling down in pink streaks through the makeup she'd put under her eyes to hide the dark circles made everything all the more pathetic. Ma would have been embarrassed by the service. She would have pursed her lips and hissed, *Great turnout.*

Daddy came in then and I got up to pour him a drink. Vodka

and ginger ale. That's all he ever drank besides beer. He hugged Rosey from behind as she used a spatula to scoop the cheesy enchiladas onto the paper plates we found in one of Ma's cupboards.

"This is the real reason I came," Daddy winked at me. And I knew that he was telling the truth.

We sat in the living room with plates on our laps and cocktails resting on the armrests of our chairs, trying not to spill anything on Ma's carpet. After we had folded the dirty paper plates in half and stuffed them into the wastebasket under the sink, we returned to the living room and everyone made their excuses for leaving. Lily, who had come bleary-eyed out of the bedroom when Rich called for her, said she still had a headache and wanted to lie down again. Rich fell asleep on the couch with Violet sprawled across his chest, and Daddy and Rosey left together. Rosey's grandchildren were coming for dinner and Daddy was going to drive down to Phoenix and stay the night with Eddie Grand and his wife. His flight wasn't until tomorrow morning.

"Thank you for coming, Daddy," I said and leaned into him.

"You're welcome, honey. Please call me if you need anything at all. Okay? And maybe you can talk Peter into getting on a plane and coming to visit me soon?"

I nodded and smiled, but after his car had disappeared through the trees, I felt my throat grow thick with tears. I have never gotten used to saying good-bye to Daddy.

In Benny's room, I took off my stockings and shoes and curled up in a spoon with Peter on the small bed. And only then, with the familiar warmth of Peter behind me and his beard tickling the back of my neck, did I start to feel sad. Only in the sweet pine circle of his arms with his fingers reaching to brush the hair out of my eyes, did the tears come. And even then, my body didn't tremble. I held my breath to keep my shoulders still and turned my face so that the tears fell into my hair.

. . .

I dreamed about Ma. I dreamed her gestures and slivers of her expressions. A wave, the way her hand flew to her throat when she was nervous. A half-smile, the blankness of her disappointment. But no matter how hard I tried, I could not dream a whole picture of her. She came to me in fragments that slipped through my fingers like sand. I dreamed the way she shrugged her shoulders, and the corners of her smiles.

I woke up cold and disoriented. Peter was still asleep next to me, but he had come uncurled from my body and was facing the wall. His shirt was twisted, and the cuffs of his jeans had ridden up around his calves. I thought for a minute about straightening him out, but then realized it would probably only wake him.

I got out of Benny's bed and opened the door to the hallway. The lights were off, and the hallway was dark. It could have been the middle of the night; it could have been just before dawn, but when I looked at my watch, I saw that it was only seven o'clock. The door to Ma's room was open, and Rich was sprawled across Ma's bed, still wearing his dress pants and starched white shirt. Violet wasn't in the crib next to the bed, and Lily wasn't in the room either.

My heart started to pound as I walked quickly down the hallway into the dark kitchen and into the living room. My eyes were adjusting to the darkness. I could see the shadows and outlines of furniture and walls, appliances and sharp corners. I walked on tiptoes to the living room, afraid of what I would find. It was too quiet. *Not even a breathing sound.*

Lily was sitting on the couch, holding a blanketed bundle in her arms. She and the bundle were motionless. She could not hear me, could not see me, here in the doorway. It was too dark. I felt a scream rising in my throat, instinctual and fierce. My knuckles tightened on the door frame when Lily's head lowered and she leaned over, kissing Violet's pale head.

"Lily," I said, a warning.

Lily looked up and fear flashed in white streaks across her face, through her eyes, made her hands tremble. The muscles in her neck tightened as she spoke, "Indie, please . . ."

"What are you doing?" I said, moving slowly toward the couch. "What did you do to her?"

Lily shrank and clutched Violet tightly. "Indie, please don't tell him, please don't . . ."

I sank to my knees in front of her and reached for Violet. *It might be too late,* I thought. *Oh God, she may already be gone.*

But as my hands closed around the edges of her blanket and Lily's hands tightened around her, Violet let out a small cry. Irritated and annoyed. We'd woken her. We'd only woken her from sleep. She blinked twice, hard, and then her eyes closed sleepily again.

"Indie, please don't tell Rich. I only wanted to hold her."

Still kneeling, I sat back on my knees and looked at Lily's terrified face. I didn't understand.

"He won't let me near her. But I just wanted to hold her. I just wanted to watch her sleeping." Lily was crying, harder than she had cried at Ma's funeral. "I promise," she sobbed. "I won't hurt her."

My knees were numb. I couldn't move.

Lily reached for me with her free hand, her fingers imploring. They clutched at my arm, begging for me to understand. To forgive. And this gesture, these fingers asking forgiveness, were unfamiliar. They didn't belong to Ma. They belonged to Lily, and they thrummed *I'm sorry, I'm sorry, I'm sorry* against my skin.

The sounds trapped in my throat, the animal sounds of protection and warning, dissolved. All of the anger and fear were like sugar in warm water. Metal becoming liquid, the solid pang of tin turning into smooth mercury. I put my fingers across Lily's and looked for Ma in her face. But there was only the soft blue of Lily's eyes. And in the dark living room with Violet sleeping quietly between us, I thought, *This is all I wanted*. All of this time. I only wanted an apology. I only wanted someone to acknowledge that something had gone terribly wrong.

"Did you do it?" I asked quietly, quietly. "Did you?"

Lily's fingers dug into my wrist and then she let go of my arm, her eyes open wide. She pulled Violet to her chest and shook her head.

"You bitch. You goddamned bitch," she whispered.

And in that one moment, all of the fragments of my dream, the recollected slivers, Ma's gestures fractured into glass, suddenly realigned themselves. The corners of her mouth, her clenched jaw, and the defiant flat circles of her eyes became Lily's face. She looked at me in disbelief and hissed, "How can you believe that shit he's telling you? What kind of person do you think I am? What kind of mother would do that?"

I stared into the empty blue of her eyes, but she was already gone.

"A mother like ours," I said. "Someone like Ma."

THERE IS ALWAYS A SMALL gentle gesture that confuses every-thing. There is always a sliver of kindness more painful than glass or fragments of bone. Like the way a hand becomes suddenly tender after fingers unravel from a fist. The simple swell of a tear in an eye that used to be unforgiving. We cling to these acknowl-edgments, these small apologies, trying to make sense, but it's no easier or more realistic than holding water in your hands. Colored sand or wind.

I used to love the hems of my mother's dresses. On the floor where Benny and I played with pots and pans and wooden spoons, I could touch them sometimes when she walked by. They felt like wind, I thought, the way they brushed across my fingers and then were gone until she moved across the room again. When she stood in the bathroom, peering in the mirror at her face, I could sit on the cold linoleum forever looking, touching the bottom of her dress. Benny preferred the soft brown boots that zipped up. Her animal legs of coffee-colored suede. When she left them on the floor, unzipped and open, he put his hands inside to the feel their warmth. But it was the crisp edge of cotton or the loose sway of rayon that thrilled me. If she had let me, I would have held the edges against my cheek, put them in my mouth and tasted them.

Before the lightning threw me into the sky and flung me down again, there was tenderness. In the hems of Ma's dresses and in the way she brushed Benny's hair out of his eyes. But afterward, gentle fingers curled into fists again. Fists that hung at her sides, threatening when my fingers reached to touch that part of her that reminded me of wind.

When we came home from the Foodmart, Ma called Daddy at the bar. *I was leaning inside the car, looking for Indie's Crissy doll. She was fussing in the shopping cart. I knew she wouldn't stop until I found the doll. Lily was in the back. I only leaned in for a second. Less than a second. That's when it happened.*

After she hung up the phone, she turned around and held on to my shoulders.

"Where's your Crissy doll?" she asked, her voice shaking.

I shrugged. I had stopped playing with her after the button that controlled her long red hair broke. She was useless with her ponytail stuck inside her. I closed my eyes and tried to think of where I had put her.

"We have to find her," Ma said and ran down the hallway to my room. I heard the creaky lid of my toy chest and the *thump, thump, thump* of my other toys on the wooden floor. "Damn it. Where is that stupid doll?"

On the back of my eyes I saw her red hair before she broke. I saw her outside in the field behind the house. I saw Benny twirling her pink arms around and around.

"Her button broke," I said walking down the hallway to my room.

"This is very important. Do you know where she is?"

I shook my head. "She only has one arm. Benny twirled the other one off."

"Where did Benny put her?"

I shrugged my shoulders again, sat down cross-legged on the floor next to the open toy box and picked up an alphabet block. The red paint was worn to a soft pink. When Ma started to walk away, I looked up at her polka-dot dress, at the sharp hem dotted black and white, and I reached for her. I wanted to feel the crisp cotton between my fingers. I wanted to hold on to her.

The sting of a slap. It was sharper and more painful than the lightning rushing through my body. I pulled my hand away from her and enclosed it inside the one that wasn't wounded.

When I looked up, I saw Ma standing over me, her face colorless and blank.

"She's in the flowers," I said, my throat constricting and my hand stinging still.

"Outside?" she asked, her face brightening. She knelt down next to me, her skirt swirling around her like a fortress of polka dots. "In the backyard?"

I nodded and sucked my bottom lip in to keep from crying.

When she leaned over to kiss my cheek, I recoiled. I'd cut my fingers on the sharp edges of her. I wasn't about to let that happen again. But her lips were warm and soft and her skin smelled like Lily's: powder and sweet lemons.

I followed her back into the kitchen and watched her through the open back door as she walked to the field to find my Crissy doll. She bent over, searching through the tangled grass. She could have been picking flowers. She could have been making a bouquet of purple asters to put in a coffee-can vase on the kitchen table.

When she found the doll, she turned to face me. Standing in

the middle of the field of wildflowers, holding my broken doll by her remaining arm, she hollered, "Indie, look! I found it!"

I didn't care about the doll; I only cared that Ma's expression had changed. That her face was smooth and smiling again. When she came into the kitchen she handed me the doll and picked me up. My legs dangled at her sides and she held me close. I felt warm and happy. I even felt tenderness toward the doll I had neglected and left outside in the rain. Nothing in the world mattered in Ma's arms with Crissy in my hands and my legs embracing the polka-dot breezes of Ma's dress.

That night, Daddy helped me put on my blueberry nightgown and piled blankets from my bed on the couch. I would go to the doctor in the morning to make sure everything was okay, but for now he wanted me close so he could keep an eye on me. In the kitchen, I could hear the *clink, clink* of Daddy's fork on the plate, the *glug, glug* of milk being poured from the gallon jug. He had brought the TV tray into the living room and set it up for me. But my mouth was full of too many new strange tastes. The lightning had made my tongue confused.

"I just don't understand why you left her in the cart while it was raining," Daddy said softly.

"I was in the car looking for her *damn* doll," Ma hissed. "I can't have my eye on her every second. When I turned around, it had already happened. If I hadn't been there, *she* wouldn't be here now, would she?" Ma's voice mixed in my mouth with Daddy's like orange juice and toothpaste.

I tried to separate the tastes. Meat loaf, cheesy scalloped potatoes, wax beans from a can. Ma's lies and Daddy's acquiescence. It only stopped when the room fell silent. And even then, there was the faint bitter of Daddy's sigh on my lips. Of Ma's insistence and the hint of sugar in Lily's cooing. Benny was the only quiet one. The only one who didn't leave a terrible taste in my mouth.

I held the Crissy doll tightly to my chest. I pushed the button hard and tried to pull her hair out of her head. But the button was broken and her ponytail was stuck somewhere deep inside her plastic body.

THE RESULTS FROM THE environmental toxicity tests arrived in Ma's mail the day after the funeral. I had called the radon guy already and told him not to bother coming back, but I'd forgotten about these. I threw all the other mail addressed to Ma (sweepstakes entry forms, magazine subscription renewals, Sears sale catalog) on the kitchen table and held the envelope from the lab.

I could hear the shower running. Peter had been in there for almost a half hour already. He did this in Maine sometimes to get warm on colder days, as if the heat of the water might penetrate his skin and stay inside of him after he turned the faucet off. I imagined him using Ma's shampoo, not bothering to read the label that said it was for colored hair. Using her lavender soap, her mint dental floss, and her clean white towels. Peter didn't notice these things the way I did. Everything I saw, now, seemed to reveal a little something more about Ma. The disposable things of her life seemed to say more about her than anything else did.

I'd brought the kittens to the Humane Society reluctantly. The mother was healthier and more affectionate now. I'd grown more attached to them than I had ever intended. When the girl with braces and a lazy eye took the cardboard box from me, I felt sad and guilty.

There was still some Coke left in the two-liter bottle that Rosey had brought over. I took it out of the fridge and unscrewed the plastic top. It made a weak hiss, and when I poured it into a cup and sipped, it was too sweet and almost completely flat. I sat down and looked at the smudged postmark on the manila envelope from the lab. It was dated the day that Ma died.

In the bathroom, the shower had stopped running. I could hear Peter brushing his teeth. He would be wearing just his jeans, a towel around his neck like a bib. He brushed the top teeth first and then the bottom, in the circular motions they teach you in those first early visits to the dentist. He would floss and then brush again. Quickly, just using water instead of toothpaste.

The girl had braces and a lazy eye. She was probably no more than sixteen. One of those girls who decides to become a veterinarian after her first pet dies. I see her with a cat, long-haired and gray. She might have stood barefoot in the blood-speckled snow after the car passed, staring at the scene of the accident.

Funny. Mail keeps coming long after a person dies. It takes a while for your name to disappear from all of the computers that have, at some time in your life, stored your name and address. After Chuck Moony's mother died, he had to forward more than thirty magazines to his address, and for years afterwards, they kept trying to get her to renew.

Peter's habits are as familiar to me as my own. Clothes are put on left to right. Sleeves, pant legs, shoes. He's done this since he was a child, and he doesn't remember anymore why he started, but he insists he can't stop now. It is his ritual to ward off danger.

Left then right. Gloves. Socks. Shoes. The one day he did it wrong, there was a horrible accident on the road. The motorcyclist in front of him ran into the back of a semi and was decapitated. Just like that. Left to right. It's just easier that way.

I thought about the kitten that died. The one I'd buried in the backyard. The ground had been too hard, and I wasn't able to make a proper grave. I hoped that it would be okay out there after I was gone again. I tried not to think about coyotes or hawks or vultures. They all descended when you weren't looking. I could turn my head for a second, and its body might have been ripped from the earth. I didn't tell the girl at the animal shelter about the one that died. How do you explain something like that to a teenage girl with braces and a lazy eye?

I wanted the results to be positive, for the tests to reveal that there was poison all through the house. I wanted there to be lead in the water and walls. I wanted there to be asbestos, radon, and arsenic. I wanted the poison to have been here all along, lurking in everything she drank and breathed and touched. I wanted all of what she'd said to be true. For once, I wanted to believe. But instead of tearing at the sealed flap, I folded the envelope and stuffed it into the trash can.

Peter flushed the toilet and ran water in the sink. He would run it until there were no little hairs in the basin. He would even wipe a clean towel across the top of the faucet so there would be no spots. Everything in Peter's world was clean and bright. Precise. The stars in Peter's sky were perfectly aligned.

Rich said he would take care of everything. He was putting Ma's house up for sale. He had a friend who was a real estate agent in Mountainview. He would sell all of her things. He said, *Take what you want, Indie. I'll take care of the rest.*

I whispered, "What do we do?"

He took a drag of his cigarette and when he exhaled, it looked like ghosts escaping from his mouth. "I don't know."

I nodded and took the cigarette he offered me. I inhaled and then made my own, smaller ghosts.

Later I went through the drawers and cupboards and filled a small box with the things I wanted to keep. A corkscrew, some Tupperware, a giant black mohair scarf. The things I really wanted I couldn't take home with me: the smell of snow through Benny's window, the sound of wind chimes Ma had hung out back years ago, the glow and chaos of the constellations on Benny's ceiling at night.

After everyone was gone, Peter and I went for a walk in the woods behind the house. I wrapped Ma's scarf around my neck and breathed the chemical smell of mothballs. We held hands, but we didn't say anything. I pretended that we were walking though the woods behind our house. That we were already home instead of here. The sky was bright blue, like the inside of a robin's egg, a color you couldn't possibly know about unless you'd seen a robin hatch from its shell. Peter walked slowly so that I could keep up. His legs were longer than mine, and despite his limp, he usually walked much faster than I did.

"You cold?" he asked, squeezing my hand. I'd forgotten to bring mittens.

"Nah," I said, stepping over a branch.

"You sure? We could go back to the house and get some mittens."

"I'm *fine*," I said.

Peter raised his eyebrows and said nothing.

"What?"

"Nothing," he said.

I scowled at him, suddenly angry. He stared straight ahead. The only sounds were our feet slapping against the layers and layers of wet leaves and the sounds of our breaths.

"Why are you pissed off?" I pushed.

"I'm not pissed off. I was just thinking we could go back to the house and get you some mittens. Jesus. Forgive me."

"I guess I just don't understand why you always have to save the day. You know? *Indie, do you need this? Indie, do you need that? I'll take care of it. Don't you worry. Blah blah blah.* I can take care of myself you know." I didn't know where this was coming from, but it had already been said.

"What are you *talking* about?" Peter said. He stopped walking and reached for my hand.

"I *mean,*" I said, yanking my hand away, "that I'm tired of being taken care of. I'm tired of you always having to pick up the pieces. I'm tired of being the one who's always a mess."

Peter sat down on a fallen tree and stared at his hands.

"I lose my job and you hand me a spoon and some muffin batter. I lose my mother and you're on the next plane. I lose my mind and there you are. *Have a new one, Indie. Don't worry, it's on me.*"

"You're not making any sense," he said.

"I'm making perfect sense. You don't need *me.* You need me to be a mess."

"I'm sorry, I thought that's what people do for the people they care about. I must have been crazy," he said and hit his forehead with the heel of his hand.

I sat down cross-legged on the damp leaves, waiting for him to tell me that my pants would get wet, that I'd get a cold, that I was making another mistake. "You never need me to pick up the pieces for you. You never even *have* pieces," I said.

"Of course I do," he said and reached again for my hands. But he and I both knew he was lying. That's what people *really* do when they care for each other. They say what they're supposed to say. They'll say anything to the keep the balance even, even when it's not.

We walked back to the house quietly.

Inside, I closed the curtains in the living room so there was only a sliver of light. Peter sat down next to me on the couch and took my hand, hesitantly, almost afraid. His caution made me feel terrible. I squeezed his hand, felt the bones in my fingers. The rhythm of blood in his veins and the tensing ropes of his tendons. I squeezed until my own hand pulsed with pain. Peter's expression did not change. He only looked at me, his face a question mark, asking when I would be back to normal again.

Peter's eyes were wide and scared when I pushed his back against the couch and pulled his jeans down around his ankles, but he closed them when I put my legs on either side of him and pressed my own bare chest against his. I pushed my whole body into his, until there were no spaces between us. I put him inside me and wished that I could swallow him, fill my entire body with him, until the only part of me that was left was a thin layer of skin, like the skin of a snake ready to shed, or the transparent husk of a cicada. For one terrifying moment, I touched his thigh and through the blur of tears thought it was my own.

I WAS MISTAKEN ABOUT BEING far enough away. I thought that geography alone could separate me from my childhood. I didn't understand then about time. I was naive. I believed that a suitcase alone was evidence of certain departure.

Here I am at nineteen, wearing a pair of Levis from the Salvation Army worn soft and blue by someone else. This was the other uniform I wore at the Birches. I liked the way the soft denim felt on my pelvic bones, which pushed against the front pockets when I leaned against the step railing on the porch outside the rec room. I wore boys' V-neck T-shirts that I bought in plastic-wrapped packs of three at Wal-Mart before I came here. This one, today, was fresh out of the package with creases in the shoulders and waist. I wore a choker I'd made out of jade beads strung on a black leather lanyard. Low-top navy blue Converse sneakers, tied loosely so I could slip them on and off with ease. My ankles were sockless and brown. I smoked cigarettes and had an antique silver lighter engraved with someone else's initials.

Both of my roommates were working the breakfast shift. I'd woken to the starch and hair spray of their voices. I had the whole day off, so I didn't mind being woken. It would make the day seem longer. Sun streamed through the mist of hair spray. I looked out the window at the impossible blue of the lake and incredible green of the golf course and manicured miles of lawn. I was hungry and swore I could smell maple syrup and pancakes and bacon.

I got dressed and walked out of the girls' dorm and across the parking lot to the building where we ate and did our laundry and watched TV. This early in the morning most people were either working or still sleeping.

I'd been at the Birches for two weeks. Two weeks was long enough to learn the nature of mornings. Sunlight and the *clank, clank* of the dishes and glasses and silver utensils in the hotel dining room. Children in booster seats spilling syrup on the floor. Grumpy hotel guests in pastel clothes wiping sleep from their eyes and complaining about the color of their toast and the texture of their juice. I preferred mornings like these, outside the dining room. In my jeans and sneakers. A cup of coffee on the porch steps and a cigarette. I didn't read the newspaper here. Here, the rest of the world could have been the figment of someone else's imagination.

I had only talked to Ma once. When she realized that the number I'd given her was only a pay phone in the hallway of my dorm, she stopped calling. I never got her messages. She couldn't find me here. She was angry that I hadn't come home for the summer. I could hear it in the words she didn't say.

I told my roommates that I was born on the reservation near Flagstaff. That my father was white and my mother Navajo. That she died when I was four. That the only thing I remembered about her were her hands, laden with turquoise. Silver-edged skies or lakes circling her fingers. I told them my name was *Indian*. I told them about the lightning, but in my version of the story, it happened in the desert of my imaginary childhood instead of in the Foodmart parking lot. I made Lily and Ma in her polka dot dress dissolve in the rain, like pink baby aspirin spilled on the pavement.

I went inside the cafeteria and poured a cup of coffee from the silver canister, shaking clumpy powdered creamer into the paper cup. I scanned the steam table looking for pancakes. I'd been wrong. There was only baked egg and vegetable casserole, shriveled bacon and donuts. I took my coffee outside, sat down on the porch steps, and lit a cigarette.

A guy in a tall white chef's hat and apron rolled a block of ice out of the kitchen's back door and into the parking lot. He was tall and thin. The white chef uniform was too big for him. When he took off his hat, I could tell that he was also a college kid. A summer employee like me. The Birches advertised at all of the northern New England colleges. I'd torn the number off the sign from a bulletin board in the English building.

He went back into the kitchen and came out with a chain saw. He pulled the goggles that were hanging around his neck up to his eyes, leaned over, and pulled the cord until the chain saw roared. He could have been chopping wood; there was nothing delicate about this. But instead of wood chips, slivers of ice flew off the block. He circled the ice, revving the chain saw and whittling away at it until its edges were rounded and almost smooth. He turned the chain saw off and inspected the ice, touching the edges with a gloved hand. I was fascinated.

When he turned the chain saw back on, he began to the make small strikes at the ice, touching it with the blade and then moving away. Each touch evoked a new angle, a new sharp edge in the ice. Precise and certain. There was no hesitation, only the quick agile movements of his wrist and the trembling machine in his hands. I rested my chin in my hand and watched.

The block of ice was now split halfway down the middle, two triangular points reaching upward from the rounded center. He made three more circles around the table and then turned the chain saw off. Then he pulled a metal pick out of his apron pocket. The sunlight caught in its sharp edge for a moment and found me, blinding me, on the porch. When he moved his wrist, I could see again, and in the now-quiet parking lot, he began to whittle the ice.

For almost an hour he chipped away. His concentration was absolute, his movements ginger but exact. From each tick-tick of the pick against the ice emerged another minute detail. Soon, the cold arch of a neck. Its head lowered, but its posture almost arrogant. Transparent but remarkably strong wings beat underneath his fingers until the swan ascended from the center of the table.

I set my coffee cup down as he pulled the goggles back down around his neck and began to roll the table back toward the kitchen door. I stood up and ran toward him.

"Hey," I said just as he was about to close the door.

"Yeh?"

"That was amazing," I said. "What you just did."

He pushed the table into the kitchen and one of the chefs took it from him.

"Thanks, Peter," the chef said.

"No problem." Peter smiled.

He closed the door and stepped back outside with me. Beneath a mop of black hair, his eyes were the same blue as the lake.

"I mean," I said. "I've never seen how they're made before. I guess I thought they came from a mold or something." Lunch was always a buffet. Every day for two weeks, in the center of the silver platters of cold cuts and cheese and fruit, a swan sat perched in a lake of parsley and spinach and chard. I had only seen the finished product. I'd never seen its birth.

He nodded and put his hands in his pocket.

"My name's Indie," I said, reaching out to him.

His eyes brightened and he took his hand out of his pocket to shake my mine. "Indie, like *indie-pendent?*" he asked.

"Sure." I smiled and shrugged.

"That's a great name." His cheeks were flushed pink from working next to the cold ice.

"Thanks," I said.

"I've got to get back to work," he said, reaching for the door.

I felt my heart sink a little, and I stared at my feet. Kicked a piece of gravel.

"I'll see ya," he said and stepped into the doorway.

"Hey," I said after him. "What happens to them afterwards?"

He raised an eyebrow.

"To the swans?"

"They melt," he said, shrugging.

"Oh."

He looked at me for a minute and then grinned. "They let them melt in a giant silver box, which they freeze again. That's where the ice comes from." He winked and started to close the door. "It's the same swan. My job is just to find it every day."

Leaving was easy. Before we went to bed, Peter and I locked all the windows, unplugged all of the appliances, and pulled the blinds. When we got up the next morning to catch the early bus to Phoenix, it was still dark outside, and closing the door was simple. Peter locked the deadbolt and put the key in his pocket. I stared straight ahead at the road where the taxi's headlights were shining like dull stars fallen to the ground.

"Ready Freddy?" he asked, opening the cab door for me.

I nodded, handing the cab driver my suitcase and the box of Ma's junk. He put both in the trunk along with Peter's bags and then he got in and drove us to the bus station.

Rich had asked us to come by the house in Phoenix before we left. I didn't want to see Lily again. I didn't think I could bear to look at her hands, not now that I knew what they were capable of. I had been telling myself I must have imagined everything. I must only have still been dreaming about seeing Ma in Lily's face. But there was desperation in Rich's voice. A high-wire voice, the voice of someone teetering high above the world, staring down at the threatening ground. I reluctantly agreed, *But only for a minute,* and he, relieved, said he'd pick up some Chinese, that we could have an early lunch.

I used to get carsick, nausea in sick waves every time I was in a car or bus. I hadn't felt that way since I was a child, though. I thought I'd gotten over it, grown out of it at least. But as the bus lurched out of the station and the diesel fumes reached my nose, I felt the familiar roiling of my stomach and I reached to turn the vent over my head.

"You okay?" Peter asked. "You look a little green."

I nodded and leaned my head against the cold glass of the window, riding the waves of nausea with my eyes closed. When we stopped at the casino to pick up a load of passengers, I nudged Peter and said, "I've got to get off. Just for a second."

We only had a few minutes, but I felt suddenly panicky, as if my life depended on getting off the bus. I pushed past the other passengers to get to the door.

"I'll just be a minute," I said to the driver and walked quickly down the steps outside.

The air was not as brisk as I had hoped it would be. I put my hands on my hips and walked back and forth as if I were trying to walk off a cramp. The ocean of nausea had followed me, though, and the still ground beneath my feet didn't feel still at all. The only other time I felt this way was once when we spent a day with Peter's father on his boat. We'd been out during a terrible storm, and I could feel the storm in my legs for the rest of the day.

I walked back to the bus and leaned my head in.

"Excuse me, I just need to run into the gift shop and get some Dramamine. Can you wait just a couple of seconds?" I asked the bus driver.

He looked at me and shook his finger. "This bus pulls out in three minutes, ma'am."

"I'll be right back," I said, swimming through the waves to the front doors of the casino. It was just past dawn, but there were several people sitting wide-eyed and alert at the slot machines, cups of coffee perched next to their plastic cups of quarters. It looked like Christmas inside the casino. Like an electric parade.

I found a gift shop near the entrance and went straight to the cashier. An old Native American woman was manning the register. Her face looked like a baked potato, dark and deeply lined. She was wearing a T-shirt with the casino's name in glittery letters across her chest, a squash-blossom necklace heavy around her neck.

"Excuse me, do you sell Dramamine?" I asked.

She turned to the shelf behind the counter and pulled down a box. "You sick to your stomach?" she asked.

I nodded grimly.

"Lots of people get sick inside here. All the lights, I think," she smiled. "These are the chewable kind. My kids like these the best. Eat them up like candy."

"Thank you," I said, shoving a five-dollar bill across the counter and tearing at the cardboard box. I popped the pink pills out of their plastic bubbles and into my mouth. The taste of childhood middle-of-the-night stomachaches filled my mouth.

When I got outside, my head was still spinning with the sounds and lights of the casino, but it was still and quiet, the silence of an early, high-desert morning. Peter was standing outside with the bus driver. He must have convinced him to wait. He shook his hand and muttered, "Thanks," before he followed me onto the bus.

"You okay?" he asked. He had also gotten a pillow and a scratchy blanket from the driver and had made the seat up like a bed for me.

I felt suddenly too tired to resist his kindness, and slept the rest of the way with my head in his pillowed lap.

Phoenix was still unseasonably hot. My body took the shock of the heat like a punch in the stomach. The Dramamine had made me sleepy, but I woke up feeling almost as sick as before, and the blast of hot air that hit when we stepped off the bus downtown almost knocked me over.

Rich was waiting at the bus station for us with Violet and her stroller.

"You look terrible," he said.

"I think I need to barf," I grimaced.

"You can barf at the house, just not on me. Violet's already done that today." He motioned to a wet shoulder.

"It's a deal," I said, and he took my bags from me.

When we got to Rich and Lily's house, remarkably, I started to feel better. The artificial air felt good this time. Clean and pure. I took a deep breath and let it fill my lungs.

Lily was in the kitchen, writing on a yellow legal pad. There were Chinese food cartons all around her. The smell of lo mein made my stomach flip-flop again.

"Hi," she said, looking up from the list. "Thanksgiving. Can you believe it's almost here already?" There was nothing in her expression to acknowledge what had happened between us at Ma's house.

Rich carried Violet's car seat into the kitchen and set her on the table. She was fast asleep, her eyes flickering beneath their lids in a dream. "Okay, Bunk," he said, lifting her heavy body out of the seat. "Off to bed for you."

Lily stared at the legal pad.

"What are you making?" Peter asked, sitting down next to Lily.

"The usual stuff," she smiled. "This is my first time. Usually we go to Ma's house." She stared at the legal pad. "I've never made Thanksgiving dinner."

"I have a great recipe for oyster stuffing," Peter said. "I'll give it to you once we get home. My mother used to make it when we were growing up. Esmé called it ostrich stuffing. For some reason she didn't have a problem eating ostrich, but she wouldn't touch it if she'd known there were oysters in it." He was trying to make her smile.

"Unfortunately, it's not as easy to get good oysters in Phoenix as it is in Maine." Lily frowned.

I stood in the kitchen doorway, waiting for something to explode.

Rich had gone to the nursery with Violet. I could hear her Pooh pull-toy playing the Winnie-the-Pooh song.

"I've got tons of recipes I can E-mail you if you want," Peter said. "I could put together a menu for you if it might make things easier."

My head was pounding.

"I'd like to have Thanksgiving at home this year, too," I said suddenly.

"Really?" Peter asked.

We always went to Peter's parents' house for Thanksgiving. We'd leave before sunrise. Outside Peter would start the car and scrape the inevitable ice from the windshield while I stood inside watching him through the window. When the car was warmed up and the pies Peter had made were already in the backseat, he would motion for me to come, and I'd get in. He'd have brought my favorite tapes to listen to and would stop at the 7-Eleven for a cup of the hazelnut coffee that only I liked. The drive took three hours, and by the time we were close to Bar Harbor I could smell the ocean. I could practically taste the salt when I rolled down the window. Esmé would already be there, home from school for the long weekend. The entire house would smell of oyster stuffing and turkey and cloves.

"Yeh," I said. "I really feel like staying home this year. Esmé can come down if she wants, but I'd like to stay home." I looked at Peter, knowing that he loved spending the holidays with his family. I looked at him and waited for him to argue. To remind me that our little kitchen table wasn't even big enough for three people. I waited for some spark of resistance or reluctance, but he only nodded.

"Good idea," he said. "We can do it at home this year. That'll be nice."

I frowned and Lily said loudly, "I was thinking of making that lemon Jell-O mold that Ma used to make. The kind with Cool Whip."

I stood up from the table. "I still feel a little sick. Can I use your bathroom?"

I left Lily and Peter in the kitchen and walked down the hall, passing by the nursery on the way. Rich was sitting in a rocking chair in the corner holding Violet, who was still sleeping.

"Hi," I said softly.

"Hey."

"How's Violet?" I asked, reaching and touching her hair, which was beginning to grow in thicker.

"Good," he whispered. "Look."

I knelt down and looked at Violet's small face. Her eyelashes were dark and long; her eyes closed gently.

"I'm taking a leave of absence from work," Rich whispered. He rocked slowly back and forth in the rocking chair.

"For how long?"

He shrugged and tucked Violet's blanket around her. "I suppose I could set up shop here, if I needed to. Just until everything settles down again."

I took my hand away from his arm and picked up a stuffed bear that had fallen from Violet's changing table. It looked like it had never been held.

"Last night she came in while I was feeding her," Rich said, staring absently at the bear in my hands. "She just stood in the doorway watching. The hall light was shining through her night-gown, and I could see how small she was. Her hair was all mussed up, she was wiping her eyes, and standing there in her nightie, watching me. It was like looking at a little girl."

Despite the chill in the air, I could feel cold beads of sweat running down my arms underneath my shirt.

"What happened to her?" Rich said, suddenly looking me in the eyes. "What did your mother do to her?"

I looked at Rich and then glanced down at the bear in my hands. My fingers were clutching the fur, trying to hold onto something as hard as I could. When I looked at Rich, his eyes were still pleading with me for answers. And for a moment, I almost felt like I could say the words that had piled up in so many unspoken syllables. As if the answers he wanted were right there, waiting only to be uttered.

I set the bear down and looked at Violet, sleeping in his arms. He wanted me to tell him that *yes*, all of this was Ma's fault. That now that Ma was gone, the strange spell of medicine and poison and hands held over small mouths until breathing stopped would be broken. That Lily was free now, that Violet was safe. But what he didn't understand, and I had no words to articulate, was that we inevitably inherit our mother's gestures. The certain sway of hips or slow blink of an eye. The way of buttoning a child's sweater or leaning into a man's chest. What he didn't understand was that the subtleties she passed on to us were what he should fear. That the simple way of telling a story before we turned off the light at night was more revealing than the way we held a child.

I leaned over and put my head between my knees to fight the waves rolling under my skin, in my blood.

"I can't . . ." I said.

"It's okay," he said. "I shouldn't have . . . I'm sorry. This isn't your problem." His voice was flat, almost angry.

I felt terrible, but there was no way to explain that silence is also inherited, that Lily wasn't the only one with a legacy from Ma.

Lily didn't want to come to the airport with us. She didn't even argue when Rich strapped Violet into the car seat instead of leaving her at home. She stood in the doorway when we left, her face colorless in the sun. She shielded her eyes and watched us drive away, but she didn't wave.

Rich dropped us off at the airport just before our flight was scheduled to take off. He knew that we didn't want to sit in the airport longer than we had to. It would have given us too much time to think. We carried our luggage on, shoving it in what small spaces were left in the overhead compartments, despite the angry glares of the flight attendants, and sat down, exhausted, in our seats.

Peter and I pretended that we were not afraid of flying. But I could feel my heart thumping in my head even after we had risen through the white ceiling of clouds. And Peter would not open his eyes even after the seatbelt light went off. Miles above my old world, we pretended for each other that the possibility of falling did not exist.

FOUR

COTTON CANDY AND caramel–apple fingers. Benny dropped his SnoCone on the pavement, and I offered him mine. I would have given him anything that night. It was warm, the sky teasing us, insinuating summer with bright sun all day and now, tonight, with the leftover glow of the first really hot day. School was out for the summer. Ma and Lily were gone for another whole week. And Daddy had paid five dollars for me to enter the pool tournament at Rusty's.

Summer in Mountainview officially began with the carnival in the park. With the rickety Ferris wheel and trailers steaming and stinking of sausages and french fries and Indian fry bread. With another five dollars for Benny and me to share on anything we wanted. I told him I would hold on to the change. His pockets were always full of holes that led nowhere; the money was safer with me.

They blocked off all of Depot Street and set up tents where the Navajo women brought their jewelry and laid it out on colored sheets. Where local potters displayed their plates and mugs. Dishes as deep as pie plates. Oil lamps and bowls. Where you could get your picture taken and within minutes it would appear on a T-shirt or a wall hanging or a coffee mug. I was so happy, so filled with the prospect of summer, I agreed to spend one of our dollars on a photo of Benny and me. Nothing fancy, just one of those black-and-white strips you could get at the drugstore booth. Three photos, a ribbon of our faces.

When the strip shot out of the slot, Benny grabbed for it with his strawberry-stained hands. "Let me see, let me see," he said.

"I told you to hold still," I said. "Oh look, this one's good, though."

The first photo on the strip was full of Benny's smile. Our heads leaning together. Both of us grinning. But in the middle one, Benny's face was a blur, and in the bottom one only my face appeared. If you looked close, you could see Benny's ear and a lock of his hair.

"Can I keep it?" Benny asked. "I could put it in my wallet with my library card."

"Okay," I said. "But don't lose it. Why don't you give me your wallet?"

Benny handed me his wallet and I carefully tore the good picture from the strip. I shoved the other two photos in my pocket and slid the good one into the sticky plastic picture holder. You could barely see through the plastic; it was too thick and linty. Benny's library card was perched in one of the slots. A bicentennial quarter was loose inside the zippered pocket.

"We have a dollar left," I said. "And we need to be at Rusty's by nine for the tournament."

"A ride?" he asked. "Can we ride the wheel?"

"Is that what you want?"

"Oh, oh, maybe I would like a taco," he said, his eyebrows furrowed with the weight of this decision.

"We can get a taco from Rosey," I said.

"Maybe I would like one of the tacos here," he said, putting his hands on his hips. "But then *you* don't get anything."

"Whatever you want, Benny. But make up your mind, because we've only got a half hour."

"Let's ride." Benny smiled.

We bought the tickets and approached the metal ramp to the Ferris wheel. We stood there waiting for it to stop, watching each of the swinging carts as they descended. Then Starry and Heather Potter were in the cart in front of us.

Heather Potter was in the eighth grade. She normally didn't talk to anyone but eighth graders. She was into gymnastics and at recess did penny drops from the high monkey bars until her hands were red or the teachers stopped her. She had a turned-up nose and what she called a "pixie" haircut. I thought she looked like a little pig.

"Hi Indie," Starry waved.

Benny was jumping up and down on the ramp. "Hi Starry!" He was waving at the cart.

"Shhh," I said.

"Who's *that?*" Heather asked. And then they were rising upward again, looking down at us.

They kept rising up slowly, and Benny kept jumping on the metal ramp until my head ached with the pounding and I was dizzy with the colored lights. Then the man operating the Ferris wheel stopped the spinning and pointed to an open cart.

Above us, Starry and Heather leaned their heads together. Starry whispered something to Heather, and Heather's laughter rained down from the swinging cart above. Benny waved and

Heather pointed. Through the lights and the pounding of my head I could taste her words, *vinegar, vinegar, vinegar.*

"Get in the seat, Benny," I said, squeezing his arm and pushing him gently toward the cart.

"That's Starry up there!" Benny said.

"Get in," I said, my face hot and my head pounding.

Finally, Benny stopped waving and sat down in the seat. I sat down next to him and the man closed the rusty metal bar across our laps. And then we were moving backwards, then rising, and then at the top of the world, looking down over the entire street. I watched Starry and Heather get off and go running toward the place that would put your picture on a T-shirt for five dollars. And I knew that they'd probably get matching shirts with their faces, leaned in together, printed across their chests.

"If I wanted a taco without any of the hot sauce, do you think Rosey would make it for me? I don't like lettuce either. But sometimes I do," Benny said.

"Sure, Benny."

"Let's look at the picture again," he said, tugging at me to pull his wallet out of my back pocket.

I watched Starry and Heather disappear into the photo booth.

"The other ones came out blurry, but this one is a good one," Benny said, pulling the little picture of us out of the plastic. "See?" He was holding the picture in front of my face, but my eyes were blurry with tears. "See it, Indie? That's me and you in the picture. The other ones came out blurry, but this is a good one."

"I see," I said, forcing the tears back inside my eyes. Blinking so hard the lights all melted into one mess of color.

But Benny kept holding the picture in front of my face, close to my face, and his stupid grin and my stupid grin were right there. Clear and sharp as this early summer night.

"Enough," I said and grabbed his arm, moving it away.

When the photo slipped out of his fingers, the Ferris wheel stopped. It fluttered down, down, down and landed in one of the empty seats.

"Oh no, oh no, oh no," Benny said, shaking his head like he sometimes did when he didn't know what else to do. "Oh no, no, no."

"Stop it," I said, covering my ears with my hands. "Please just stop it."

"We have to get the picture out of there. That's the only one that came out. The rest of them was blurry." Benny was leaning over the metal bar, staring at the cart below. The bar was pressing into his stomach.

Finally we were down on the ground again and the man lifted the bar, letting us out. I took Benny's hand and pulled it as hard as I could. But he was bigger than me, his hands and arms stronger.

"Indie, we gotta get that picture."

"Benny," I said, digging my nails into the soft palm of his hand, "I said stop it. If you don't stop it this second I am going to Rusty's without you. I'll leave you here."

Benny kept looking at the Ferris wheel. "Don't leave me here," he said. "Please don't leave me here."

"Then come *on*," I said and tugged one more time.

And we walked away from the park, turned down a side street so I wouldn't have to see Heather and Starry in their matching T-shirts, and into the heavy doors at Rusty's where the pool tournament was ready to the start.

Cigarette smoke swirled around my head like ancient halos. The chaos and cacophony of jukebox and flirtation and tortillas crackling in vats of hot fat. Benny tugged at my sleeve even after we closed the door and stepped into the loud room. My chest pressed into the bar, my heart beating against the dark polished wood.

The vinyl seat of the stool swiveled under me. I could not keep still. *Indie, we got to get that picture back. The other ones is blurry.* Little Ike smelled like Old Spice and black licorice. Sheila was balancing a round tray in the palm of her small hand. Her stomach was pink. Sunburned. She had probably spent the day sprawled across the flat, smooth rocks by the creek. I almost wanted to touch her to see if her skin felt like the sun. *Hey, Indie. Good luck tonight. Your Daddy is so proud.* Daddy had opened up a whole new box of blue chalks. They were lined up on the edges of each pool table like blue candy. The felt had been brushed clean and smooth. The light bulbs in the lamps hanging over the tables had been dusted. The cues were lined up like wooden soldiers in the rack along the wall.

Benny tugged at my sleeve again. *I need a quarter. You got a quarter for the jukebox?* I pulled away from him and walked to the rack, remembering the Spalding personalized two-piece pool cue, feeling vaguely sad. Ike said that a good pool player could play with a bamboo pole if he had to. I'd never seen bamboo, but I was pretty sure it looked a lot like the warped sticks on this rack. I carried the stick back to the bar and sat down, waiting for it all to begin. A Shirley Temple, glass sweating grenadine, a gift from Daddy. Rosey had come out from the kitchen to watch. She'd left someone else in charge of the enchiladas. Someone coughed, someone put a quarter in the slot and released the balls from their pockets, a thunderous cascade, the opening game in the men's tournament. Then at the other table, the same for the women's. When the cue balls cracked against the perfect triangles and the balls shot across the table like miniature colored cannonballs, Benny reached into the pocket of my sweatshirt and grabbed at the loose change. *Indie, gimme a quarter for the jukebox.* I turned to him and slapped his hand as hard as I could. The slap was louder than the crack of ball against ball. *Stop it. Leave me alone*, I said.

240

And Benny's wounded hand flew upward, into the cave of his open mouth. He sucked on his fingers and his eyes grew red. *Just stop,* I whispered, afraid Daddy might have seen what I'd done. But when I turned around, Daddy was busy watching the women's game, his elbow resting on the bar, his chin in his hand.

I wasn't used to playing against girls. There seemed to be a different set of rules. Not about the game so much as about the etiquette. All of the policies of respect that Ike had insisted upon did not seem to apply here. When I won the first game against the woman with the tight ponytail and tight jeans, I could hear her hiss under her breath. She didn't shake my hand, but turned on the heel of her cowboy boot and walked over to her friend in one of the booths and started whispering and laughing. I imitated her military clip and went straight to the bar, where Daddy reached over and gave me a high-five. Benny was eating a hamburger, dipping his french fries in a white glob of mayonnaise.

"You won?" he asked, holding up a french fry to his mouth. Mayonnaise hung dangerously over his lap.

"Eat it, Benny," I said. "Quick!"

His mouth hung open as the white blob landed on his pant leg.

"Oh no, oh no, oh no, Ma's gonna be so mad," he said, shaking his head.

"Ma's not even coming home for another week," I said, annoyed, and sat down at the stool. Sheila plopped down another Shirley Temple in front of me and smiled, "I saw that bank shot you made with the thirteen."

There were a lot more men than women who signed up. To speed things along and have both tables open for the men, they decided to use single elimination with the women. There were only eight of us, so by winning the first game I was already a semifinalist. If I could win two more games I would be the winner. I watched the next three women's games, paying close attention to the players. Not so much at their shooting, but at their personalities. Ike said that knowing how an opponent's mind worked was as important as knowing whether they shot left- or right-handed. That way you could second-guess not only their shots, but what made them nervous or angry or cocky.

Ike sat down next to me while I was waiting for the next game. He was wearing his lucky shirt, a blue cowboy one with white pearly snaps. There was blue embroidery in the shape of a lasso across the front. I'd already heard one of the women make a rodeo midget joke, but he either didn't hear or didn't care.

"How do they look?" he asked, shaking the ice in his glass.

"Mean," I whispered.

He nodded his head.

"What's your poison tonight, Ike?" Sheila asked. Her face was sunburned, too; the whites of her eyes were bright in contrast.

"Water," Ike said, handing her his empty glass. He never drank beer or liquor when he was playing in a tournament.

"Another Shirley?" she asked me.

I shook my head. I was starting to feel a little sick from all the grenadine.

"How you doin', Benny?" Ike asked.

"Fine," Benny smiled. His french fries and hamburger were gone. He was wiping his finger through the remaining ketchup and mayonnaise. Benny was almost twice Ike's size. When Benny got up to use the bathroom and Ike went back to the men's table, they looked like the pictures in the *Guinness Book* of the World's Tallest and Shortest, side by side.

Finally it was my turn to shoot again. This time, the woman was not quite so mean. She'd seen me shoot earlier, so she was nice enough not to make any jokes. She shook my hand and called herself Chloe. She was one of those gentle pool players; every shot was precise and smooth, even the ones that had to travel all the way across the table to reach their destination pocket. But sometimes you have to be aggressive. Ike had taught me this from early on. Sometimes you need to hit the cue ball hard, leaving it standing as the ball it hits goes soaring into the pocket. She still had three balls on the table when I sank the eight.

I had never felt so happy. Ike came over to pat me on the back. Daddy saw me and winked all the way across the bar even though he was busy making drinks for about fifty people. Benny was clapping his hands and spinning on the bar stool. His legs were so long, his feet dragged on the floor.

I couldn't do anything but chew on my nails while the other two women played to determine who would shoot against me in the finals. It was Ponytail's friend, a woman who was wearing black leather pants and a purple tube top, and a woman who looked old enough to be my grandma. Tube Top had a funny way of shooting, but it seemed to work. She crossed her legs when she leaned over, one leg perfectly straight and the other bent at the knee. It didn't matter what the shot was, this was always her posture. She won the game by shooting three in a row and then sinking the eight in the side pocket. She almost scratched; the cue ball was teetering on the edge of the corner pocket, but finally it just sat there. She threw up her arms and Ponytail came over and hugged her. I knew that if Ike had been watching he would have decided that she was the kind of woman who lived on the edge, that she'd take risks, making her vulnerable if you left her with shots where she was liable to scratch. I kept this in mind when the final game started.

I won the coin toss to decide who would rack and who would break, so I opted to rack. Tube Top leaned over so far when she lined up the cue ball, I could almost see her nipples. I blushed a little, and then realized maybe she was doing that to make me uncomfortable. After that I tried to ignore her boobs.

She didn't make anything in on the break, but all of the solids were nicely dispersed around the table while the stripes were clustered together at the top. I knew that if I could get a solid in then it would be an easy game. The first shot was hard, but the seven ball squeaked into the corner pocket. I made the next three shots, too, and I thought for a minute that I might be able to win the game in one fell swoop. I missed the next shot though, because I hadn't chalked up my cue. I shook my head and went back to my stool.

"Nice work," Daddy said.

I just sat there, watching to see what she would do next. First she took a long drink from the tall glass (a Long Island Iced Tea, Daddy had told me), and started to plan her strategy. Ike would have been right about her tendency to take chances. But despite her risky shots, she got in four of her balls before she missed. We were tied. I was starting to feel nervous. That was the worst thing, Ike had told me, but I couldn't help it. I wiped my hands on my pants before I picked up the stick to shoot. I made one ball in and then missed an easy shot. Tube Top didn't even look at me when she got up to shoot again. Ponytail was standing up, leaning against the booth. She shot me a look that was mean and drunk when I glanced over her way.

Benny was nervous too. He was rocking back and forth on the stool.

"Indie, after can we go ask the man at the ride if he found that picture?" Benny whispered.

"Shhh," I said.

She called a combo shot, ten, thirteen in the corner pocket. She could have cut the thirteen to the side, but she made the shot anyway. She smiled and yanked on her purple shirt, as it had slipped down dangerously low. She made the ten ball, and my heart sank into the pocket with it. She had a straight shot on the eight ball. The game was as good as over.

Benny was tugging at his earlobe, rocking in his seat.

"Stop it, Benny," I said softly. "You're making me nervous."

Benny looked at me, his eyes red and mad. He kicked at the metal bars on his stool and rocked harder.

Tube Top walked over to the chalk and rubbed her right hand over it, making sure it got between her fingers.

"I mean it," I said, as Benny kept rocking.

"I'm all blurry in them other ones," he said.

She checked the alignment of the cue ball and the eight ball with her eyes as she walked around the table. Then she leaned down to shoot. She wasn't the kind to spend forever lining up the shot. She worked on instinct, this I could tell. So when her arm pulled back the first time, I knew it would be the only time.

I pinched Benny to keep him quiet. My nails dug into the soft skin of his arm.

"I hate you, Indie!" he screamed then and shot off the stool, grabbing at his hair and running toward the door.

At the same time, Tube Top looked up just as the tip of her stick met the cue ball. It hit the eight and both balls went rolling toward the corner pocket. The eight ball sank and then the cue ball followed it. Tube Top watched in disbelief, her face and chest as red as Sheila's sunburn.

"That's not fair," she said.

My face was hot, my ears buzzing. Benny was standing near the door, stomping his feet.

"You won!" Sheila squealed. "Fair and square."

Tube Top was standing with Ponytail, swilling her drink. "That little bitch only won because I was distracted. What is this, some sort of scam? Get the retard to make some noise and win the game?"

Daddy came out from behind the bar and grabbed onto Tube Top's bare shoulder. "I think you need to leave now," Daddy said.

"Excuse me?" she said, twirling around.

"I said, I think it's time you two went home."

"I am not going home without the pot," she said. "I would have won that game if he hadn't screamed like that."

"Okay," Daddy said. "Let's go."

"Fuck you," said Tube Top, and then she splashed the Long Island Iced Tea in Daddy's face. Eddie Grand, who had been in the bathroom for almost half an hour, came out then and seeing Daddy standing there dripping wet, escorted the two women out the front door.

"Fuck you! Fuck you! Fuck you!" Benny screamed, now happy, now jumping up and down.

"Shhh," Eddie said as Daddy disappeared into the kitchen. "Come on, Benny, sit down."

"You won, Indie?" Benny asked, cocking his head and looking at me. All the mad was gone from his eyes. "You won the pot?"

And I hated Benny. I hated him more than I hated Ma sometimes. I hated him even as I put the envelope with the winnings in my underwear drawer and put the little silver trophy on my shelf. Because I knew that she would have scratched anyway. I had seen it in the way her stick was aimed too high. That's what happened when you were careless with an easy shot. It didn't take a retard screaming to make that happen.

HOME. CHUCK MOONY picked us up at the airport, bringing a paper bag with two live lobsters wriggling inside. We squeezed into the cab of Chuck's truck, and I held the lobsters on my lap.

"I figured they probably didn't have lobsters out there in the desert," Chuck said, starting up the truck.

"Nope," I smiled, peering into the bag. They were good-size ones. Probably two- or three-pounders.

It was almost twilight by the time we pulled into our driveway. My knees felt like liquid as I climbed up the porch steps. Jessica was in the window, staring out at us. Chuck was still in the truck, the engine still running.

"What are you doing?" Peter asked, leaning into the driver-side window. "Come help us eat some of this lobster."

He was afraid to be alone with me.

"Nah," Chuck said, shaking his head.

"What's Leigh up to tonight?" Peter asked.

"She's over to her mother's house. Planning the baby shower with her sisters. I think it's a little early, but they don't seem to think so."

"Then come in and help melt the butter. Indie always burns it," Peter laughed, opening up Chuck's door.

"Don't you guys want some alone time?" I heard Chuck whisper.

"Stay for dinner," he said.

There was a little bit of snow on the woodpile and in the boughs of the trees, but it hadn't gotten cold enough yet to really stick. We didn't usually get our first big snowstorm until after Thanksgiving. The cold air had loosened the lock and my key, which was usually fussy, slipped right in.

The house smelled deserted. It felt as if we'd been away for a year instead of for just a couple of weeks. I'd forgotten the way a place as familiar as your own home can seem foreign and abstract after even a short absence. The proportions of this kitchen were different from Ma's. The darkness of late afternoon even darker. I turned on the light over the kitchen table and set the lobster bag down. Jessica jumped off the windowsill and went straight to her food bowl, meowing.

"Hold your horses," Peter said, reaching into the cupboard for the box of cat food.

"I fed her this morning already," Chuck said, closing the door behind him.

"Manipulative little wench," Peter said, rubbing Jessica's back. Her spine raised up in response, her tail curling upward.

The hairs on the back of my neck bristled.

"I started a fire too, but it feels like it's gone out," Chuck said, rubbing his hands together and blowing into them.

"I'll go get some wood," I said, glad to leave the stagnant air of the cabin for the familiar woodsy smells of early winter outside.

I picked a few good-size logs from the woodpile and carried them back into the kitchen. Chuck was still standing in the doorway.

"Excuse me," I said, and he stepped to the side to make room for me. "Take your coat off, Moony. Stay awhile."

Chuck untied his work boots and slipped them off at the door. His wool socks were mismatched and stretched-out at the toes. He yanked at the heels and then padded across the kitchen to the table, where I had set the lobsters down. He peered into the bag and pulled out one large lobster. It moved slowly, hindered by the bands around its claws.

"Anybody want a drink?" I asked, reaching for a dusty bottle of bourbon in the cupboard over the sink.

"Pete used to hate lobsters," Chuck said to me, grinning. "Remember, Pete?"

"Nope, don't remember," Peter said.

"Hated 'em." Chuck nodded and winked at me.

"I'm having a drink. Anybody else?"

"Beer," Chuck said.

Peter shook his head.

"The day that Liz and Gary moved into the house up the road from us, I was so excited that there might finally be a kid my age in the neighborhood, I spent the whole day riding my bike back and forth in front of their house trying to get a peek in the windows."

"It was a scooter," Peter said and sat down at the table, staring at his hands.

"I never had a scooter," Chuck said, shaking his head, cracking open his beer.

"Moony, it was a *scooter*."

"Whatever, anyway I was just thrilled about there being another kid to play with. But the first time I saw Pete, I almost turned my bike around and went home."

"Scooter," Peter said wearily.

"Why?" I asked, taking a big swallow of bourbon.

"Complete geek," Chuck said. "He was helping his dad unload some boxes from the back of their truck, and his face was all red, and he had these dorky glasses, duct tape holding them together or something."

"It was hot and my glasses were not held together with duct tape, thank you very much."

"Paper clip, scotch tape, who cares. Point is, I knew this was the last kid I needed to buddy up to. It was the summer before seventh grade. End of summer and I hardly needed to start junior high with this goon as my new friend."

"Thanks," Peter said.

"So I turn my bike around and ride all the way home."

"Scooter."

"*Bike.* But when I get there, my dad is just coming home from the docks and he's got a bag full of lobsters. *Bring these up to our new neighbors,* he says. And my ma's standing there with her hands on her hips waiting for me to take the blueberry cobbler she made with my other hand. There wasn't any saying no to my pop, so I took the grocery bag and the cobbler and walked out the door.

"I thought for a second about dumping the lobsters over the cliffs near our house, but I knew there was no way to get rid of the blueberry cobbler without my Ma sniffing it out. So I started to trudge up the hill to Pete's house. Well, it's Liz that answers the door, of course, and next thing I know she's got a pot pulled out of a box and is boiling water for the lobsters on the stove. And Pete has lured me up to his room to show me some bug collection or some such thing . . ."

"Shortwave radio," Peter said, crossing his arms and laying his head on the table, only one eye on Chuck.

I finished the glass and poured another shot. My insides were warm.

"Whatever. And then we're sitting at their kitchen table and Gary's talking to me about my Dad's boat and Liz is unwrapping the cobbler. I remember they had this classical music on really loud. Mozart or something."

"Beethoven."

"Anyhow, Liz puts a big lobster on each of our plates, and Pete just stares at it. A fisherman's kid, and he won't eat seafood. *Too messy.* You know how Liz is about company, though. If I'd brought live frogs over for dinner, she would have made him eat them.

"Finally Liz gives him one of her looks and Pete knows he's in trouble unless he opens that thing up pretty soon. So he cracks it open, and its insides go *splat* all over his glasses. All green. Looked like throw-up."

"All right, enough," Peter said, lifting his head.

"He's staring at me through that green mess like it's my fault or something," Chuck said.

I laughed.

"Just about cried. He wouldn't even wear that pair of glasses afterwards. Turned out to be a blessing though. Between ditching the nerd glasses and hanging out with ol' Moony for a couple of weeks, I had him all undorked by the time school started. If it hadn't been for me he'd have spent the whole school year dusting his bug collection."

"Shortwave radio. And you rode a scooter, Moony."

Then, quietly, Chuck and Peter started to make dinner. It looked as if they'd done this a thousand times. It was so easy between them. Like brothers. I felt my heart pull with each easy gesture. I kept swallowing from my glass, softening each pang with bourbon.

"You guys going up to Bar Harbor for Thanksgiving?" Chuck asked.

Peter turned to look at me, his face a soft question mark. "I think we'll do it here this year," he said. "Esmé might come down. What are you and Leigh doing?"

"We were going to go to her folks' house, but they decided to go to Florida this year."

"Why don't you come have dinner with us?" Peter asked. "Leigh hasn't been over for ages."

I imagined us sitting at the table trying to find something to talk about.

"Leigh makes amazing mashed potatoes. Lots of garlic," Chuck said.

Peter nodded, "I'll do the turkey and pies."

"I'd offer to the help with the turkey, but you know how anal repulsive he is," Chuck said, winking at me.

"You mean anal *retentive?*" Peter asked.

"Repulsive, retentive, whatever. I'll let you deal with that bird, Martha Stewart."

They boiled the lobsters in Peter's silver pot, and I opened up a can of green beans. There wasn't any fresh food in the house; Peter had been careful to get rid of anything that would spoil while he was gone. Chuck had also brought a loaf of bread from the Swan and two sticks of butter. Chuck and I tore our lobsters apart, divided up the claws and tails, and deposited the clean white meat on Peter's plate. Peter picked up his fork. He ate one bite of lobster first, then speared his beans, then tore of a small piece of bread. *Lobster, beans, bread.*

I was suddenly starving. I couldn't seem to eat fast enough. Butter dripped down my hands first and then down my arms. I wiped the back of my hand across my mouth and sucked on the legs and claws until the meat slithered out in clean white pieces.

It was so salty, and the more I ate, the thirstier I got. I knew I was getting drunk, but I didn't care.

I looked at Peter's plate. *Lobster, beans, bread.*

Chuck dipped everything in butter: lobster meat, his hunk of bread, a forkful of green beans. He had crumbs and glistening butter in his beard.

Peter finished and folded his napkin into quarters, setting it in the middle of the plate. There were empty red shells in front of me, butter in yellow pools. Peter stood up and carried his plate to the sink quietly. He turned and reached for ours.

"Leave them until tomorrow?" I said, grabbing his wrist.

He looked at my hand.

"Please?"

He pulled away, and it felt like a slap.

"Fine," I said, standing up. I was dizzy, my head was thick. "You stay here and *clean.* Moony and I will go catch the last of the sunset." I reached for Chuck's arm, noticing how much hairier and thicker it was than Peter's.

"You need any help?" Chuck asked.

"No, go ahead. Get some fresh air," Peter said.

I scowled at him and grabbed my coat.

Chuck shrugged his shoulders and I handed him his jacket. I went back into the kitchen and found a flask someone had given to Peter for Christmas years ago, filling it with the last of the bourbon. I stuffed it into my coat pocket and pulled Chuck's hand.

The woods behind the house are thick, but there is an old logging road that leads straight through them to a small pond about a mile away. We trudged through the mud and new snow along the ruddy path.

Chuck pulled his hat down over his ears. Inside I was warm with bourbon, but I could feel the wind rushing through the deep canals of my ears and settling there, making my head ache. I wrapped my scarf around my neck and up over my ears, but the wind still found its way through the porous fabric.

"You okay?" Chuck asked as we reached the pond's edge.

"What do you mean?"

Chuck shrugged.

I walked to the edge of the pond and tested the ice with the toe of my boot. It wasn't cold enough yet to make the ice strong. One step would send me into the cold water. I stepped away from the ice and sat down on the embankment, staring westward to where the sun was almost finished with its orangey pink descent behind the hills. It would be dark soon. It would be too dark to find our way home.

"Good to be back?" Chuck asked.

I shrugged.

I pulled the flask from my coat and unscrewed the cap. I took a sip, letting the fire spread across my cold lips. I offered the flask to the Chuck, but he shook his head.

Wind blew across the pond, making small tornados of snow on the surface. I could feel the bourbon in my throat and chest.

"Were you ever mad at your dad?" I asked, pulling my hands inside the sleeves of my coat. "When he . . ."

Chuck's eyes opened wide and he looked out toward the water blankly.

"I'm mad at my mother," I said. It felt good. "I'm pissed as hell." I could have screamed it into the trees.

Chuck was still staring at the sun. It colored his freshly shaven face in pinks and orange.

"She fucked everything up. She always fucked everything up." I could feel the warmth of bourbon behind my eyes.

Chuck yanked his hat further down over his ears.

"Peter, Peter is so . . ." I said, liquor buzzing in my ears. "He just doesn't know. He hasn't . . . you know?" I nodded, remembering. My throat was thick. "Everything is so tidy for him. So clean."

Chuck took my hand and looked at it as if it weren't a hand at all but something fascinating. A miniature teacup, or a strange bird.

He spoke softly, his breath warm in the cold air between us. "I *was* mad. At my pop. I was mad at her too, I think. For dying. For making him so sad that he'd do what he did."

My heart beat hard in my chest; it felt like I'd accidentally swallowed a cough drop whole. He understood. He knew what it felt like to be broken.

I reached for him. Drunk. And pulled him close to me. I reached with everything I had to offer, searching for something he couldn't possibly give. But the moment that I felt the new stubble of his cheeks touch my lips I started to cry. He pulled away from me sharply, leaving me leaning toward him.

"We best get back to the house," he said, standing up abruptly.

"I'm sorry," I mumbled. I pressed my palm into the sharp pine needles carpeting the forest floor.

"S'okay," he said, offering his hand to help me up. The sun had set behind us. It was dark, but Chuck knew the way back. He led and I followed his silhouette in front of me, leading the way. And in the cold darkness, the ache in my ears spread down my spine, into my knees and my ankles. My wrists and my empty hands.

Peter had finished washing and drying the dishes already. The discarded shells were on top of the nearly frozen compost pile. Everything was bright in the kitchen. Everything was clean.

"Give Leigh a smooch," Peter said, seeing Chuck out the door. I watched them through the window.

Peter didn't come back inside until after Chuck had pulled out of the driveway. He was shivering when he came back in.

"Hi." He smiled.

He reached out for my hand tentatively, and I accepted it. And then I followed him, up the stairs to the bedroom where we curled around each other in our familiar bed. I tried not to think about Chuck, about the sharp sting of pine needles in my hands. I tried to concentrate on the way Peter's chest rose and fell in a rhythm that was perfect and predictable.

The trip and the bourbon had made me exhausted, and I was grateful for the need for sleep that descended on me like the weight of too many blankets. I don't remember my head touching the feather pillow. I don't remember closing my eyes. I only remember the phone ringing, pulling me out of sleep like a reluctant anchor out of a watery dream. I only remember my head pounding with too much bourbon and Peter's words.

Peter was sitting at the edge of the bed, with the phone to his ear. He was pulling on a pair of long johns and wool socks.

"What's the matter?" I asked, pushing against the heaviness of sleep and quilts, trying to make sense of the shadows in the room.

"I'll be there in twenty minutes. Just hang on," Peter said and hung up the phone.

"What's going on?" I asked. My heart was thudding hard in my chest, as if I'd been running instead of sleeping.

"It's Leigh," he said. "She just lost the baby."

We were the only car on the road. It was three o'clock in the morning, and for a moment it felt like we were only driving to the café to start baking bread and muffins. But by the time we got to the hospital, I wasn't able to trick myself anymore. The hospital lights glowed green on Peter's skin as he walked purposefully across the parking lot to the emergency room entrance.

Chuck was standing outside, smoking a cigarette. His boots were untied, his wool hat sitting crooked on his head. When he saw us coming, he snubbed the cigarette out with his boot and reached for Peter. Peter held on to him, patting his back with both gloved hands. I stood quietly watching.

Peter stepped back, still holding on to Chuck's arms. "How's Leigh?"

"Okay, I guess. They had to do a D and C; she's pretty groggy." Chuck shoved his hands in his pockets and stared at his feet. "It happened on the way home from her ma's house. She could have been in an accident. I shouldn't have let her go by herself."

I shook my head and reached for Chuck's arm. "It's not your fault. . . ."

At the same time Peter put his arm around Chuck's shoulder and steered him toward the door. I stood there with my arm outstretched toward nothing. I walked behind them. Followed them. Matched my footsteps to theirs, identical on the white tiled floor.

MA AND LILY PULLED INTO the driveway just after I'd gone to bed. I could hear the tires crushing gravel, the trailer carrying Lily's stairs dragging wearily behind. It was too early to turn in, only eight o'clock, but I had hoped to be sleeping when they got home. I had hoped I wouldn't have to see either of them until the next morning. But there was no way to feign sleep when Ma threw open the kitchen door. There was no way to keep my eyes pressed closed when she started screaming.

"Get your father on the phone now!" she said in the empty kitchen. Her voice had not been forgotten but had been missing for so long now it sounded like a phantom voice in the other room.

I lay on my back staring at the ceiling, knowing that as soon as I relented my whole world would be turned upside down again. I tugged at my nightgown, which had ridden up my legs. I'd used one of Ma's rusty pink razors I found in a drawer and my legs were covered with little red itchy bumps.

"Indie!" she insisted, somehow knowing that I was lying awake in my bedroom just after twilight.

The trophy from the pool tournament was sitting on my bureau. I could make out its outline among the shadows of old perfume bottles, music boxes, and rolled-up socks. I'd left it there to put away later. I squeezed my eyes shut and listened as Benny's heavy feet fell across the kitchen floor, as he leaned into Ma, whose arms remained heavy at her sides, as he started to whimper in the way that sounded like the train coming. I thought he was only crying because she wouldn't hug him, but when the rumble of his sobs became the metal on metal sound of the tracks and the warning whistle of his cries became the scream of steam, I knew something much worse was happening in our kitchen.

As I ran down the hall, my legs brushed against the nylon of my nightgown, the damaged skin of my legs burning. I leaned down and pressed my cold palms against them to squash the fire. The only light on was the one over the stove; its fluorescent green glow made this an underwater scene, as if the linoleum were the floor of the ocean, and Benny, cowering in the corner by the refrigerator, was a creature instead of a boy. Ma stood by the kitchen table with her hands hiding her face. When she moved them away, there were dark, bloody hand prints on the pale green of her skin.

"What's the matter, Ma?" I asked softly. Afraid.

She didn't answer me, but picked up the phone and dialed the number for the bar. "Sheila, this is Judy Brown. I need to speak to my husband."

I imagined Sheila in her halter top. I thought of the way she had stroked Daddy's hair when he hurt his knee in the backyard dancing like John Travolta. I thought of the way her words tasted like stale peppermints. She would roll her eyes and hand Daddy the phone. She would maybe touch him by accident when he took the receiver from her.

In the deep-sea kitchen, Ma's words swam softly. "Lily's hemorrhaging. She was feeling sick yesterday during the awards ceremony, but she didn't have a fever so I thought we could wait until we got home so she could see her regular doctor. But then she started bleeding just past Camp Verde." Ma pressed her free hand onto the table and stared at the red mark it made. "I've got the rental car with the trailer. I need you to come get us."

I saw Sheila go back behind the bar while Daddy curled the long cord into the kitchen. I smelled Rosey's enchiladas and heard the basket of onion rings descending into the crackling fat. I felt Sheila's sigh on Daddy's neck.

Ma closed her eyes and raised her voice. "Your daughter is bleeding to death in the backseat of a car. If you don't get here in five minutes she will die. Do you understand?"

Benny had sunk to the floor and was crawling toward the table. He looked like a man instead of a boy. He looked like a giant slithering across the sea floor. When he got to where Ma was standing, he bumped into her accidentally. His eyes rose up to meet hers, knowing probably that he'd made a terrible mistake trying to hide. Because no sooner did his soft eyes meet hers, trying to explain in a glance that he hadn't meant to bump her, that he only needed to be safe, that she kicked. Like she was kicking a dog, and I covered my ears when she hung up the phone and started to yell at Benny.

Benny held one large hand to his side, wounded but not dead, and kept crawling through her liquid words toward the table. The cave under the sea. I thought for a moment of joining him. Of living inside that cave forever. But then her attention shifted to me, standing in the doorway with my hands over my ears and razor burn on my legs. She came at me as if she might be gentle, as if she might pull me into her arms and hold me there softly. That she might be sorry.

And she did. Inside my chest my heart bumped and thumped, awkward and scared. But her arms made a circle of softness around my bare shoulders. Benny was silent, hidden now and safe under the table and Ma was holding me. Tears grew hot and wet in the corners of my eyes. And she didn't let go. This was the closest I had been to Ma in so long that I'd forgotten the way she smelled of lavender. I'd forgotten that her ribs made a cage around her heart. I'd forgotten that her hands were smaller than mine on my back. And in this lavender moment I could forgive her for kicking Benny. I could understand. The night at Rusty's was still vivid in my mind. The metallic taste of hate in my mouth. But there was only tenderness here. Ma was holding on to me for dear life.

But when Daddy came into the kitchen, Ma let go.

"Where is she?" he said.

"I told you she's in the car," Ma said, turning to face him. All that softness turned to the hardness of bone and the sharpness of breath.

"Indie, stay here with your brother," Daddy said.

I nodded and Ma followed Daddy out the door.

I left Benny under the table. I walked past him, pleading with me to stay, and into my room, where I picked up the trophy and stared at the brass plate with tiny screws holding it onto the marble base. I hadn't even asked if Lily had won the Little Miss Desert Flower contest. I hadn't asked because I already knew. I knew this like I knew when there was electricity in the air. I knew that if there were a banner and a crown and a trophy fifty times the size of mine that there would have been no blood. It was a simple as that. If Lily had won the contest, Ma wouldn't have made this happen again.

THE DAY BEFORE THANKSGIVING, I got up to go to the café with Peter. I got up while he was in the bathroom, startled him when he came back into the dim light of our bedroom.

"Go back to bed. You don't need to come with me today," he said, running his long fingers through his hair.

"I want to," I said, and went to the bureau for something to wear. The floor was cold underneath my feet. When I breathed, cold clouds escaped from my lips.

"Really, Indie. It's okay," he said, reaching for my hand.

I ignored him and pulled a pair of jeans out of the drawer.

"I said I *want* to." My eyes were stinging.

"Okay," he said, backing away from me, his hands raised defensively.

"What's *that?*"

"What?"

"That," I said, imitating his gesture.

"Nothing. Sorry."

I pulled the jeans on and turned away from him to pull my nightgown off. I was shivering, but I lingered like this, my naked back turned to him, for several moments before I slipped my favorite bra on and then a worn T-shirt over that. When I turned around again, he had already gone into the living room to rekindle the fire.

We rode silently through the woods to the Swan. The streets were empty. White Christmas lights in the trees were like fallen stars trapped in cold branches. It was beautiful. Strange. But today Peter didn't linger inside the truck. He opened the door and slammed it shut again, walking briskly to the door, his keys ready in his hands as I followed quietly behind him.

He went straight to the kitchen, leaving me to navigate the dark stairs to the bakery alone. I flicked on the light, pulled an apron from the starched and newly laundered pack, looped it over my head, and pulled my hair away from my face with a rubber band. I found three buckets marked *Wet* in the refrigerator (milk and sugar and eggs floating on top like miniature suns), and three marked *Dry* on the counter. I found a note written by Peter with instructions for triple berry, maple walnut, and chocolate cheesecake muffins. Anyone could do this job. This message could have been left for anyone.

I pulled three mixing bowls from the shelf and lined them up along the smooth wooden counter. I turned the oven to 325 degrees and blew flour off the radio. But when I turned the radio on, the knob came off in my hands. I tried several times to re-attach it, but it no longer seemed to fit. Frustrated, I hurled the knob into the sink and it reverberated against the stainless steel sides.

I measured blueberries, raspberries, and strawberries into one bowl. Chocolate and sour cream, maple syrup and walnuts into the others. I dumped the *Wet* and *Dry* buckets' contents into their respective bowls and stirred purposefully until my arm ached and the batters were smooth. I lined three tins with paper muffin cups, pretty, blue miniature accordions. The nonstick spray saturated them, beaded up on the exposed tin. The batter was thick, streaked with berries and chocolate and pure Vermont maple syrup.

Above me, I could hear Peter's feet walking across the kitchen floor. I could hear the sink. The doorbells as Joe came in, his bicycle rolling across the floor and then out the back door to the alley where he would lock it to an old set of pipes.

After I put the muffins in the oven, I went to the office and turned on the lights, looked at Peter's desk. I pulled open the drawers and stared at the carefully organized tray filled with tacks and erasers and rubber bands. The employee schedule hanging on the bulletin board was organized into shifts, names penciled perfectly into their time slots. Pencils sharpened like daggers, erasers free from ink or dirt, were lined up like soldiers on the lefthand side of the desk. A blotter without doodles. An empty wastebasket and a file cabinet without a single file out of place.

When I picked up the phone to call Lily, I also picked up a black magic marker. As the phone rang, midnight Phoenix time, I took the cap off and let the strong scent of poison, of toxins, linger under my nose. As Lily answered the phone, her voice frightened, I started to make black Xs all over Peter's things. Instead of speaking, instead of demanding answers, instead of stopping her with my words, I marked the blotter, the employee schedule, the walls with black ink. I made Xs on the backs of my hands. I hung up the phone and made marks on the clean white apron, on my jeans, and on my T-shirt. I didn't stop until the marker ran dry in my hands and my tears ran wet down my cheeks. Upstairs I could hear Peter dragging the Daily Special easel outside, and I stared at the mess I'd made and cried. It wasn't until I smelled the muffins burning that I realized what I'd done.

Peter came down as I was pulling the blackened muffins from the oven. Smoke poured out of the door making us both cough.

"Let me get it, Indie. Please," he said, and tossed the burning muffins into the sink.

I sat down on the floor next to the giant bread dough mixer, leaned my cheek against the cold metal base and closed my eyes.

Peter turned on the giant fan near the doorway and sat down next to me on the floor. He pulled me into him, fought me.

"What's going on?"

I looked at his face, his eyes wide and filled with sorrow.

"Please help me," he said.

I felt the cool metal against my skin, allowed my chest to rumble as it expelled the last few breaths of smokey air. "I'm like one of those cans you won't buy at the grocery store," I said.

"What?" he asked.

"One of those cans they always pile into a grocery cart and charge half price for. They're the ones that someone dropped, the dented ones. Remember? Remember that time I put one in our cart? Tomatoes or something. You made me put it back. You said that a dented can is not just a dented can. You said that it makes the insides go bad. Remember?"

"No," Peter said into my hair.

"It's true, Peter. God, just give me that much."

*H*ERE I AM AT NINETEEN. *Swimming inside a borrowed sweater at six A.M. watching Peter coax the same swan from ice each morning for a week. The sweater was made on the wrong size needles by someone's great-aunt. It is gray, thick with cables, and falls well below my hips. I have to roll the cuffs to keep my hands from disappearing in the long sleeves. Inside the borrowed sweater I imagine myself a swan trapped inside ice. I even feel my neck begin to arch in the same cold and precise way.*

Finally, he asked if I would like to take a walk with him later in the day. If he might show me something he'd found. I remember nodding shyly; I had been quite content just to watch him chipping at ice with a chain saw. I imagine now we must have looked like any other pair of gangly teenagers scuffing our feet as we walked down the winding dirt road away from the Birches. In my memory of this day, a spectacular backdrop of paper castle and mountains jutting into the clear summer sky adds a strange effect to our silhouettes, but the truth is we could have been any other couple of kids on a hot summer afternoon. He had a way of walking a few steps ahead. I could see that he had to concentrate not to leave me behind. His legs were long and he knew where he was going. I didn't know then that he was also counting his steps, like a metronome, keeping time. Didn't understand yet that counting kept him safe.

The Birches charged employees a dollar an hour for bicycle rentals. The bikes were red and had one speed, more appropriate for beach boardwalks than for these mountain roads. But we made do and I followed behind Peter, my heart and legs pumping to keep up as we climbed hills and avoided the locals' cars that sped along the dangerous asphalt curves. It took nearly an hour until we came to a bridge that overlooked what people here called a *notch*, what we might call a *canyon* out west. We left the bikes untethered and climbed over the guardrails, being careful not to tumble into the ravine below. Peter held out his hand to help me and I accepted. His backpack was bulging with something. I thought for a minute that he might have brought a picnic lunch for us, but when we got to the bottom where the stream was wider than it had appeared from the bridge, it was only a pair of binoculars and a blanket that he pulled from his pack.

The nest rested precariously in the higher limbs of an old maple near the water. It took me several attempts before I could even see it through the thick summer leaves.

"No," he said, gesturing to the place I'd been looking. "*There.*"

Finally, I saw movement and held still until I could discern the heads of three infant robins, their heads peeking out over the top of the nest. They were small and nearly featherless. They craned their necks and opened their mouths, but no sounds came out.

"I found the mother's body in the stream yesterday," Peter said, sitting down on the blanket he had spread out on the grass.

I kept looking at the nest through the binoculars.

"I thought I'd try to get up there and bring them down. But the limbs are weak. They probably wouldn't hold my weight."

I stared through the binoculars at the limb jutting out over the cold water. I looked up at the tree and back at him. He was looking through the binoculars now, quiet. And I thought about saying, *I'll do it. Just help me up.* But as I looked again at the fragile limb, I shivered inside that giant sweater.

Peter shrugged his shoulders and put the binoculars back into his pack. "It's too dangerous."

He didn't mention the birds again. He still smiled each morning when I got my coffee and sat on the porch to watch him work. And sometimes in the late afternoons we would go swimming or ride a pair of rented bikes into town for pizza. We always bought the largest one and ate until our stomachs hurt and our fingers were greasy. He was careful not to touch me for too long, though, and I always blamed this on the birds. And so at night while my roommate snored softly in the bunk beneath me, I dreamed it over again. I felt the bark in my hands as I shimmied out on the limb. I dreamed my palms holding the prickly nest. I gave the three scrawny and featherless birds voices. The blue eggshells I offered him were the same color as my imagined sky.

By the end of July, I started to hate those birds. Each time he walked a few too many steps ahead of me or dismissed my offered hand, each time he said he'd rather stay in and read a book than drink beer on the employee beach with me at midnight, I resented their straining necks. I hated their mother for building her nest outside of my reach. Each time I waited for him to kiss me and instead he squeezed my shoulders and walked up the dimly lit wooden steps of the boys' dorm, I was glad the birds had died.

I kept watching him carve the swans, though. No matter how hard I tried to stay in bed each morning, I couldn't resist pulling on my jeans and wandering into the parking lot, where I always knew I could find him. And then, finally, one morning I decided to give up. The night before I had dream-tipped the birds' nest over, spilling them like pebbles into the ravine below.

When the sun fell across my face I pulled the covers over my head and willed myself to stay inside.

I know now that I was responsible. That my simple willful absence must have been what upset him, what made his hands slip. I had inadvertently become a part of his intricate routine, and my absence that day distracted him. As he freed the swan from its cold prison, he might have been glancing toward my window. He might have lost his concentration when he turned his head to see if the sound behind him was me instead of a mosquito humming or just a strong late-summer breeze through the tops of the trees.

I remember only that the familiar buzz and hum of the chain saw had stopped. And the silence that followed was louder than Peter's screams. Louder even than the sound of my heart and my feet pounding against the indoor-outdoor carpeting in the dormitory hallway as I ran to see what had happened.

The cuts were deep. The blade had slipped and traveled across the shin of his left leg and then sliced into the calf of his right. He had carved from his flesh a mangled sculpture of bone and muscle and blood.

The next day, I packed my things and got a ride into town, where I bought a bus ticket to Hanover. I had made almost a thousand dollars already, enough to rent a room in a Dartmouth sorority house that was almost empty for the summer. And every day for an entire month, I walked across the campus to Mary Hitchcock, where Peter's legs were healing.

He didn't seem surprised to see me the first time I arrived at the door of his hospital room. He never even asked why I'd left the Birches or where I was staying. He only smiled and held my hand when I read to him and brought him smuggled hamburgers. He only kissed me when I left him at the end of visiting hours each day. And in this way, Peter and I fell in love. In this way, I made him forget that I'd let those birds die. In the clean white room that smelled of Clorox and wilting flowers, I had never felt so needed. Or loved. Or forgiven.

WHEN WE GOT HOME from the café, I went straight to the bathroom to run a bath. I dumped a handful of powdered bubble bath under the faucet and watched the bubbles multiply. When the tub was full, I took off my clothes and sunk into the soapy water up to my neck. With a brand new bar of soap, I started scrubbing at the black marks all over my skin. The water quickly turned gray with ink.

After a while, Peter knocked on the door.

"Come in," I said.

He came in and stood next to the tub, looking down at me in the water. Then he rolled up his sleeves, kneeled down, and put both of his hands in the dirty water. I could see how hard this was for him. But he didn't wince, he just leaned toward me, kissing my forehead.

"Peter, I'm a mess."

"I don't care."

"Not this," I said, motioning to the murky water. "I mean, everything."

He closed his eyes and opened them again.

"It's too much . . . You shouldn't have to deal with this shit."

"I'm still here," he said. "I'm not going anywhere."

"Why not?" I asked.

The cuffs of his sleeves dipped into the water.

"Careful," I said, pulling his sleeve up over his sharp elbow.

Peter looked at me, his eyes intent, his face serious. "We're all damaged, Indie," he said softly.

"I don't want to hear this," I said, shaking my head.

"Listen to me," he said. "Please."

He sat back on his knees, but his arms stayed in the water. "Everybody's dented. Everybody's been dropped and slammed."

"How are *you* damaged?" I asked.

He looked at me intently. I knew he was thinking about his legs.

"What? Because you have scars?" I said, snorting. "It's hardly the same thing. I've never met anybody more normal than you."

Peter pulled his arms out the water and ran one wet hand through his hair. "You think I'm *normal?* You think the way I live, counting every step, afraid of doing anything out of order, is *normal?*"

I looked down at the gray water.

"When I was six years old, I thought that I had to count to a thousand every night before I fell asleep or something bad would happen to my mother. She found me once, interrupted me, and I was terrified. I tried to explain, it made perfect sense to me, and she just kept reassuring me. I started over after she left my room. I was so afraid. Later it was other things. Left to right. All these rituals. And when the accident happened, it was like some sort of proof. It got worse. I must have spent hours trying to figure out what went wrong that day . . . whether I put my right shoe on first instead of my left? I almost drove myself crazy trying to figure out what I could have done. But finally, I had to let go. I had to just let it be an accident."

"I don't see what this has to do with me."

"Everybody's got scars. But there's got to be more to us than the accidents in our life."

"*Accidents?*"

I wiped my eyes with the back of my hand. It made everything wet. When I squeezed my eyes shut, I saw the stars on Benny's ceiling.

"You lasted, Indie. Bumped and bruised, but you came out alive. Isn't that worth something to you?"

"I didn't survive, Peter. I ran *away*." A sob caught in my throat like a knot in a rope. "I ran away and borrowed somebody else's life. And now, it feels like . . . like an overdue library book or something, and every day I'm afraid somebody will ask me to give it back." I was crying so hard now my chest was lurching forward with each sob. "And they weren't *accidents*. Nothing that happened was an accident. Accidents are things you can't stop from happening. Somebody could have stopped it."

Peter came toward me again and held onto my shoulders, gently, keeping me steady. Keeping me from sinking underwater.

I looked down at the gray water, at my pale body trembling in the cold.

"Ma could have stopped it, Daddy . . ." I said, looking at him hard. "I could have stopped it. That's the difference, don't you see?"

Peter helped me out of the water. He wrapped me in his old robe, bandaging me in flannel.

He brought me to our bed and stroked my hair until my chest stopped heaving. And then he unwrapped me from the robe like a gift and kissed all of the sore places: the lids of my tired eyes and the palms of my hands.

"I don't want to make muffins anymore," I said, later, as I was drifting off to sleep.

"That's fine." And he didn't seem to notice that his arms were stained gray from my bathwater.

Peter had to pick Esmé up at the bus station at midnight. He asked me to come, but I told him I wasn't feeling well. I offered him vague symptoms and hoped that it would be enough. He felt my head with the back of his hand, and even though I didn't have a fever, he brought me two aspirin and a cup of chamomile tea.

After he left, I curled up in our bed (sheets so clean they still smelled of soap) and wished I had gone with him. It would have been nice to drive through the woods, which were now laced with snow from an early storm. It would have been nice to watch for Esmé coming down the steps of the bus into the hot and smelly bus station, to have offered her a hand with her heavy backpack. It would have been nice to be anywhere but here, alone. If Jessica had curled up in the bed with me, I might not have felt so lonely, but she refused to get off the dryer, which was warmer than the woodstove. She'd made a nest out of Peter's boxer shorts and my pajamas. I was glad when they finally came home. But I told him I still didn't feel well when he breathed questions into my bare breasts. And I stayed in bed with my imagined fever the next morning, listening to them making pies and bread in the kitchen.

Peter had brought the TV into the kitchen so he could watch the Macy's parade while he made Thanksgiving dinner. I could hear the sounds of a high school band from the bedroom when I finally reluctantly pulled myself out of bed. I could also hear the faint twinkle of Esmé's sweet voice, rising like a parade balloon.

THANKSGIVINGS. Mountainview, Arizona. *Benny liked cranberry sauce in a can. He loved the sound it made as it broke the vacuumed seal and came slithering out of the can into the bowl. He would push his finger into the ridged cylinder until it pierced through the gel.*

Leigh Moony was still in the hospital. There had been some complications because of an allergic reaction to one of the antibiotics they'd given her to ward off infection. I was alarmed by how small she looked inside the hospital bed. Chuck had said she could carry a keg of beer all by herself. She could carry a whole keg of beer but not a baby. I wondered how she felt now in a hospital, and empty.

The Macy's parade sounded like memories of other Thanksgivings. The last parade I went to was when I visited my father in San Diego. Christmas lights strung in palm trees, lighting the way of surfers and VW buses and Harley Davidsons decked with antlers. In the kitchen Esmé was running cold water through the slimy, hollowed-out bird as the announcers glowed pink before Broadway understudies costumed and lip-synching in the city streets.

Ma's Thanksgivings were made from boxes and cans. Stovetop Stuffing and cranberry sauce and crispy fried onions sprinkled over uniformly shaped green beans. Benny had a headdress he wore. A forgotten Halloween costume turned him from a boy into a savage. What he didn't know was that there were Indians everywhere around us. When he dreamed Thanksgiving, he dreamed Technicolor tomahawks and Tonto on TV. The feathers fell out one by one, littering Ma's kitchen like autumn leaves.

Chuck Moony married Leigh because of her strength and stoicism. He told us he loved her because she was unbreakable. She wasn't fragile the way some girls are. You didn't need to worry about her falling to pieces in your hands.

When Esmé was a little girl, Peter used to bring her everywhere. She liked to ride on the handlebars of his bike when they went out to visit their father at the docks. He carried her piggy-back around the house. He let her ride in the front seat of his car when he first learned to drive. Peter's face lit up when she was around. He missed her when she was gone.

Benny's laughter might have sounded maniacal to anyone who didn't know him. He threw his head back and opened his mouth and let out a sound that could pierce eardrums, break glass. His skin flushed red with the effort of laughter. I think he knew even then that in our family joy was hard work.

I brought Leigh a bunch of yellow daisies, which she seemed to like. When she took the bundle from me, the plastic crinkled in her hands and I noticed that her veins were like fishing lines. It must have taken several attempts to puncture her skin with the IV needle. Chuck says that Leigh is like a good tree. Not too beautiful and not too tall but trustworthy and strong. A little wind wouldn't do much but whistle through her branches. I wondered if she felt hollow. The rotten pulpy insides gone now.

Peter was almost thirteen when Esmé was born. She was an afterthought, Peter says. *Accident*, Esmé always laughs. Usually siblings with that many years between them lack the shared childhoods necessary for bonding, it seems. The closest brothers and sisters seem to be the ones who were necessarily allied in the great childhood war against their parents. But Peter and Esmé have that closeness. I can see it in the way they easily curl around each other, in the speech patterns that sound like music when they tell stories. I think it's difficult for Peter to understand that Lily and I have never been allies. That it was always she and Ma. Even after Benny died and Daddy left, it was still Ma and Lily. Impenetrable and united. Sometimes I still think of myself as an only child. A *lonely child,* Chuck Moony once described it. He was one, too; his brother was more than ten years older than he. I could hear Peter asking Esmé to preheat the oven to 425 degrees. Cymbals and trumpets and horns. Marching bands and majorettes, cold instruments and batons.

I wonder sometimes what would have happened if Benny had lived. I like to think that he would have kept growing until he towered over us: over me, over Lily and Daddy, and over Ma. That he wouldn't have been able to fit under the table or porch or even inside the house anymore. That his hands would have eventually become as big as the silver sleds we dragged up the neighbor's hill to slide on. That his smile would have become as big as a canoe. That he could have carried me away in the palm of one of those giant hands.

I got out of bed and realized that I had talked myself into a cold. The fever Peter had been looking for in my skin had become real. I stuck the thermometer in my mouth and sat on the toilet waiting for the evidence. 102 degrees. I shook the glass tube and dipped the end in peroxide. The bubbles hissed as they fought whatever germs I'd left there. I splashed some water on my face and pulled on my favorite slippers.

In the kitchen Esmé and Peter were peeling potatoes.

"Hi Indie!" Esmé said, setting down her half-peeled potato and reaching for me. I took her hand and she squeezed it. "You look horrible."

"I *feel* horrible," I said. And as I said it, it became true. I felt a chill and the scratch of a cold at the back of my throat.

Peter sliced his potato into perfect cubes and dropped them in a large pot of water on the stove. He smiled at me.

"Do we have any Vitamin C?" I asked.

"In the fridge."

I reached into the refrigerator past the covered casseroles and pies. I knocked a bag of cranberries to the floor as I pulled out the family-size bottle of vitamins. I felt shaky, my hands and knees unsteady.

"You can leave those out," he said. He grabbed another potato from the wicker bin and ran it under the cold water.

Esmé said, "Peter was saying you might start doing some writing on your own. Do you miss the paper much?"

I hadn't thought about the paper or about writing for a long time.

"I'd love to read your stuff. I have E-mail at school. You can send me anything you want to."

"Thanks." I smiled. "I will."

"Do you want a scone? Peter made the maple ones I like." She smiled.

"That's okay," I said.

Esmé is beautiful in a way that suggests complete ignorance of her effect on the eye. She blushes easily. She has bad posture and will not take a compliment. She is enthusiastic about everything. Trusting and eager and sincere. She reminds me sometimes of Benny, strangely, in small things she does. In her laughter. In the way she loves Peter. Benny loved me like that.

Esmé rested her head on Peter's shoulder. My head was pounding, my legs felt weak.

"I'm going back to bed," I said. "I have a little bit of a fever. Wake me up when it's time for dinner."

"I'll come jump on the bed," Esmé said without moving away from Peter.

As I was walking back down the hall, Peter came up behind me.

"Don't forget the vitamins," he said and offered me two pills in his outstretched hand. His eyes were soft and scared. "Feel better."

. . .

I fell asleep and didn't wake up until Esmé crawled in the bed next to me.

"Are you okay?" she asked.

I nodded.

She curled up next to me and hugged me. Her skin smelled faintly of cinnamon, probably spilled while making pies.

"I'm so glad I'm here," she said. "I love your house."

"You do?" I said.

"I'm so happy when I'm here. It's easy, you know?"

"Really?"

Esmé sat up and pulled the covers back over me. "He loves you," she said.

"What?" I said.

"Peter. He really loves you."

Esmé, like Peter, sometimes knows the exact thing to say.

Chuck Moony arrived just as we were sitting down to dinner.

"I'll get it," I said, as he knocked on the door. I shuffled to the door in my slippers. I hadn't bothered changing out of my jammies.

He stood outside shivering, his hands in his pockets, and his face tired. He had shaved his beard and underneath the scruff he looked younger. His cheeks were hollow and his jaw determined. "Sorry I didn't call. I came straight from the hospital. Turkey noodle soup wasn't quite my cup of music," he sighed.

I grinned and ushered him in, helping him off with his jacket.

Peter had gotten a couple of sawhorses and a piece of plywood from the shed to extend our small table, and covered the whole thing with one of his mother's tablecloths. He had set a place for Chuck next to Esmé. Chuck pulled off his boots and sat down.

Yams, mashed potatoes, creamed spinach, artichoke hearts, salad with brilliantly red hothouse tomatoes, and cornbread circled the golden turkey in a parade of colors and smells and tastes. My throat was thick with the cold, but I piled the food onto my plate.

Chuck helped himself to several scoops of spinach. One long strand reached from his plate to the casserole dish. He looked apologetic when it stained the white tablecloth. "So what are you studying in school now, Ez?"

Esmé blushed and finished chewing the piece of turkey she had in her mouth. "Still books," she said. "Stuff nobody else reads anymore."

Peter quietly cut another piece of turkey off the beautifully garnished bird perched on a yard-sale china platter. He offered it to me, and I accepted. The homemade gravy was thick and delicious. I ate until the chills in my shoulders had subsided. Until I felt better. Until the tickle in my throat was just a recollection.

Peter made us vanilla lattés to have with our pie. Chuck and I took ours out onto the back porch while Peter and Esmé built a fire and watched *It's a Wonderful Life* on TV.

Outside the sun was setting, leaving only traces of pink and gold in the trees. We sat in the porch swing, resting our cups on the end of the tables Peter had fashioned out of two tree stumps.

"I'm sorry," I said. "For that." I motioned vaguely to the woods where I had stupidly, drunkenly kissed him.

"It's okay," he said. "Water under the road."

I smiled.

"I'm sorry about the baby too," I said.

Chuck stared into his coffee cup. "Once I bought this brand-new car. It was the only time I've ever had a new car in my whole life. I drove it up to Canada to go to the bars with some friends.

When we came out of the bar it was gone. Just like that. I'd hardly even driven it."

I looked into Chuck's wide-open face, into the dark ponds of his eyes.

"Sometimes things get stolen," he shrugged.

I nodded, and I thought about things stolen from me. I thought about the thieves I had known.

When Chuck and I went back inside, Esmé had fallen asleep on the couch with her head on Peter's lap. Peter motioned for us to be quiet as we came in the door, shaking mud and snow off our boots and out of our hair. He had built a fire and the living room was warm, all the smells of the dinner lingering like ghosts in the air.

"I should be getting back to the hospital," Chuck said.

"Take some pie for Leigh?" Peter whispered.

"That's okay. She's still on the IV."

"Take some home for yourself at least," I tried. I pulled the tin foil from the pumpkin and apple pies. I pinched a little piece of crust off and popped it in my mouth. It was buttery and sweet.

"She'd kill me if she even smelled pumpkin on my breath. I'll stop by for leftovers tomorrow," Chuck said.

"Let me walk you out, then," I said.

I smiled. He hopped into the truck and turned on the headlights. He rolled down the window and leaned his head out. "Don't let Pete eat all that apple pie."

By the time I went back inside, Peter had fallen asleep too, his fingers wound into Esmé's long black curly hair. They looked alike in this light. Both tall and thin. Long fingers, eyelashes, and narrow feet. Esmé was curled up, and Peter's head was leaning against the back of the couch. There was a faint smile on his face. I got an extra quilt from our bedroom and laid it across Esmé.

Her curly hair spilled across the blanket's edges. Jessica, after trying futilely to the fit into the neat little mountain of quilt and legs and hands on the couch, gave up and followed me into my bed, curling up at my feet.

In the middle of the night, I crawled up into the attic study and picked up the phone. When Lily answered, I felt butterflies in my throat. Wings beating, threatening to choke me. A cold breeze blew through the cracked woodwork across my bare shoulders.

"Lily, I want to talk about Violet."

I could hear her breathing on the other end of the line. Her throat was filled with butterflies, too.

"And I want to talk about Benny," I said.

Lily was silent for several moments, and then she whispered, "That wasn't Ma's fault."

My eyes stung.

Silence. And then, quietly, the sound of her hand brushing across the soft skin of her cheek, wiping at tears.

"You're going to lose Violet *and* Rich because of what you're doing. It's the same thing. Don't you see?"

*H*ERE IS BENNY. *As tall as Daddy and wearing a pair of his rubber fishing boots. Lying on his stomach on a rock at the creek, staring into the water. He reaches deep into the current, trying to change the water's direction with his hands. A leaf catches in his fingers. Frustrated, he shakes it loose against the muddy ground next to him.*

It was July, monsoon season, and the creek was high from all the rain. Too high for swimming. Even for Benny. So instead, after Daddy went to work and Ma went to visit Lily in the hospital, I brought Benny to the creek to go fishing. I found a pole in the shed, and because of the rain there were worms everywhere in our muddy backyard. I didn't know the first thing about fishing, or even if there were any fish to be caught in the creek. But I did know this—since Ma and Lily came home from Phoenix and Lily went to the hospital, Benny and I were better off outside the house. Inside the house, Ma's storms were worse than any monsoon. Her anger came on just as quickly, dark clouds passing through the rooms of our house, the only warning a muffled sigh or the sound of her feet gaining momentum until she was standing at your bedroom door. But the monsoons left as quickly as they came, and the air was cleaner afterwards. There was a stillness after these storms that never seemed to come after one of Ma's fits. Daddy said not to worry. That Ma's head was full of concern over Lily, and that as soon as Lily came home everything would be back to normal. I didn't remind him that there was no such thing inside our house.

This morning, I didn't wait for the storm clouds to come. I woke up when the sky was still bright and hopeful and crawled into bed next to Benny.

"Benny, get up. Let's go fishing," I whispered.

His eyes popped open, alarmed and then soft. "We're going to the creek?"

"Yeah. But you gotta get up quick while Ma's still sleeping. And be real quiet."

I found the pole in the shed and a rusty old tackle box. I dumped some old nails and screws from a coffee can and filled it with moist dirt and a few worms that I had plucked from the ground. Benny came outside, wearing Daddy's gaiters, and closed the screen door softly. I smiled at him and motioned for him to follow me toward the woods.

We ran to the spot in the woods where we knew we were safe, and Benny let out a big sigh. "I didn't make a sound. Not even the door."

"I know, Benny," I said. "That was good. Now come on."

I pulled him by the hand and we continued through the early morning forest until we got to the tracks.

"Listen," he said, dropping to his knees and pressing his ear against the ground.

"It's fine, Benny. One just passed. I heard it when we were in the woods." I was eager to get to the creek. He looked at me suspiciously and then scrambled to his feet when I stepped over the tracks and wooden ties to the other side.

"You should be more careful," Benny said.

"I know," I nodded. "Let's go."

The sky was bright and sunny. It was early in the morning, though, and the air was still, clean, and cold. By the time we got to the creek, the sun was warm on our backs and I knew it was going to be a hot day. Benny wiped the back of his sleeve across his face. He was sweating in his flannel shirt.

"Why don't you take your shirt off, Benny?" I said. "You've got an undershirt on, right?"

He nodded and unbuttoned the heavy flannel shirt and pulled it off. He hung it from a tree branch that was jutting out over the rock where I was sitting. Then he stretched out across his stomach on the flat rock.

"What kind of fish are in there?" he asked, staring into the water.

"I don't know," I said, opening the lid of the tackle box.

"I ate a fish once that was rotted inside."

"Hand me the pole?" I said, motioning to the pole I'd left leaning against the tree.

He reached for the pole and handed it to me. "I took one bite and I almost barfed."

"It wasn't rotten. It was just frozen still. Remember? It was a fish from the grocery store."

"I hate fish sticks."

"I know," I said.

"I really hate 'em."

I found a hook in the tackle box and tied it to the end of the fishing line. I didn't really know what I was doing, but it seemed like it would work okay.

"Can you pass me the coffee can?"

"What's in here?" Benny asked, peeling back the plastic lid.

"Worms. Now give it."

"Gross. Worms!" Benny squealed and shoved the can toward me.

"Shush," I said, looking up toward the overlook to make sure there weren't any early-morning tourists spying on us.

I'd never put a worm on a hook before. It wasn't as easy as you'd think. The first one was wriggling so hard it slipped right out of my fingers and fell into the water. I was able to do it the second time around, though, and then all we had left to do was to wait.

Here is Benny. Leaning into the creek, staring at the way the water changes the shapes of his hands. The creek is so full of sun that it could be colored glass. He is quiet here. Quieter than he has ever been. When he closes his eyes the sun is warm on his eyelids.

I knew we wouldn't catch anything. But that wasn't why we were here, anyway.

"Want to see what I found?" Benny asked.

"Sure," I said.

He stood up and went to the tree where his shirt was hanging. He reached into the front pocket and pulled something out.

"It was on the floor to my room this morning." He opened up his hand and sitting in his palm was a moth. It was one of the big ones that came in at night if somebody left the screen door open. They were clumsy, beating their big wings against the walls, looking for light. Sometimes there were six or seven of them hovering near the bare bulb that hung over the back porch.

"I'm gonna give it to Lily when she comes home from the hospital. She likes butterflies."

"That's not . . ." I started and then stopped.

He was looking at the moth in his hand and stroking its papery wings with one of his large fingers.

"That's nice, Benny. She'll like it."

"She's very sick," he said, looking at me. "She might die."

"She's not going to die," I said.

"She *might*," he insisted, and I let him.

"Put it back in your pocket," I said. "You don't want to lose it."

Benny returned the moth to his shirt pocket and sat down next to me on the rock.

"I don't think there's no fish in there," Benny said, shaking his head.

I shrugged.

Benny wanted to go swimming, but the current was too strong and the water was too high. "Put your feet in if you want," I said. "But we gotta wait for the water to go down before you go swimming."

"Will it go down today?" he asked hopefully, tugging at the rubber gaiters.

"Not today."

After a while I gave up. I looked at my watch and saw that it was 11:30. Ma would be leaving for the hospital any minute. We could go home soon.

"What do you think?" I asked. "Call it a day?"

Before he could answer, thunder cracked above us. Like a slap. Benny's hands flew to his ears.

"Let's go," I said. I yanked the pole out of the water. The worm was gone. I could see it being carried away by the current, white and limp, several feet away. I closed the tackle box and thunder rumbled deep and insistent. Closer and louder this time. It was a warning.

But before Benny had even pulled the giant rubber boots back on, rain began to fall in hard sheets. Guillotines of water sliced through the tops of the trees. Benny stumbled, falling forward onto his hands. When he stood up again his hair was already plastered to his head. He opened his mouth and let the hard rain fall into his throat.

I scurried to my feet and pulled his hand. "Come on, Benny."

We ran up the slippery embankment. Benny's boots made sucking sounds on the wet grass and mud. By the time we got to Highway 79, we were soaking wet and covered with mud. A couple of cars whizzed past us, their headlights shining through the darkness.

"I don't got my shirt," he said.

"That's okay," I said. "We'll get it later."

"I gotta get Lily's butterfly."

"We'll find another one," I said. His face was fallen, serious. "I promise."

Benny hit his temples with his fists. His undershirt was so wet you could see his ribs through the ribbed cotton.

"Stop it," I said.

Another car whizzed past us, splashing cold water close to our feet.

"It's the only one I had," he cried, pulling the hair at his temples.

"I said *stop it*," I said, angry now. The rain beat and beat, like a thousand small fists pounding my skin.

Here is Benny. Standing at the edge of the road in rubber gaiters, in a tired undershirt drooping like a second layer of skin. Fourteen years old and as tall as Daddy. Crying like a baby. Tugging at his hair. Through a passing car window it might not make sense. Through rain-splattered glass you might think he was a man instead of a boy. Only when you slow down can you see that he is only a child. Only when you roll down the window can you see that the rain distorts things.

The woman was wearing a baby-blue shirt with embroidered silver flowers on each pointy collar. Her lips were the color of peaches. She smiled when she rolled down the window.

"You okay, honey?" she asked Benny.

Benny kept crying and tugging at his ears and hair.

"He's fine," I said.

"You sure?" she asked. "He doesn't look okay to me."

"He's fine. I'm just taking him home."

"Maybe I should drive you home," she said, shaking her head. Her hair was frosted. White streaks on top of dark curling iron curls.

"That's okay," I said, blinking away the rain that had settled in the corners of my eyes. "We live just over that way."

"You're Indie Brown, aren't you?" she asked then, reaching her hand toward me. "I'm Starry's Aunt Cathy. Remember? I met you once when you came over to spend the night at the A-frame."

I remembered her now. She and Starry's mom were planning a Tupperware party that night. She was the one who showed Starry how to use liquid eyeliner. She also gave Starry a brand-new record player for Christmas last year.

"Oh, hi," I said.

"Let me give you a ride."

Benny was tugging at my elbow now. "Let's go see Starry," he said softly.

"No Benny," I said.

When lightning split the sky in two, Benny covered his ears and started to twist his body back and forth.

"Thanks anyway," I said and turned to Benny. "Let's go."

"Okay then," Cathy said and started to roll up her window. "See you later."

"I said *let's go*."

Cathy's car drove away and I walked ahead of Benny all the way home. And after we were inside the house again, I didn't offer him a clean dry shirt from the pile of clean laundry I found on top of the dryer. And I didn't drag a clean towel across the top of his wet head. I just locked myself inside the bathroom and ran a hot bath. I would stay there until Ma came home. I would stay there until my skin was loose on my bones.

I turned the water on full blast and as hot as it would go. I stared at my face in the mirror until it disappeared behind a film of steam. I opened up Ma's drawer and found her favorite bath crystals, the pink ones that smelled like roses. I dumped them into the running water and watched them melt at the bottom like hard candies.

I turned the portable radio on as high as it would go and peeled off my wet clothes. I put one foot into the tub, yanking it out when my skin turned bright red with the heat. Then I put it back in, biting my lip. Enduring the heat. I sat down and let my body get used to the water. The tub filled almost to the rim because Daddy had filled the drainage holes with caulking when we got a leak last year. Then I leaned my head back and went under.

On the backs of my eyes I saw the frosted tips of Starry's aunt's hair. She looked a little like the lady in the tube top at Rusty's who had lost the tournament to me. I squeezed my eyes shut tighter until both of them disappeared. I imagined them rising like steam. Only transparent ghosts now. It was so hot inside the bathroom, it was almost hard to breathe. But I didn't want to stand up to open a window. I didn't want to get out of the water. I sunk deeper, the edge of the tub sharp against the bones of my shoulders. The water was cool enough now that it didn't burn when I opened my eyes. Through my watery lenses I saw Lily's sequinned costume. Silver sparkles and her baton slicing through the air like a sudden streak of lightning. I saw the silvery wings of the moth that Benny found, dead and dusty on his bedroom floor.

I sat up and wiped at my eyes, stinging from hot, watery roses.

I reached for a towel and pushed it against my eyes to try to make the stinging stop. I opened the window and let the cold air rush in, let the steam slither out. It was still raining outside. I could hear thunder, far away now, but persistent.

I knew before I walked into the quiet kitchen that Benny was gone. I knew before I dropped the towel and pulled on my jeans and sweatshirt and a pair of flip-flops by the door. I knew the way I knew that the storm was almost over. That the sky would become benevolent again.

I let the screen door slam shut behind me. I ran through the rain-drenched field of heavy sunflowers to the woods. I cried as I ran, following the fresh footprints made by Daddy's gaiters in the wet ground. I let each of my breaths resound like thunder in my chest as I reached the clearing and the train tracks.

JULY 28, 1978. Mountainview, Arizona. *Here is Benny. Stumbling down the embankment to the spot where he'd left his flannel shirt hanging on a limb. Reaching into the pocket for the butterfly. He would leave it on Lily's pillow so that when she came home from the hospital it would be there, waiting for her with silver wings. He is careful not to crush it when he puts it back into his pocket and puts his shirt on. It isn't raining so hard anymore. It feels good on his neck and his hands. He climbs back up the embankment and walks along the road until it is safe to cross. And then he runs as fast as he can across the pavement. At the tracks he kneels to the ground and listens for the train. But it is only distant thunder that he hears. He presses his ear harder to make sure. Distant thunder, the passing storm. It is quiet. Only the sounds of his breathing. The sounds of the moth's wings beating against his chest. And so he crosses the tracks, careful not to slip and fall. The light coming toward him could only be the sun emerging from the darkness of the stormy sky. The whistle, only wind through the trees. The rumble of the train only thunder beneath his feet. And then it is quiet. Not a sound. Not even a breathing sound.*

After Benny was gone, I found the photographs that he and I

had taken in the photo booth crumpled in a pocket. In the first photo, Benny's face was a blur. In the second, he was completely missing from the picture. I lament the lost photo, the one that fluttered down from the top of the Ferris wheel. But it's rare that there is clarity in recollection. Most memories are like the blurred photo of Benny's face. Moments of bright light are rare and precious. This is what the lightning taught me.

IT WAS COLD AND SUNNY and the streets were filled with people loaded down with shopping bags. Esmé ran ahead of Peter and me, peering into windows. She had a Christmas Club account this year into which she'd been putting five dollars a week. She clutched a brightly colored envelope filled with her savings. Peter and I always go shopping the weekend after Thanksgiving. Usually we are in Bar Harbor with his family, and I wind up bringing home bags full of tacky souvenirs: ladies made of seashells, rubber lobsters, music boxes with decals that say *Bah Hahba*. But this year we took Esmé into town. She thought this was perfectly wonderful; Bar Harbor was about as thrilling to her as going to the dentist, she said. We took her to the places we knew she would love: the stained-glass store, a vintage clothing shop, the bookstore. When it was time for lunch we decided to go to the Swan so that she could see Joe. She rushed into the kitchen as soon as we walked in, Peter went down to the office to pick up some paperwork to work on later, and I picked out a table for us near the window, facing the busy street.

I stared out the window at the streets filled with Christmastime. It was warm in the café. I took off my coat and went to check out the specials on the chalkboard.

"Hi Indie," Julia said. She was one of those few employees who lived in town and got stuck working through the holidays when all of the students went home. She was wearing a bright red-and-green sweater and had a sprig of holly in her hair.

"Hi," I smiled. "What's good today?"

She leaned across the counter and said, "Don't get the minestrone. Joe went crazy with the cloves."

"I heard that," Joe hollered from the kitchen.

"Can I get a bowl of cheddar broccoli soup and an onion roll?"

"The minestrone is perfectly fine," Joe shouted.

I'd seen his bike out front this morning. The dusting of snow hadn't stopped his daily trek.

I brought the soup and roll back to the table. Peter and Esmé joined me with steaming plates of Joe's white lasagna: spinach and Alfredo sauce with three kinds of cheese. Peter brought a bottle of wine from the walk-in and we drank the whole thing. We had rum cake for dessert and Esmé announced that she wanted to go back to the bookstore to look for a Christmas present for her roommate. "You guys stay here," she said. "Indie looks like she's ready to drop."

It was true. Though the cold had subsided, I was still tired.

"What's playing today?" I asked.

"What do you feel like?" Peter smiled and reached for my hand. It was the first time we'd touched in days.

"How about *Roman Holiday*?" I said.

There were a few people in the theater, mostly husbands taking breaks from their shopping wives. Peter and I sat in the back in two chairs we'd found at an antique store in Portsmouth, New Hampshire. The stuffing was coming out of the arms, but they were the two most comfortable seats in the theater.

I have always loved this movie. I like the idea of a princess trying to be a normal girl for a day; usually it's the other way around. I suppose everyone needs to escape their lives sometimes. To pretend they're something they're not. Even princesses.

Peter held my hand through the whole movie, stroking the space between my index finger and thumb.

Esmé was in the café having a beer with Joe when the movie finished. Outside the sun had set and the trees lining the street were laced with sparkling white lights. The flower store across the street had put up their obnoxious electronic Chipmunks display. Their squeaky voices sang Christmas carols at high speed. The restaurant was empty and Julia was putting the chairs up on the tables to mop the floors.

"Closing early tonight?" I asked.

Peter nodded. "Everybody go home and get some rest. Christmas season has officially started and there will be no rest for anyone from now until New Year's. Wanna beer, Indie?"

"Sure," I said. He brought a six-pack out of the walk-in and set it down on the table.

Joe opened up the beers with a bottle opener from his apron pocket and Esmé made a toast.

"To breaking tradition," she said. "This beats the hell out of Mom's mulled wine."

"Hear, hear," Peter said.

I had to agree. Peter and Esmé's mom had a tradition of hot and spicy wine that I'd never quite taken to.

Peter leaned over and kissed me and my cheeks felt hot. *This is home,* I thought. *This is mine. Not borrowed. I made this.*

Peter had locked the front door and flipped the sign to CLOSED. A few people came by, checked their watches, and peered through the glass. Normally Peter would have let them in, but today was a holiday of sorts. He merely shrugged and smiled, waving at them through the glass. When a man so bundled up it looked like he was carrying blankets under his coat came to the door, I figured Peter would do the same. The man tried the door and when he realized it was locked, he began to the pound on the glass. Around him snow was starting to the fall in thick white flakes. His shoulders and hood were covered with it. But instead of smiling apologetically and waving him away, Peter stood up and went to the door.

"Tell him we're closed," Julia sighed. She'd seen Peter let in tired and cold people long after closing too many times.

But Peter reached into his pocket and quickly unlocked the door. When the door opened and the man stepped in, I could see that it wasn't blankets he was carrying inside his coat. It was a baby.

"Rich," I said, my heart catching in my throat. "My God."

LATE NOVEMBER, 1999. Phoenix, Arizona. *Lily Hughes of Phoenix, AZ, after months of denial, has finally admitted to repeatedly smothering her nine-month-old infant, Violet Hughes. After an extensive phone conversation with her estranged sister, Miranda Brown of Echo Hollow, Maine, Mrs. Hughes was allegedly discovered by her husband, Richard Hughes, late on Thanksgiving night (midnight-dark night) in the child's cold nursery, holding a pillow over the infant's face. When confronted by her husband, Mrs. Brown is reported to have stared at her hands in disbelief, as if they did not belong to her. As if they were not her hands at all. But soon, they became familiar again, and she held them* to her face, whispering, "Save her," or "Take her." It could have been either request, she said it so softly. It could have been, "Blame her." In her nightgown, she looked small and scared. A girl offering a woman's apologies.

I UNDERSTAND LIGHTNING. I'm not afraid when the sky opens up and blinds my eyes with rain. I am not afraid of its white fingers. Of its electrical kiss. I have an agreement with the sky. An understanding.

After Benny was gone, after the train, I learned to dance for rain. In the backyard junkyard playground behind our house, I stomped my feet, demanding that the sky show me the sympathy of a storm. I wore Benny's headdress and willed my feet to remember the moccasin movements of the field trip, Indian tribal dances in the junior high school auditorium. I braided my black hair into the braids of my imagined Indian mother and painted my face with lipstick signs of who I should have been. I made circles around the rusty swing set, making red clouds of dust, crying in the voice of my imaginary ancestors. And soon enough, the sky answered back with thunderous apologies. Clouds first blinded and then strangled the sun. When the rain came, and the first streak of light divided the sky, I held my arms out and spun. My bare brown legs were wet and cold. Rain pooled in my open mouth, filling my throat and eyes. Then, the sky opened up and showed me its insides. I stared into its belly and touched the light.

Daddy found me in the field of sunflowers, curled up and wet, the feathers of Benny's headdress stuck to my skin like a strange crimson bird's. He picked me up in his arms and carried me back into the house, stroked my wet hair with his fingers and didn't ask why. Perhaps he knew that lightning wrote words to explain that only I could read. That the electric story it told was more vivid and real than any story anybody could make up to explain.

Peter got up at three o'clock to go to work. It felt strange to be back inside our old routine. I listened with my eyes closed to the almost forgotten sounds of his waking. The creak of springs beneath him as he sat up and turned on the small lamp on the night table. The silence of waiting for his eyes to adjust to the light. The swish of jeans being pulled on, socks, and the woolly scratch of a sweater unfolding. When he sat back down and then lay down next to me, I could smell the woods in him. In his clothes, in his skin, and in his breath.

"I love you," he whispered. Words that tasted like pine. His arms folded around me like wings. I pulled his wrists to make him hold on tighter.

"Do you mind?" I asked. "Are you sure it's okay?"

"Promise," he said, his words getting tangled in my hair.

It would only be for a week or two, just long enough for Rich to get settled into his brother's place in Boston. Rich's brother ran the East Coast division of their dad's construction company.

He told Rich he could do work for him out of their home. That way he could be with Violet. That way he could keep an eye on her all the time.

After Peter left, I got up and tiptoed into the living room, where Rich and Violet were still sleeping. Peter had stoked the fire to keep them warm. I stood with my back to the woodstove and let the warmth penetrate my flannel pajamas. Outside, the sky was still completely dark. Moonless, starless, a prelude to snow.

Violet was snoring softly, lying on her back with her arms raised over her head in the crib we had assembled the night before. The white blanket I'd found in a box marked *Bedding* was at her feet, probably thrown off soon after Peter put another log on the fire. Rich was sleeping similarly, his arms thrown over his head, his mouth slightly open. He was too long for the couch, and his feet stuck out from under the heavy quilt. He would be sore when he finally woke. His back might bother him all day. But now, everything was peaceful. Still.

In the kitchen, the coffeepot was still hot. I poured a cup of coffee and looked at Violet's things stacked on the kitchen table. Boxes carefully labeled *Onesies, Pajamas, Diapers, Toys*. Her car seat and playpen on the floor. A stroller and a puffy pink baby bag. Boxes of bottles and cases of formula.

I imagined Rich like the woman who begins hiding the change from the grocery bill in a secret drawer. Who packs a suitcase with a week's worth of clothing, underwear, and shoes. Who practices crawling out of bed and walking to the front door while her husband lies sleeping, his fingers still clenched into fists. Waiting until he strikes again before she makes the trip for real. He must have been ready for this. He must have known all along that it would happen again.

And I imagined Lily waking to find that he was gone. I imagined her listening for the sounds of anything besides the hum of the air conditioner, besides the sound of her own breaths. But like the man whose wife finally leaves, Lily must also have known that he was planning his escape. Because the expression on her face is not one of surprise, of astonishment. Remarkably, it looks strangely like relief.

It was Violet who woke first. I could hear her stuttered breath, the first soft sobs of hunger. And then Rich was in the kitchen heating formula in a saucepan, wiping sleep from his eyes.

I made buckwheat pancakes from a mix that Peter put together and left for me, labeled with instructions, in the fridge. Rich ate hungrily, as if fueling his body for a marathon. With one hand he shoveled the thick brown cakes into his mouth. With the other he held on to Violet.

When it began to snow he looked out the window, scowling. "I haven't got snow tires or anything," he said. "I should probably head out soon."

I nodded, and he offered me Violet. I took her, surprised by how heavy her small body was. I held her against my chest, her head instinctively resting on my shoulder.

Outside Rich checked the bungee cords holding his things to the roof of the car. He scraped ice off the windshield and started the engine. Exhaust rose in white sighs into the morning air. The sky was filled with snow clouds, making everything white.

Rich stood in the doorway of the cabin, reluctant to let go of Violet's small finger. His face was tired, but easy. Relieved.

"Are you sure this is okay?" he asked again.

"Go," I said. "We'll take good care of her."

"I'll call when I get to Boston," he said, releasing his grasp. "It shouldn't take me more than a week to get settled in. If you need me, my brother's phone number is on the list. So is his work number. I'll keep the car phone on, too. That's probably the best way to find me."

"Don't worry," I said again. "She'll be fine here."

"I know," Rich said, pulling his coat on and sticking his hands in his pockets. "Thank you."

I closed the door after I couldn't see Rich's headlights through the trees anymore. I shivered from the chill that had found its way into the warm cabin. It didn't take long. Winter can sometimes penetrate even the thickest walls.

I carried Violet into the living room where Peter's fire crackled hot inside the cast-iron stove. I laid her down in her crib and went to the phone in the kitchen to call Lily. Rich had asked me to. He knew, like I knew, that she was too weak to argue. She had inherited a lot of things from Ma, but not her tenacity. Lily knew how to let go. When I thought of the words I would say to Lily, I thought *don't worry, safe,* and *take care.* I also thought *sorry.* I also thought *forgive.* But when she answered the phone, I had lost all the good words.

"It's me," I said.

I could hear her breathing, but she didn't speak.

"Violet's here . . . Rich wanted me to tell you. . . ."

Silence.

"Lily, he wants you to know . . . he wanted me to tell you that he loves you, but he's afraid. . . . He's afraid for Violet. Maybe if you see someone, maybe if you can get better . . ."

Her voice was soft, like a child's, but it startled me. "After Benny died she stopped, you know."

I nodded, closing my eyes.

"And I felt like she didn't love me anymore. Sometimes she'd go days without even talking to me. Without touching me. All that sadness in our house. Remember?"

I remembered. We held on to that sorrow. We clung to it. It defined us.

"I felt invisible."

This was something I could understand, this imprecise invisibility. The gossamer feeling of childhood mornings when Ma could walk past my open bedroom door and not remember I was lying there, waiting to be woken. The footstep stutter of remembrance and then the knock, *Up, Indie,* and the empty sound of her feet on the floor moving away from me. How could Lily know this transparency? Was it possible she, too, had felt like a clear windowpane at the moment a bird breaks its wings or neck against it?

"Indie, she was the only thing I ever had. That belonged to me. You had Benny, and I had Ma. But when Benny died, I lost her too. And I hated you for what happened to Benny. I hated you for leaving him alone."

"It was Ma that left us alone, it wasn't *me,*" I said, my throat aching. And I realized for the first time that it *wasn't* my fault. It never had been.

"*Listen,*" she said louder. "I hated *myself.* I hated myself, and then I hated Ma."

I looked at Violet sleeping in the crib.

"I knew I would be a terrible mother," she said. "But Rich insisted. He wanted a big family. Like his. I told him I wouldn't know what to do with a baby. I told him." She was crying now.

And I thought of the way Peter once touched my stomach when I told him I was late, his eyes wide with forbidden hope, and how his expression changed when I pushed his hand away. Her fears were no different than mine.

"It's good," she said, her voice stronger, more certain now. "What he's done."

Violet stirred in the other room.

"What can I do?" I asked. And for the first time, in a long time, I felt purposeful. Like I had something important to do. I felt needed.

Lily paused and then whispered, "Please tell Violet that I love her. That I'm going to get better. That I promise."

I nodded, squeezing my eyes shut to keep my own tears from escaping. This was an apology; this was *sorry*. Here were the words Ma never said.

After I hung up the phone, I went to Violet's crib and picked her up. I sat down on the couch with her, carefully, and curled my feet under the quilt that, remarkably, still held the warmth of Rich's sleep. She wriggled in my arms, pulling her head back to look at me. I held her out so that she could see me, and she opened her eyes wide. I could see Lily in her face. She was in the small bones of her nose. In the depth of blue in her eyes.

"Hi," I said.

She looked at me and thrust her head and body forward. She fell into my chest and rested her head against my neck. I pulled my hair away from her face and leaned back. Soon her body relaxed and became heavier. She was sprawled across my chest, sleeping. She didn't stir, even when I uncurled my legs and stretched them out in front of me. She only held on to my hair with her fists and breathed slowly into my shoulder.

The phone rang, and I knew it must be Peter calling to make sure everything was okay. I could see him in the kitchen waiting for me to answer. Tasting the beef barley soup that Joe made every Sunday in winter. He might think I was sleeping. He might think we'd taken a walk. But he wouldn't worry, and that's why I loved him. Because he really did trust that I could take care of myself. That I was safe alone. I let the phone ring. I didn't want to disturb Violet's deep slumber. I would call him later and ask him to bring some of the soup home for dinner.

ALMOST WINTER. Echo Hollow, Maine. *Outside, the sky slowly fills with light, the bright white light that accompanies snow. A gentle offering from the sky this time. White light illuminating a child's fair skin and the instinctive circular motions of my hands on her back. And the story I tell her begins after the Wolf has come to the village. After he has come and just as easily gone. When all that's left to do is to mend things broken, to return things stolen, and to forgive.*

About the Author

T. GREENWOOD is the author of *Breathing Water* and the recipient of the 1999 Sherwood Anderson Foundation Award. She lives in Ocean Beach, California, with her husband, Patrick Stewart.